Man
with a Mission

by

RUTH CLEMENCE

Harlequin Books

TORONTO • LONDON • NEW YORK • AMSTERDAM • SYDNEY

Original hardcover edition published in 1977
by Mills & Boon Limited

ISBN 0-373-02158-5

Harlequin edition published April 1978

PRINTED IN U.S.A.

CHAPTER ONE

DAVINA was doing her best to imitate the pace of an Olympic runner despite lunchtime window shoppers when a firm hand on her arm halted her in mid-flight as a laughing voice above her remarked, 'I might have guessed it would be my pint-sized cousin trying to cut a swathe through these long-suffering pedestrians. Where are you going in such a hurry?'

Davina was out of breath as she looked up to meet teasing brown eyes. 'Oh, James, I can't stop. There's a sale on at Selfridges and I want to try and get something special for Grandmother's birthday shindig before all the best things are snapped up. If I stop and chat I might miss a bargain.'

'You and your stupid pride! Grandmother would buy you fifty dresses if you'd let her,' James replied, keeping a firm hold on his cousin's arm. 'And haven't I just heard on the family grapevine you'd got your degree? Surely you or one of your girl friends could come up with an original design.'

'We've all been too busy with Finals for dressmaking sessions, and in any case it was English we studied, not dress design, you idiot. And you know perfectly well I can't go to Grandmother every time funds are running low. Dad would turn in his grave. After all, she did give me an absolutely wonderful trip for my twenty-first present. Now I've qualified, I simply must pay my way,' and Davina tugged her arm free at last.

'Hence the dash to the sales, I suppose? Okay, off you go,' James said, 'but since I've not set eyes on you for months let me cook you a meal this evening. Paul's away, my bird's got to work tonight, so I'm at a loose end. We'll have the flat to ourselves and you can tell me all your news while I grill the steaks.'

Davina's face broke into an enchanting smile. 'You're on. I seem to have fed on nothing but baked beans and eggs for weeks. By the way, where are you and Paul living? Still in that fabulous place in Wapping?'

When her cousin nodded Davina with a brisk 'see you later,

then' was soon lost to view on the crowded pavements and with an indulgent smile, James Brehm turned to go on his way.

She had to ring his bell several times, changing her shoulder bag and the plastic carrier bags containing her purchases from hand to hand before James answered the door. He had obviously hurriedly dragged on a dressing gown and was rubbing at his wet hair with a small hand towel, but his frown miraculously cleared as he stood back to let Davina in.

'Trust you to arrive when I was in the shower! I only got back from the office ten minutes ago and wasn't expecting you here for another hour. I fancied after a shopping spree in hot weather like this, you'd have wanted to go back home and bath and change.'

'So I would,' Davina said as soon as her cousin paused for breath, 'but if I was to be here in time for that steak, I couldn't go all the way out to Harrow. You remember my old flatmates Jane and Peggy? As soon as exams were over they decided to hitch their way around Europe. I couldn't afford to keep the flat going on my own, so I've moved into a bedsitter. I thought if I asked you nicely you'd lend me your bathroom while you got supper ready,' she finished, giving James a dimpling smile.

He responded by giving her a familiar smack on the seat of her jeans. 'Let me get you some clean towels, and the shower's all yours,' James said as he led the way into a bathroom with mirrored walls, sea green fittings and a closet in one corner from which he took a couple of fluffy towels and tossed them towards Davina. 'Don't stay in here all night,' he warned her as he went away. 'If you're not out by the time the meal's ready I swear I'll start without you.'

Davina laughed as she slammed the door on her tall cousin and dumped her belongings in an untidy pile on the carpeted floor. She and James did not meet often, but she liked him the best of all her many relations. Stripping, she stepped under the shower and proceeded to wash away the city grime, taking advantage of limitless hot water and James's expensive shampoo to wash her curly dark hair at the same time.

Wrapping a bath towel around herself sarong-fashion, she tucked her wet hair in a smaller towel and hurried along the corridor to ask James if he possessed a hair-dryer. But as she entered the living room the question died on her lips. Dwarfing her tall cousin to the size of a midget was a positive giant of a man, and he was examining her from head to toe with a curiously unnerving look in his hooded eyes.

'Sorry if I'm interrupting . . .' something in the stranger's glance made Davina blurt out an apology as the blood came up to stain her cheeks. Quick to recognise her confusion, James covered for her by saying smoothly, 'Don't go. I'm sure Mr Fitzpaine will excuse your rather bizarre appearance since he's only come to return some keys. He found the office closed and didn't want to risk simply dropping them into the letter box. May I introduce my cousin, Davina Williams. She's come to dinner, but as you see, decided to make use of the bathroom beforehand. Perhaps you'd care to join us,' James added with a grin, 'for dinner, that is,' and Davina's flush of embarrassment deepened as the newcomer's eyebrows started to rise.

Her cousin was doing nothing to remove any false impressions from the stranger's mind and Davina let out an inward breath of relief as the man turned away. His voice when he answered James, however, surprised her, for it held a faint but unmistakable accent. Mr Fitzpaine was undoubtedly an Australian. What was he intending to buy from Brehm & Co.?

'Thank you, I have a dinner engagement, but I wouldn't say no to a cold beer.' The voice was deep and musical. I wonder if he sings, Davina was pondering as James answered, 'Coming up. What can I get you, Dav?'

'Nothing at the moment. I'll go and dress.' Davina, curious or no, was eager to escape those curiously searching eyes. She took her time, but when she eventually went back to the living room, now respectably attired in jeans and a new shirt blouse, she was disconcerted to discover her cousin's unexpected visitor lounging in an easy chair and apparently in no hurry to keep his dinner date.

As Davina curled up in a corner of the wide settee tucking her bare feet beneath her, she found herself the target of yet another disquieting scrutiny. She gave back stare for stare, deciding that for all the no-nonsense look in his eyes, the air

7

of supreme physical fitness and confidence was curiously attractive. 'Have you been in England long?' she asked on impulse, then before he could reply, 'I know you're Australian and since you're returning keys, I guess you must be looking at houses and intend staying some time.'

The corners of the straight mouth twitched as if her undisguised curiosity amused him in some way. 'Not a house exactly, but what I think you Brits call a smallholding, though there is a house on the property. As to a long stay, now that depends.'

'On what?'

'On several things. I've had it in mind for some years to take time off to run a small experimental farm—what I think you'd call a sort of sabbatical, I guess. Now seemed as good a time as any.'

'And James has been helping you find what you're looking for?'

'Stop asking so many questions, brat,' James ordered, 'and tell me what you want to drink.'

'Bitter lemon, please, and I don't think Mr Fitzpaine objects. Do you?' Davina asked, and favoured the visitor with one of her dimpled smiles.

There was a gleam in the eyes watching her, but she was at a loss to interpret it. 'No, I don't mind setting your curiosity at rest. Your cousin has really been most helpful. I believe I've found just the very place for my purpose. Now all I have to do is agree a price, find myself suitable breeding stock and a housekeeper not afraid to live in the wilds.'

'A housekeeper?' Davina could not keep the note of eagerness out of her voice. 'Have you anyone in mind and what would she have to do?'

'Clean, cook reasonably well—and yes, I did have someone vaguely in mind, but nothing's settled yet.'

'Oh, I see.' Davina's voice was sadly wistful, and James, who had been listening to the exchanges of comments, laughed as he asked, 'Why the gloom, Dav? With a degree under your belt you're surely not looking for a domestic post?'

'That's just it, James.' Almost as if she had forgotten the man sitting watching in the easy chair, Davina turned her eyes on her cousin. 'I didn't have time to tell you earlier, but the editor of one of the teenage magazines thinks I can produce the sort of material he wants and he's asked me to submit some short stories for a start. The trouble is I won't get a penny until I'm in print, and I need a part-time job. Something that will keep me in bread and butter but with enough free time to do my writing as well. As soon as Gran's party was over I'd intended to look around.'

'Independent little thing, aren't you,' James remarked, 'but I wouldn't have thought keeping house was quite your scene.'

'Why not?' Both cousins turned as their argument was interrupted. 'I take it you can cook?' James's visitor had turned to look directly at Davina. At her nod he went on, 'Then don't worry about looking any further for your part-time job. In a month or less the legal side should all be settled. What about coming North with me, then, when I go to take over? I reckon six months should be long enough.'

Davina's forehead in a slight frown. Long enough for what? Was this strange man talking about his experimental farm or her short stories? And what about the other prospective employee he'd had in mind?

But the Australian was getting up to leave and Davina concentrated on saying goodbye. He held her hand briefly in his as he said, 'I'll be getting in touch with you through your cousin. If you're really serious I'm willing to give it a go if you are. But remember, the place is well off the beaten track. No shops just round the corner.'

He let go of her hand as he turned to bid her cousin goodbye and Davina wondered if she imagined the hint of quiet satisfaction about his farewell smile. Had she been over-impulsive in offering her services to a comparative stranger? But after all, if he were doing business with Brehm & Co. Uncle Giles would undoubtedly know a good deal about his background.

Her mother's brother, Giles Brehm, was James and Paul's father and head of a prosperous London real estate business. He was much too astute a businessman to do a deal with anyone from overseas unless he was absolutely certain they were a safe risk. Davina, smilingly content at this evening's fortuitous meeting, was unprepared for her cousin's, 'Taking a bit of a chance, aren't you, Dav?' when he returned from seeing the visitor out.

'That's right! Tell me I'm too impulsive for my own good,'

Davina defended herself. Then, 'Honestly, James, I'm not a child! In any case, I'm sure your Mr Fitzpaine is perfectly respectable.'

'Oh, sure. He came recommended by our associates in Sydney, Australia, with the very highest possible references. But that's not the point. One of these days your fond illusion that the whole human race are angels in disguise only needing a helping hand to sprout wings is going to make you come a cropper. In fact I understand it already has. Come into the kitchen while I see to the meal and tell me all about the on/off engagement you had with that fellow you met on your birthday trip. I never did get you alone long enough to hear the whole sordid story.'

'Must I?' Davina gave a grimace of distaste as she followed her cousin into the well equipped kitchen with its dining area beside the window, giving a panoramic view of the river and the buildings on the opposite bank of the Thames now lit with a rosy glow as the sun slowly dipped over the chimney pots. 'There's very little to tell,' she went on as she watched her cousin slip their steaks under the grill and begin to mix a French dressing for the salad.

James dipped a finger into the big wooden bowl and licked it thoughtfully. 'Aunt Marjorie told Mother that you all had a wonderful time in America but that on the boat you took pity on some Australian lad and that by the time you docked in Sydney, he just about thought he owned you. Then two days later you were knocked out by seeing your engagement to him in the local newspaper. When you issued a denial Aunt Marjorie said there was a nasty little scene with your "intended's" mother.'

'That's an understatement!' Davina gave a reminiscent shudder. 'She called me every name under the sun. What I can't understand is how Barr could have misunderstood my feelings. Yes, I know ...' she added as James turned a sceptical glance in her direction, '... it's not the first time my plain honest-to-God sympathy has been misconstrued, but poor Barr looked so lonely and out of things on the boat. No one else bothered to try and cheer him up, so when Uncle Martin booked us on a day trip in Honolulu I asked him to include Barr. It simply never occurred to me he'd think I seriously fancied him. Apparently as soon as he was home he told his mother he'd be bringing his fiancée to meet her. When Aunt Marjorie and I went to tea, I couldn't understand why she was so friendly. I suppose she'd made it her business to find out all about Uncle Martin and thought because I was his niece, Barr was on to a good thing.' Davina chuckled. 'She may still imagine I'm an heiress, for I certainly didn't tell her about Grandfather disinheriting Mum when she ran away to marry a penniless Welsh schoolmaster.'

'That, my dear cousin, must be where you get your impulsiveness,' James observed as he began to uncork the wine. 'I love your mother, but there's no doubt she lets her heart rule her head. Grandfather was as mad as fire when he found his favourite daughter preferred love in a cottage to the life of luxury with the Italian count Grandfather had so carefully picked out for her. I don't believe even Aunt Pamela's extremely advantageous marriage did anything to reconcile him to Aunt Helen's elopement. She was always the apple of his eye. Small as I was even I knew that, and I shall never forget arriving in Switzerland for the wedding just when the grandparents discovered your mother had upped and left only forty-eight hours before the ceremony was due to take place. Not that in the long run things didn't turn out for the best. It was plain your father made her very happy.'

Davina sat, her eyes full of memories, as James filled the wine glasses. 'Dad made us all happy and Mum has been like a lost soul since he died last year, for all she pretends otherwise. I can't help feeling sorry, though, for Grandfather. He seemed such a sad old man at the end—first a disappointment over Mum, then your father and Uncle Martin deciding Swiss banking was not for them and setting up a business here in London. Do you think he blamed it all on Gran insisting all her children had an English education?'

'Shouldn't imagine so,' James replied carelessly. 'After all, we've all kept in close contact. But you're straying from the point. You still haven't explained why your shipboard acquaintance thought you were prepared to make an honest man of him.'

James placed a loaded plate in front of Davina and slid into a seat opposite. As she helped herself to salad she said,

'I wish you wouldn't take the mickey when you talk about Barr.'

'He must have been pretty wet to take so much for granted,' James answered with brutal frankness, and Davina was immediately on the defensive.

'Aunt Marjorie must have given you quite the wrong impression. Barr Patterson simply suffered from an overprotective mother, as I discovered to my cost,' she finished ruefully.

'Hence the nasty little scene you told me about?'

'It was worse than terrible. According to Mrs Patterson I was Jezebel, Delilah and Helen of Troy all rolled into one.'

'And you'd led her poor defenceless son on. Don't worry, I know the type,' James remarked dryly. 'Put it down to experience and let it be a lesson to you not to feel sorry in future for every man who spins you a line. I daresay your Barr was so uptight when you met him simply because he was on his way back to that possessive mother of his. Maybe he saw you as a way of escape. Whatever the reason, forget about it and eat your steak. Is it cooked enough?'

'Just right,' Davina answered, her mouth full. She looked across the table and smiled affectionately. 'Now it's your turn, James. What have you been doing since I saw you last? I expect you've got a smashing girl in tow—you usually have.'

For the rest of the evening the conversation veered from girl-friends to Paul Brehm's holiday in Greece and finally round to the forthcoming family party for Grandmother Brehm's eightieth birthday which was to be held in the house outside Lucerne where she lived. As James was driving Davina home later he asked casually, 'How are you and Catrin getting there? I suppose Aunt Helen is already dancing attendance on Grandmother?'

'Yes, Mum went out as soon as her school broke up. You know she's taken a living-in job as a matron and has let our cottage to one of the masters at Dad's old school? When Catrin started her nursing there was no point in leaving the place empty, and anyway it gives Mum a bit of extra money. Her salary isn't all that generous and Dad's pension doesn't add up to much. Catrin and I try to live on our grants, so we've decided to travel on cheap student's tickets. We'll go to Zürich where Mum has said she'll meet us in Gran's old Rolls. After fourteen hours in trains it will be rather nice to do the last few miles in style.'

James briefly took his eyes off the road ahead to give his cousin an admiring glance. 'You, Catrin and Aunt Helen are a shining example to us all. I shall feel almost guilty as I go up the steps of an aircraft in ten days' time thinking of you girls sweating it out somewhere below in a stuffy train.'

Davina smiled back mischievously. 'No need. You, my dear affluent cousin, will doubtless be flying on a daytime scheduled flight. To qualify for cheap rail fares, Catrin and I have to travel overnight—no sleeping cars, no buffet, no nothing. Still, the thought of what we'll be saving will keep our spirits up, and one usually meets quite a few kindred souls travelling in the same impecunious way. It's so long since you were a student you've forgotten what it's like to have to count every penny.'

Before they said goodnight, James made a note of Davina's telephone number, 'Just in case that Fitzpaine character is rash enough to take you up on your offer,' he teased, 'for I bet you'll burn all his shirts and shrink his socks.'

'Which just goes to show you don't know me as well as you think,' Davina retorted. 'Mum brought Catrin and me up to do our share of the household chores. And don't forget, the cottage didn't have all mod. cons. until about five years back when Dad put in central heating and had a modern bathroom built on. Before that we'd made do with one that first saw the light of day in Victorian times, by the look of it.'

Before she put out the light and climbed into bed, Davina wrote her mother a long letter telling her of the meeting with James's Australian client and the job he had offered her. 'It would suit me beautifully,' Davina ended, 'because I shall be back in London after Gran's party just about the time Mr Fitzpaine gets possession of his farm. With only one man to look after I should have lots of time to get on with my writing. I'm hoping to get at least a dozen short stories done, not to mention making a start on that children's book I've always had a hankering to write.'

Three days later Davina was heating a can of ravioli when her landlady came to tell her she was wanted on the telephone.

When she picked up the receiver, James's voice sounded in her ear.

'Hello, Dav. Haven't dragged you away from anything important, I hope.'

'Not unless you consider tinned ravioli important,' Davina teased. 'What's on your mind?'

'You and this job with friend Fitzpaine. We've agreed a price and the deal should be completed in about three weeks. If you're still interested in working for him, he wants you to give him a ring at the Inn on the Park. I still think you're taking a chance if you agree,' James finished warningly.

'Honestly, James! Stop judging everyone by your own sorry moral standards,' Davina exploded. 'He doesn't look to me the type who walks in his sleep, but if he is I'll buy a strong bolt for my bedroom door. Thanks for letting me know he hasn't changed *his* mind about offering me the job. I'll get on to him right away.'

'I suppose you're old enough to know what you're doing,' James replied. 'Incidentally, I think I'd better warn you Grandmother phoned me this morning to ask me for Fitzpaine's telephone number.'

'Grandmother! What could she want it for?'

James chuckled. 'Come on, Dav, you know Gran. I suppose you've written and told your mother about Fitzpaine's proposition. Aunt Helen will have shown Grandmother the letter and she'll be checking his credentials.'

'I wish the family would mind their own business,' Davina said angrily. 'You'd think I was about two years old! I hope Gran hasn't messed up my chances.'

'Cool it, Dav,' James's voice held friendly warning. 'Just be thankful you've a family who care what happens to you and are not a poor little orphan Annie.'

'I'm not sure sometimes that wouldn't be preferable,' Davina grumbled, then added quickly, 'sorry, that was a mean thing to say. Thanks for ringing, James, and for warning me Gran may have contacted our friend from Down Under.'

But if Davina's grandmother had been in communication with her granddaughter's prospective employer, he did not enlighten her. When the hotel telephone exchange connected them, he thanked Davina for getting in touch and asked if she was still prepared to take the job he'd offered. At her 'yes' he asked for the address of her digs and with a laconic 'be seeing you' rang off.

Davina stood in the draughty hall and stared blankly at the telephone for several minutes and her face was thoughtful. She was unused to being treated in such a cavalier manner, but suddenly remembering she had left the gas on, she hurried to rescue her meagre supper.

After she had eaten, she began the mammoth task of sorting out her belongings. Like most students, Davina's wardrobe was adequate without being lavish, but in addition to clothes during three years at college she had accumulated a considerable amount of other possessions, from books down to mundane necessities such as pans and crockery. When she moved from the flat she had simply brought everything haphazardly packed into cardboard boxes, but she could hardly travel two hundred miles with her belongings in old grocery cartons.

She was sitting staring glumly at the piles of clothes and goods when the landlady knocked. Mrs Styles smiled at the chaos which met her eyes.

'Doing a bit of sorting out, I see. I came to ask you when you'll be moving out, because I've had several people enquiring about the room.'

Davina sighed. 'My job starts in about two weeks' time, but I'll pay until the end of the month. I guess I'll have to leave my things with you until I get back from my grandmother's.' She threw her arms out in a gesture of despair. 'What *am* I to do with all this, Mrs Styles? All I possess is one suitcase.'

'Now I may be able to help you there. My hubby has an old trunk we never use out in the shed. I've been on at him to get rid of it, so you'd be welcome to have it for say two pounds.'

Davina was pleasantly surprised by the size and condition of the cabin trunk stored in the tidy garden shed and handed over the asking price before the landlady could change her mind. By dint of pruning down to what she thought she would need at the farm, Davina managed to squeeze everything except clothes for the journey to Switzerland into the capacious trunk. True, saucepans jostled old walking shoes, but to part with these would be madness. Davina had not been raised in a country district without knowing that unmade roads and muddy farmyards were no place for fashion footwear.

On the day they were to leave for their grandmother's house, Davina met her sister in at Paddington and after a good meal they made their way across London to catch the overnight train from Victoria. It was due to leave at seven and they arrived in good time to get corner seats in the carriages reserved for students. Catrin looked tired and when Davina turned a questioning glance on her sister Catrin smiled ruefully.

'Yes, I know I look a mess, but a good night's sleep should put that right. I've just finished three months on nights. What can have made me take up nursing? It's all work with little pay.'

Davina laughed. 'You know why. Since we were old enough to play hospitals you've never wanted to do anything else. Anyway, it can't be all bad.'

Catrin smiled, a secret, almost a self-satisfied smile. 'It isn't. Oh, Dav,' she went on as if words were bursting out of her, 'I've met the most fabulous sailor! He was brought in off a minesweeper with a burst appendix and he's got the bluest eyes you ever saw. He got some sick leave before he had to report back to his ship and I've been seeing him every free moment.'

'I thought you nurses weren't supposed to date your patients. Medical etiquette or something,' Davina replied, smiling at her sister's dreamy expression.

'But I didn't—see him socially until he was discharged, I mean,' Catrin replied, her voice quite shocked. 'In fact I tried hard not to get involved with David at all. But when you've nursed a man for nearly three weeks and he's just your type—well, I simply couldn't say no when he rang me up. Not that I wanted to. Somehow or other you get to know people much more quickly when you're with them all night.'

Davina laughed, genuinely amused. 'I imagine you must, but don't let anyone but me hear you say so! It's the sort of comment very easily misconstrued. Particularly if they don't happen to know you're in nursing.' She paused, then added, 'I start that job I wrote to you about in about ten days' time, so when do I get to meet David?'

Catrin sighed. 'Heaven knows. He's off on a NATO exercise at the end of this week and has no idea where his ship will dock after it's over. I hope he doesn't come back while I'm still at Grandmother's.'

'Don't worry. I know they say sailors have girls in every port, but it can't be true of them all.'

But Catrin continued to worry about her new beau and by the time Dover was reached, Davina was growing a bit tired of hearing about his many virtues. She was jerked out of her half-hearted attention by Catrin suddenly asking, 'What about you? Last year you were seeing that nice Michael, but you've not mentioned him recently.'

'Couldn't get a word in,' Davina said with sisterly candour. 'Seriously, Mike and I had fun, but when college finished we parted by mutual agreement. It never went very deep with either of us. The crowd paired us off and we simply went along with it for as long as it suited us. No, I'm completely heartwhole and fancy free, thank goodness. I've no wish to settle down for a year or two yet.'

Catrin looked dreamier than ever. 'You'll change your mind when you really fall in love. Before I met David I felt like you—thought some of the girls in my year potty the way they acted over the young doctors. Now I guess I know just what they felt.'

Davina was spared the trouble of thinking up an answer to this pearl of wisdom from her young sister's lips by their arrival at the cross-Channel ferry terminus and the bustle as they were passed through the various formalities of showing passports and tickets. The sea voyage was calm and uneventful, but Davina's hope of finding room for Catrin to lie down in the train awaiting them in Calais had to be shelved when they found the carriages already filling up.

Davina found two adjacent seats and pushed an exhausted-looking Catrin into the nearest one. As she struggled to put their suitcases on the rack she said, 'Once we get going, lean on me and try and have a sleep.'

But despite Davina's endeavours to make her sister comfortable Catrin was given little chance to catch up on her lost sleep. Their fellow travellers turned out to be an extrovert bunch of young people with every intention of talking all night and before long they were confiding their holiday plans as well as seeking information about the sisters' destination, so that by the time the train pulled into Zürich station, Davina looked almost as tired as Catrin.

Both girls simultaneously hugged the attractive middle-aged woman awaiting them at the barrier and Helen Williams smiled a welcome as she returned her daughters' embraces. 'You both look worn out. Come along. Wilhelm's waiting.'

Outside the station, a grey-haired man was reading at the wheel of a vintage Rolls, but he got out to take their suitcases as Catrin and Davina, slipping unconsciously into the local dialect learned as children, greeted him by name. After enquiring about him and his wife, they climbed into the back of the car and soon the city was left behind.

Even Catrin's tiredness seemed to slip away as they sped through the green countryside with its wooden houses, each with a windowbox of geraniums and other colourful flowers, its tidy villages and neat farms. They had done the journey many times since childhood, for Grandfather Brehm's disappointment over his daughter's marriage had not extended to ignoring the existence of his two granddaughters. Each time she was struck afresh by the charm of the country, Davina thought as they passed the steepled church in the lakeside village where her grandmother lived, saying excitedly, 'Why, we're almost there! I'm simply longing for a bath and to get out of these grubby clothes.'

'Same here,' Catrin echoed. 'Honestly, Mum, there was hardly enough water on the train for more than a lick and a promise this morning.'

'I must say you both look as if you need sprucing up, but before you do, call in on Mother. She's anxious to see you. Your Uncle Giles with Aunt Jane and James came yesterday by air and Paul's flying in from Greece this evening.'

'What about the others? Is Miranda here yet?' Catrin asked, a look of dismay beginning in her eyes.

'Martin and Marjorie are driving her. They should arrive

about lunchtime. Aunt Pamela and her family aren't coming until tomorrow since they're only an hour's drive away, and in any case, Miranda has an engagement on tonight she doesn't want to miss.'

Catrin sifled a yawn. 'Thank goodness. At least we shan't have Miranda wet-blanketing everything on our first day here. I can never understand how Francesca, who's a sweetie, came to have a first class Grade A bitch for a sister,' she ended gloomily.

She was brought up abruptly by Helen Williams saying in a shocked voice, 'I hope you two will remember this is your grandmother's birthday celebration and do nothing to antagonise your cousin.'

Catrin smiled apologetically and tucked a hand in the crook of her mother's arm. 'Sorry, Mum. It's just that Miranda doesn't exactly put herself out to please. And she's forever rubbing it in that Dav and I are her poor relations.'

'All the same, try and remember she is your cousin and we want no bickering. Mother soon senses uncomfortable atmospheres, so I rely on the pair of you to spread sweetness and light, no matter what.'

Both the girls were smilingly agreeing as Wilhelm turned the car into the narrow lane leading from the village along the lake side to their grandmother's house. Through the trees, Lake Lucerne looked placid and calm as, driving through the tall entrance gates, the car sped up the drive to the front door.

The house was built end on to the road so that its principal rooms overlooked the lake. The main entrance had a portico with marble side columns and as Davina stood looking up at the house it struck her afresh that to go from a home like this to a terraced cottage in a small Welsh village must have called for a great deal of adjustment on her mother's part.

But if Helen Williams had ever experienced a pang of regret in opting for love in a cottage her serene, still youthful features showed little evidence of the fact, and Davina could only conclude that her mother had considered her former gilt-edged existence well lost for love. It was born out by the fact that after her husband's sudden and tragic death,

Helen Williams would have been welcome back here with open arms. Instead she had stayed in Wales to live on a meagre income rather than become her mother's pensioner.

Davina and Catrin found their grandmother sitting up in bed, and she pushed away a pile of letters and telegrams as she greeted her granddaughters fondly. After hearing details of their journey she packed them off to bath and rest and when Davina returned to the bedroom they were to share she found her sister asleep on one of the twin beds, her hair still damp from the shower.

Davina smiled as she fetched a rug and covered the slim figure. Despite their disturbed night she had no intention of following Catrin's example, for the sun was shining and it seemed too good a day to waste. Slipping on a clean cotton sun dress, she pushed her feet into sandals, brushed out her hair and wandered downstairs. As she reached the hallway, her cousin James came out of the library and grinned as he saw her.

'I was just about to come upstairs and find out if you were decent. We're having coffee. Where's Catrin?'

'Flaked out on the bed. She's been on night duty at her hospital.' As James gave a grimace of distaste, Davina looked over his shoulder into the library. There were four people in the room—her mother, James's parents and one other.

'What's *he* doing here?' Davina hissed, but before James could answer she went on in an angry undertone, 'I know, so don't bother to answer. Grandmother. *That's* why she wanted his telephone number. What must he think? That Gran imagines he's not to be trusted?'

James took Davina by the arm and shook her gently. 'Stop being silly. Fitzpaine's no fool. He'll think no less of you because your family want to know what kind of a chap you intend taking a living-in job with. Come in and try to act naturally. It can't be much fun for him knowing he's been invited simply so Gran can vet him. And he could have refused, remember. I think he's pretty sporting to have accepted.'

Davina let her cousin lead her into the room, but not before angrily whispering, 'I've said it before. Why must the family always interfere?' I wish just once they'd mind their own business!'

20

James grinned sympathetically but did not trouble to reply, and in minutes they were separated as Davina kissed her aunt and uncle and replied to questions about the journey. It was some time before she could turn and face her future employer, and her thoughts were confused as she met his eyes.

The heavy lids hid his expression, so deciding to rush in where angels might fear to tread Davina held out her hand and addressed him in her usual frank and friendly manner. 'Seeing you here comes as a bit of a surprise. Believe me, Mr Fitzpaine, I'd no idea Gran planned to invite you. It must be . . .'

She stopped as she was interrupted by his 'Don't apologise' as her outstretched hand was shaken. 'I guess your grandmother sleeps easier if she knows who you are meeting, and in fact I was very pleased to accept. I was kicking my heels in London waiting for the lawyers to get cracking, and the invitation gives me a chance to see a little more of Europe.'

'This your first time here.' Davina had suddenly become aware that he still held her fingers in a firm clasp and she slipped her hand free. Half embarrassed, she added, 'Look, I can't keep calling you Mr Fitzpaine. It's ridiculous to be so formal. What's your first name?'

There was a pause and Davina looked up to meet unreadable grey eyes as the man facing her replied slowly, 'You can call me Rex if you wish.' There was something in his tone of voice which puzzled Davina, but at that moment James returned with a cup of coffee and that flickering moment of instinctive warning of danger was forgotten as she thanked him.

As she sipped her coffee and listened to James and Rex Fitzpaine discussing the plan to have an outing on the lake that afternoon Davina decided she must be imagining things. When James turned to say, 'You'll come too, Dav?' however, she found herself refusing.

'I think I ought to rest this afternoon, otherwise I'll be fit for nothing by dinner time,' she excused herself, and refused to allow her cousin's persuasions to change her mind.

By the time she awoke, the other twin bed was empty. Davina sat up and yawned. Not wishing to disturb Catrin, she had simply lain down on the bed fully clothed and felt nearly as hot and uncomfortable as she had on arrival.

There was no sound from the corridor outside and Davina decided that the boating party could not yet have returned. It seemed a good opportunity to have a swim in the indoor pool, and swinging her legs over the side of the bed she shed her clothes, climbed into a bikini and grabbing a towel ran downstairs on bare feet.

The swimming pool had been installed years before in the erstwhile conservatory at the west end of the house. Huge tropical plants still flourished along the floor-to-ceiling windows, and had it not been for the tiled surround and modern loungers, the swimmers could have imagined themselves in a setting for a Tarzan movie. Sunlight filtering through the foliage and making glittering patterns on the water revealed Catrin floating lazily at the deep end. Throwing down her towel, Davina dived in and swam the length of the pool to join her sister.

But their exclusive use of the green-tiled swimming bath was not to be of long duration. As Catrin rolled over to say, 'I was about to go and beg some tea from Frau Wilhelm,' voices approaching made the sisters turn to look towards the door leading to the living rooms. James with Rex Fitzpaine behind him strolled in and Davina had only time to say, 'I guess you'd better make that tea for four,' before a splash as James hit the water drowned out her voice.

Treading water, Davina looked across to see that Rex had taken off his bathrobe and was standing, hands on hips, watching her. Although he hadn't an ounce of spare flesh he looked bigger than ever and she was glad of the necessity to introduce him to her sister to cover the shock of excitement which had shaken her at the sight of him clad only in brief swimming trunks.

Davina found herself watching almost enviously as Catrin, an attractive figure in her green bikini, climbed out of the water to extend a hand with the utmost composure. She smiled up as Rex said, 'I see the likeness. But then you are all easily recognisable as being out of the same stable, if you'll forgive the expression.'

James had swum to Davina's side in time to overhear this comment and he said with mock anger, 'Thanks for nothing! Are you trying to say this little Welsh filly and I really look alike?'

Catrin's rippling laugh rang out as Davina tried ineffectually to duck their cousin. She was so out of practice James had no difficulty in evading her, and since she had found little time during the summer to indulge in sport, Davina soon gave up the unequal struggle.

When she swam to the side she was surprised to find Rex there ready to give her a helping hand before he dived in to join James. She rubbed at her hair with a towel as reclining on one of the comfortable loungers she watched the two men cutting swiftly through the water. Rex Fitzpaine had a deceptively lazy crawl and he had soon outstripped James, so that Davina found herself comparing his magnificent physique with her cousin's more compact build.

Almost shocked as she recognised where her thoughts were straying, Davina turned with something like relief as Catrin came back with a loaded tea tray. As she poured out and handed the cup and saucer to her sister Catrin remarked, 'I must say that sleep did me good.' She sipped her own tea for a couple of minutes in silence before adding in a low voice, 'So that's the prospective boss you wrote to tell me about? He's not a bit as I imagined him in the description in your letter.'

Davina was spared the embarrassment of thinking up a reply to this frank, sisterly remark as the two men hoisted themselves over the side of the pool and came over to where Catrin and Davina were sitting. 'Any tea for us?' James asked as he pushed the hair back from his face.

Catrin indicated the two spare cups and asked how they liked it. James took milk, but Rex, with obvious reservations about Swiss-made tea, asked, 'Is it strong?'

'Don't worry, I made it myself,' Catrin laughed, and a reluctant smile tugged at the corners of Rex's straight mouth.

'Then I'll take it black. No milk or sugar,' he instructed, and drank it standing before pulling up a chair at Catrin's side and sitting down.

Davina was conscious first of surprise, then of a sense of pique at his obvious preference for Catrin's company. The mortification which so unexpectedly gripped her was made no easier when, turning to answer a chance remark from James, Davina was inclined to think he was well aware of the feelings passing through her.

As he lowered himself to lean against her chair, James's next words confirmed that he had made an educated guess as to her thoughts. 'You'll have to get used to it, Dav. The kid sister has grown up with a vengeance!'

Faint colour stained Davina's honey-coloured complexion, for James with acute perception had hit the nail on the head. She wasn't used to competition, at least not from Catrin. In the usual course of events men gravitated as if drawn by a magnet to her side, perhaps first interested in her black-haired, brown-eyed colouring, but staying to be further captivated by her normally frank, uncomplicated approach towards her opposite sex. At no time had Davina had to resort to the more common feminine wiles, but in any case it wasn't in her nature to be devious. And so far, busy with her studies, her involvements had been of the happy-go-lucky, no strings attached variety.

But as she continued to watch Catrin and Rex from the corner of her eye, Davina awoke to the fact that the tall Australian interested her in a way no man had done before. She was actually feeling a twinge of jealousy that Catrin had his entire, undivided attention, and James was right; Catrin had blossomed almost overnight into an extremely beautiful girl. Davina was small, but Catrin was 'pocket' size, and no one looking at the black hair curling on to bare brown shoulders or the slender figure would have guessed she had either the will or the stamina to make a nurse.

No wonder her sailor patient had not wanted to lose sight of her, Davina thought as James's laughing, 'Better take that preoccupied look off your face, Dav. It's a dead giveaway,' brought her back to where she was. 'You've been singularly unobservant where Catrin is concerned,' he went on in a low voice. 'She's growing up to be the star of the family where looks are concerned. Why do you think Miranda's such a pig to her? She saw long ago that she'd have to look to her laurels one fine day.'

Davina turned her head and looked down to meet James's gaze. 'Now who's being a pig? Not that it will harm Miranda to stop imagining she's the greatest thing since sliced bread. She's been queening it over us ever since we were children —which reminds me, what time is Paul due here?'

'What made you ask that? Let me guess. Association of ideas? You're right, of course, Paul's the only one of our generation who can take Miranda down a peg or two. Let's hope he's on form if Miranda arrives tomorrow in one of her more off-putting moods.'

Davina sighed. 'We've been warned that all is to be sweetness and light during the birthday celebrations.'

'Aunt Helen's suggestion, I would guess,' James replied. At Davina's nod he went on, 'In that case we must all be on our best behaviour and I'll tell Paul to hold his fire however obnoxious Miranda is. After all,' he added with a butter-wouldn't-melt-in-his-mouth expression, 'she'll keep. Like us she'll be staying over for a few days after Grandmother's birthday.'

As Davina burst out laughing Catrin asked, 'What are you two plotting? They're the *enfants terribles* of the family,' she explained to Rex as he raised questioning brows. 'I bet you they're up to something.'

James threw out his arms in a gesture of surrender. 'Acquit us this time, Catrin. We were merely discussing the fair Miranda. In a purely cousinly way, of course,' he added.

'Shouldn't imagine there'd be anything pure about it, but you're forgiven. Who's for another dip before we dress for dinner? You know how Gran hates us to be even a minute late.'

She got up and took a header into the pool, followed almost immediately by James. Davina sat up on the lounger, arms clasped around her knees, and had decided she'd be better employed washing and setting her hair than swimming when she suddenly became aware that Rex had got up to come and stand beside her.

She had to tip her head right back to see his face and as he reached a hand down the muscles rippled across immense shoulders. Fascinated by the sheer power in this simple movement, she blinked when he said abruptly, 'Come along. Upstairs for a rest before you titivate. Judging by your efforts in the pool earlier, I would guess you're a bit out of shape—in a sporting sense, of course.'

He pulled Davina off the lounger and on to her feet as he spoke, draping a towel round her shoulders as if he took

25

her obedience for granted. She still had a long way to look up, as her head barely topped his shoulder, and a glance into his expressionless face did little to help her decide if he'd been making a two-edged remark or not. She decided to give him the benefit of the doubt. 'Too many late nights and snack meals,' she admitted. 'It will do me good to live in the country again. No temptation to sit up late there.'

'Not if you've to be up and dressed to get a meal on the table for a hungry man by seven a.m.,' Rex agreed, then at Davina's look of astonishment he asked, 'You did volunteer to come and be my housekeeper, didn't you? It's no good lying in bed when you've a flock of sheep to attend to, and I can't be in two places at once. Not that I ever did believe in keeping a dog and doing my own barking,' he added as he turned away to dive into the green-tinted water.

Davina's mouth all but dropped open. He really was the most extraordinary man! Though apparently oblivious of her presence during the last half hour he had yet observed her reluctance to follow the example of her sister and cousin and take another swim before dinner. Yet his apparent consideration might have an ulterior motive. He'd require a fit and healthy housekeeper if breakfast had to be ready by seven, and by the look of him, a pretty substantial breakfast at that. As she went slowly upstairs Davina grinned to herself as she visualised Rex Fitzpaine's reaction if she gave him the sort of thing with which she started the day. It would be a plateful of bacon and eggs he'd expect, and not half a grapefruit and a cup of coffee.

Dinner that evening was a quiet family affair, Rex being the only person not actually related to the benevolent matriarch sitting at the head of the long polished table. Davina watched her grandmother with affection as with her sons on either side she skilfully directed the course of the dinner table conversation. Without her grandmother to put a diplomatic stop to his discourse, Uncle Giles would have held forth endlessly on his current aversion. Davina much preferred her younger uncle. Martin Brehm did not lack his own brand of brain and drive, but his approach was quieter and more subtle.

Pity Uncle Martin and Aunt Marjorie had no children,

Davina was thinking, when James muttered in her ear, 'Woolgathering again! That's the third time I've asked you to pass the gravy.'

Her apology was interrupted by the arrival of James's elder brother Paul, who strode in to kiss his grandmother and add, 'Sorry to be late. The plane was delayed in Athens.'

Old Mrs Brehm accepted his apology with an affectionate smile, but as she signalled to Wilhelm to bring Paul his first course she said, 'You should have come by land as your grandfather always did. We never found the cross-continental express running late.'

Paul grinned as he helped himself from the plate Wilhelm was holding, but he did not, Davina observed, reply to Mrs Brehm's remark with the cutting rejoinder he would have snapped back at anyone else criticising his mode of travel. Like his father, Paul Brehm's tongue was in general sharp, but never towards his grandmother, with whom he was on the best of terms.

After dinner, Giles Brehm suggested a game of bridge and soon two tables had been set up leaving Davina, Catrin and James to find their own entertainment. They decided to explore the old basement games room where in wet weather they had spent many happy hours as children.

It looked neglected and desolate and running a finger over the dusty edge of the billiards table Davina said idly, 'I don't believe anyone's been in here for months. Not even to clean.'

Catrin, sorting through one of the big cupboards and emerging with the table tennis bats, replied, 'Well, what can you expect? This is a big house and Wilhelm and Frau Wilhelm aren't getting any younger. When I was making tea this afternoon they were telling me how difficult it is these days to get help, especially this time of year. Most of the village girls prefer to work in hotels. Because of the tips, I suppose.'

Catrin threw one of the table tennis bats in her cousin's direction. 'Come on, James. Bet you're so out of practice I can beat you!'

Davina hid a smile as James, never one to refuse a challenge, took off his jacket and picked up the bat. She listened to the ping of the ball and the panting efforts of the contestants as she wandered around the big room discovering old favourites in the toys and games, but her interest soon waned as she came to the door leading out into the garden.

A stroll down to the lake would be preferable to remaining in the musty atmosphere of the long-closed-up room, Davina decided, and flicking the master switch which controlled the outdoor lighting, she opened the door to climb the four shallow steps leading to the gardens. She drew in a deep breath of the sweet air before walking slowly down to the water's edge, gazing at the lights across the lake twinkling like a thousand glowworms.

She sat on a convenient bench wondering idly what the people in the houses could be doing at such an hour. Watching television, doing the last household chores of the day, perhaps even preparing to have an early night? She was startled out of her private thoughts by a slight sound and turning her head, she discovered Rex Fitzpaine had joined her and was standing rolling himself a cigarette.

The hand which had involuntarily grasped the arm of the bench unclenched. 'You must walk very quietly. I thought I'd got the garden to myself.'

Rex lit the cigarette before he replied. 'I'm sorry if I alarmed you. I mistook you for Catrin.' Then mockingly he looked around. 'No James?'

'No Catrin either. Sorry to disappoint you,' Davina snapped, for the tone of his voice had made her hackles rise. 'We're not inseparable, you know.'

Without invitation, Rex sat down beside her. 'Aren't you? I'd rather begun to think you might be. I take it they've deserted you?'

'The boot's rather on the other foot. They're having a cut-throat game of table tennis and I felt like a breath of fresh air. What about you? Bridge over?'

'Far from it—which reminds me, I'd better be getting back.' Rex got up as he spoke and extinguished his cigarette. 'I stole a few minutes to have a smoke while I was dummy. I'm playing with your grandmother and judging from her expression she had every intention of giving our opponents the trouncing of their lives. It wouldn't even surprise me to find she'd made a grand slam,' and he walked away in the direction of the house.

Davina was left staring thoughtfully at his retreating figure. He was completely different from the Australians she had met on her birthday trip with Uncle Martin and Aunt Marjorie, but their itinerary had not included what Davina thought of as the 'real' Australia. In air-conditioned hotels and mingling mostly with business people she felt she had missed out. Rex Fitzpaine gave her a feeling of a different and perhaps a rougher existence where all the conveniences of modern man were not taken for granted.

She was in bed when Catrin returned from the bathroom to get out her face cream. 'Your Rex Fitzpaine interests me,' Catrin observed, and Davina put down the magazine she was reading to glance enquiringly at her younger sister.

'In what way?'

'Well, to start with, he listens. Hadn't you noticed? He asked me all sorts of questions about the family when we were having tea this afternoon and he seemed genuinely interested in my replies, not as if he was simply making conversation. And his manners are so beautiful. He's quite won Gran over already, and the aunts, even Mum herself—well, they're practically eating out of his hand.'

Catrin paused with the pot of face cream in one hand and Davina said nothing to interrupt her sister's amazing confidences. 'Yet I feel there's something more,' Catrin went on thoughtfully. 'My guess is that under that beautiful, smooth exterior he's really a pretty tough cookie.'

'Any grounds for that masterful summing up?'

Catrin wiped her face with a tissue. 'Not really. Just a feeling I have which I hope is wrong for your sake. He'd be a marvellous person to have at your back in a tight corner, but the very devil when crossed, and won't be easy to work for.'

'I'll have to watch my step then, won't I?' Davina replied lightly. 'Come along, Morgan le Fay. Put away your crystal ball and come to bed. I don't know about you, but I'm flaked out.'

But despite Davina's assertion that she was tired, long after her sister's steady breathing told her that Catrin was sound asleep she found herself staring into the darkness and mulling over the words of warning to which she had recently listened. They brought to mind Rex's remark by the pool that afternoon. 'I don't keep a dog and do my own barking.'

Well, if he did prove to be a hard taskmaster at least she was committed for only a short time. Surely she should have no difficulty in looking after his temporary home. Though she would never win a medal for either cooking or housekeeping, from necessity she had always helped her mother, and while no perfectionist she was capable of producing an excellent meal.

Snuggling down into her pillow, Davina made up her mind not to anticipate trouble. She seemed hardly to have closed her eyes before a hand shook her by the shoulder and Catrin's voice said, 'We've overslept and breakfast is in fifteen minutes, so get a move on, Dav. Look, I had the bath last time. You take the tub while I shower. Gran's coming down early as it's her birthday and we don't want to blot our copybooks by being late.'

It was a scramble, but the girls were ready with two minutes to spare and as they dashed downstairs two steps at a time James in the hall below asked mockingly, 'Where's the fire?'

Davina was about to reply in kind when she suddenly noticed that Rex Fitzpaine, behind her cousin, was taking in every detail of their fresh cotton dresses, bare legs and sandals, and there was colour in her cheeks when she stepped on to the marble-floored hall as much from resentment at the Australian's frank inspection as from the speed of their descent.

As Catrin caught at James's arm and said, 'At least we'll not be last in the dining room,' Davina was left to accompany Rex. She gave him what she hoped was a casual, 'Good morning. Did you sleep well?' only to be warned by the look in his eyes that he was well aware his scrutiny was making her feel curiously uncomfortable.

His, 'Thank you. I always sleep well,' was conventional enough, but Davina felt an unaccustomed unease as she preceded Rex to where some members of the house party had already assembled, secretly relieved that after wishing her grandmother the customary birthday greeting she could slip into a seat at the table well away from the Australian visitor's disturbing vicinity.

CHAPTER TWO

But as she sprinkled sugar liberally over her grapefruit, Davina found her gaze inexplicably drawn to Mrs Brehm's seat at the head of the table just in time to see Rex Fitzpaine hand over a beribboned box. Davina's grandmother opened it to reveal a shawl woven in such fine wool that it looked like lace.

Hastily, Davina averted her gaze as the incongruity of the big, outdoor man and the gift he had selected hit her. He simply did not go with feminine fripperies of such elegance. Fortunately the arrival of Paul broke into these troublesome thoughts, and Davina was only too happy to push them into the back of her mind as her cousin wished their grandmother 'many happy returns'.

For the remainder of the morning there was little time for introspection as Davina helped in answering the telephone and taking in flowers and telegrams of congratulation. Soon after breakfast visitors had begun to arrive in groups of two or more to pay their respects, for Mrs Brehm had lived in the district for more than fifty years and had long ago been accepted by the locals as one of themselves despite her English background. By one o'clock it seemed to Davina that most of the neighbourhood must have decided to call and supplies of vases for the floral offerings had long since run out.

She was trying to squeeze another dozen long-stemmed roses into an already overflowing bucket in the garden room when Helen Williams peeped round the door. Spotting her elder daughter, she came right in. 'I've been looking for you. Pamela and her family have just drawn up, so I've told Wilhelm to say we're not at home should anyone else turn up to see your grandmother. Lunch is nearly ready and I want Mother to have a proper rest afterwards. At this rate she'll be fit for nothing by the evening.'

Davina laughed as she straightened up. 'Don't you believe it, Mum! Gran's loving every minute and I'll bet she's got more staying power than the rest of us put together. My feet haven't touched the ground since breakfast and I feel as

31

it I've been through a mincer. I suppose there wouldn't be time for a quick dip in the pool before lunch?'

'Certainly not!' Helen Williams's reply was prompt and definite. 'Wash your hands and come along. The caterers are due at three and I want lunch eaten and cleared away before they get here.'

Following the rest of the family out of the dining room when the midday meal was over, Davina was taken by surprise as a hand reached out to bring her to a halt. She looked from the long brown fingers encircling her bare arm and up to meet Rex's eyes.

'I hired a car when I arrived in Lucerne, and as your mother assures me she has no need of your services this afternoon, how about coming for a run? You look to me as if some fresh air wouldn't do you any harm.'

'Hardly flattering, but I know after this morning I must look a mess. There wasn't time to freshen up properly before lunch,' Davina ended apologetically, for she was well aware that her make-up had long since rubbed off and during lunch her cousin Miranda's bandbox appearance had made her feel even more untidy than she really was.

'Would there be time for me to shower and change? This dress is ready for the laundry,' and as Rex nodded she asked, 'But what about the others? Maybe I ought to see what they want to do,' Davina ended, for it had not escaped her notice that during lunch Miranda had hardly taken her eyes off the visitor from Australia, and Miranda was unlikely to enjoy the snub of having her wishes ignored out of hand.

'Are you trying to tell me you're the kind of girl who needs her family's permission before she goes out for a drive?' Rex challenged, and there was scepticism as well as disbelief in his voice.

Davina got as far as a swift denial. 'Of course not, it's just that . . .' when Rex broke in.

'If you've better things to do, just say so. I'll wait in the car fifteen minutes, no longer. If you're not down then I shall go on a sightseeing tour on my own,' and releasing her arm he strode out of the dining room.

Davina looked down at the faint marks left by his grasp on her arm and smiled ruefully at the 'take it or leave it' ultimatum. In a way it appealed to her, and the chance to get right away for a couple of hours was very tempting. Deciding to risk any possible repercussions, she ran up to the bedroom and in record time had showered, dried and dressed in halter-neck cotton top and thin coffee-coloured denim trousers. She slipped cosmetics and a comb into her voluminous shoulder bag and as an afterthought a bikini and a towel. She was back downstairs well within the stipulated fifteen minutes to find Rex Fitzpaine sitting reading behind the wheel of a large cream-coloured Mercedes.

Without getting out he reached across and opened the passenger door so Davina could get in. He made no comment as he switched on the ignition and put the car into gear. Trust him to select such a big car! Davina thought as the silence lengthened, then chided herself as she imagined Rex trying to squeeze his bulk into a Mini or one of the baby Fiats or Volkswagens. Determined not to reveal her thoughts or give him an opportunity to snub her by asking where they were headed, she turned her head to look out of the window.

But she was not a girl to remain silent indefinitely and as the village was left behind and the car gathered speed she said impulsively, 'I feel exactly as if I'm playing truant.'

Rex glanced sideways before his eyes returned to the road ahead. 'If you do, it doesn't appear to be bothering you. Did you often skive off as a child?'

'With a headmaster for a father? You must be joking,' Davina replied, then added thoughtfully, 'You sound as if you *expected* me to be a bit of a rebel.'

'Now as I hardly know you that would be an irrational and a snap judgment.' Davina sat silently, feeling as if she had been deftly put in her place as Rex went on, 'You have a very interesting family. Have I met them all now?'

At least he wasn't going to pursue the truant bit, Davina thought with relief as she answered, 'All the immediate family, yes. We've some distant Brehm cousins, but I hardly know them. What did you think of the beauty of the family, my cousin Miranda?' There was no reply and she rushed on, 'Being such a dishy girl she's much in demand and I think family gatherings rather bore her. I expect she's had to give up quite a few pressing engagements to come for

Grandmother's birthday celebrations, so it wouldn't be surprising if she were a bit fed up.'

'Is she? I hadn't noticed.'

Davina glanced at Rex through the corner of her eye. Did the ambiguous remark mean he too had spotted how Miranda's eyes had lit up at the sight of a fresh face? She asked carefully, 'You mean you don't feel she's wasting her time coming to Gran's birthday party? Miranda thinks so, believe me.' She sighed. 'I guess she's used to a lot of flattery from the opposite sex and I'm afraid James and Paul won't pander to her whims. Sorry if that sounds catty.'

'I meant I hadn't noticed she was bored. She sat opposite me during lunch and never stopped talking. In any event, I hadn't placed her as the beauty of the family. Your sister holds that title, or as she matures.'

Davina's face softened. 'Do you know, you're the second person in the last day who's told me that. I'm so used to Catrin it had never occurred to me how lovely she'd grown until James said almost the same thing last evening.' Then as Rex did not reply but turned on to the motorway she asked as the car speeded up, 'Where *are* we going?'

'Your Uncle Giles told me there's a hotel on the Bürgenstock where there's a swimming pool and the views are pretty spectacular. He assures me it's near enough to spend the afternoon there and still be back in good time for the party this evening and was good enough to tell me how to get there. The bulge in your bag suggested you'd equipped yourself for all eventualities, so I didn't bother to ask if you'd brought togs.'

Davina, a faint flush in her cheeks, turned to look squarely at the clear profile of the man beside her before dropping her glance to the strong brown hands holding the wheel. Catrin was right—beneath the calm exterior Rex hid a complex character. She said lightly however in reply, 'Trust Uncle Giles to know every five-star hotel within miles! But thank you for inviting me to share your afternoon's expedition. All those visitors this morning were a bit much.'

The hotel was the epitome of luxury, more like a grand country house than an hotel. When the car was driven off by a uniformed porter Davina followed Rex into the foyer, looking

34

was unaccustomed to asking a girl out to have her waste half the time in sleeping. But he did not strike her as a conceited man, so the unmistakenly censorious note in his voice was all the more mysterious.

They arrived back at Davina's grandmother's house to find the caterers engaged to provide the refreshments finishing the setting up of long buffet tables with Wilhelm hovering anxiously. 'He's like a hawk about to pounce as if the poor things have designs on the family silver,' Davina remarked laughingly as she and Rex went upstairs together.

He smiled at her remark, but without replying gave her a wave before going to his own room further along the wide corridor. Davina found Catrin, already dressed, was putting the finishing touches to her make-up.

'Did you have a nice afternoon? I wish you'd been here, though, to see Miranda's face when she discovered you and Rex had sneaked off on your own.'

'There was no sneaking about it.' For some reason Davina felt angry at the suggestion that she and Rex Fitzpaine had made a surreptitious assignation.

Catrin she saw looked surprised at the tart reply, but she simply said, 'If you want a bath, I'd grab it now. If you're quick I'll wait and we can go downstairs together.'

Davina did not take long, and as she dressed, Catrin entertained her with a brief outline of her own afternoon. 'Mother wanted a few extras from town, so James and Paul offered to drive me in. I think they were as glad to get away from Miranda as I was.'

'Talk about handsome is as handsome does,' Davina said as she smoothed foundation cream on to her face, 'I expect she'll be wearing something ruinously expensive tonight and shine us both down. Pity she's always so waspish.'

'Not to the men she isn't,' Catrin remarked, 'and as to shining us both down . . . well, I think your dress is super. Where did you get it?'

'Sales. It's French. Do you like it?' and Davina got up to show off the cream dress with its brown velvet ribbon ties at waist and off-the-shoulder neckline.

Catrin nodded approval. 'It's great, and that layered skirt really suits you. One thing about being pint-sized, we don't have to worry about frills making us look fat. What about mine?' and she pirouetted on her size three gold kid evening sandals. 'Laura Ashley, as if you hadn't guessed. It was the only one of its kind and probably a sample.'

The Ashley model in one of its delicately flowered prints suited Catrin's youth and dark Celtic colouring. Davina smiled in appreciation before turning back to the mirror to complete making up her face. She put down the box of eyeshadow, gave a last pat to her curls and with a sigh said, 'I should have used a mauve tint, but that will have to do. Come on, Cat, let's go and tell Gran how super she looks in *her* new dress.'

It required no affectionate stretching of the truth for the two girls to assure their grandmother she would be the belle of the ball, for even at eighty Mrs Brehm was still a striking woman. Tonight, clad in full evening dress and with her well coiffured hair and clear, almost unwrinkled skin, it was difficult to believe she was an octogenarian. And her twinkling blue eyes almost outshone the sapphire collarette around her throat as she kissed her two favourite granddaughters with affection as they complimented her.

'Away with the pair of you!' Mrs Brehm said in indulgent tones as she went to await the arrival of her first guests. 'Sixty years ago I might have given you both a run for your money, but age can't compete with youth. You'll have the young men buzzing around you like flies.'

'We don't intend to compete with you, Gran,' Davina laughed. 'In any case, in that dress you'll be the honeypot.'

Mrs Brehm smoothed the folds of her lace dress. 'I'm pleased you approve, but don't try and tell me I look twenty, you bad girl. Once everyone's here, I shan't be able to see either of you in the crush.'

Her prophecy was not far short of the mark. Mrs Brehm had invited as many friends as her house could comfortably hold and Davina and Catrin discovered among the guests many young people with whom they had played as children while here on holiday. It was the grandest affair to be held since before Grandfather Brehm's death, and until the six-piece orchestra started playing Davina was happily occupied in greeting old friends and admiring some of the gorgeous dresses and jewels of the female guests.

But as soon as the music began, she found herself on the area cleared for dancing being whirled from one pair of arms to the next. She did, however, notice that Catrin was claimed several times by Rex Fitzpaine, laughing up into his face as if they shared a secret joke.

He had made no effort to approach Davina for a dance and after his consideration in taking her for an outing this very afternoon, she was puzzled by his aloofness. She was on the floor for the second time with her cousin James when he suddenly said, 'I'm hungry. Have you had supper yet?' and as Davina shook her head he went on, 'Let's have it now, then. The first rush on the buffet should be over. It was packed when I tried to get a glass of champagne for Miranda half an hour ago.'

'Doesn't she look stunning!' Davina asked as James danced towards the door. 'That Thai silk dress looks simply gorgeous with Miranda's red-gold hair and must have cost a bomb. I bet it's an Italian model.'

'I wish her disposition was as gorgeous as her appearance,' James replied gloomily. 'Mirry did nothing but complain when I had a dance with her. Something's rubbed her up the wrong way, that's for sure.'

Davina could have given an educated guess as to what that 'something' was—Miranda's lack of success with the tall stranger from Australia. She kept discreetly silent, however, as James danced her to the door and then took her hand to lead her in the direction of the buffet room.

They were about to pass the closed door of the library when James pulled his cousin to a halt as Miranda's high-pitched voice came clearly to their ears. Davina and James exchanged dismal glances as they recognised that a full-scale quarrel was in progress and that Miranda obviously did not care if the whole house heard her accusations.

In seconds they were inside the room. Miranda, her face unbecomingly flushed with anger, was confronting a white-faced Catrin almost spitting with rage as she accused the younger girl of '... making a spectacle of yourself and embarrassing Grandmother by monopolising one of her guests. Not that Rex isn't embarrassed too. How can he ask anyone else to dance with you hanging round his neck all evening?' Miranda ended venomously.

Davina was about to spring to Catrin's defence when Paul Brehm strolled through the open French window. 'The way you're shouting, my dear Miranda, they must be able to hear your spiteful accusations as far away as Lucerne,' he drawled. 'What a dreadful bore you're becoming. But this is one evening when your tantrums are *not* going to spoil everyone's fun. You're coming with me and for the rest of Gran's party you're going to smile and behave yourself so she doesn't guess what a selfish little beast you really are,' and before Miranda could recover from her astonishment, Paul had possessed himself of her hand and had forcibly marched her through the French window into the gardens beyond.

As their footsteps faded, the three in the library could hear Miranda's agitated protests, but they too soon faded away as Paul hustled her away from the house. James chuckled as he walked forward to put his arms round Catrin. 'Good old Paul! Don't worry, he'll settle her. Now come on, Cat, no tears. It's all over. How about slipping upstairs to powder your nose or whatever you girls do, then come and have some champagne with us. I'll try and snaffle a whole bottle, so don't be long.'

Catrin gave him a watery smile and gulped down a sob. 'Thanks, James. Miranda can really hit below the belt when she sets her mind to it. I was dreading Gran or Mother hearing the row. Give me five minutes. I'll slip up the back stairs and fix my face,' and Catrin dived through the door with the words.

Davina gave a long sigh of relief. 'What an escape! I can't thank Paul, but I can thank you,' and she reached up on tiptoes to kiss his cheek. James, however, took her by her bare shoulders and smiled down into her eyes.

'It was Paul who broke up Miranda's little scene, not me, but if thanks are the order of the day, let's do it properly. I've always had a soft spot for you, dear coz,' and with the words James bent his head and laid his lips on Davina's. Suddenly, some sixth sense gave warning and she broke free, to turn and find Rex Fitzpaine framed in the opening of the French window.

There was a disconcertingly mocking smile curling one corner of his firm mouth. 'Forgive me. It seems I interrupt.'

He came right into the room to address Davina directly. 'Accept my apologies. Were you not otherwise engaged I'd have asked you for a dance,' and with the words he opened the hall door, closing it quietly behind him.

Davina's eyes met those of her cousin as he said, 'This certainly is not our lucky night. First Miranda, now him,' and he jerked his thumb at the closed door. 'What's got into everybody? Come on, let's drown our sorrows, for heaven's sake,' and Davina gladly followed him to the buffet.

While James went in search of champagne, Davina herself loaded three plates with some of the delicacies on the long tables and they had settled themselves at a small secluded table, when Catrin slipped into the third chair. She had got her colour back and reapplication of lipstick and powder had made her look more like her usual cheerful self.

When James handed her a brimming glass, however, she laughed a trifle shakily. 'I don't usually like this stuff much, but I could use a bit of Dutch courage tonight. I shan't forget Gran's birthday in a hurry. How I wish David could have come, then none of this would have happened.'

'You're not the only one, love,' James remarked, gulping down his own wine with total lack of respect for its vintage. 'But who's this David?'

'According to Catrin, he's the love of her life. He's the navigating officer on a frigate and at the moment he's doing a NATO exercise. For goodness' sake, James, don't start her off. What I can't understand is why you simply didn't tell Miranda you were more or less spoken for,' Davina accused her sister. 'That would have put a stop to all that nonsense over Rex Fitzpaine.'

'Don't you believe it,' James replied with a twinkle in his eyes. 'Didn't I say yesterday that our Miranda sees her crown slipping?'

Catrin, however, missed the implication, for her eyes were on the tall figure approaching their table. 'Here's Rex now. What shall I do if he asks me to dance again? Miranda will be more furious than ever.'

'No, she won't. Look, here she comes now,' and he pointed towards the door where Miranda, surrounded by a positive bevy of young men, was about to come in search of refreshment. Paul at the back of the group gave his brother and cousins a wink as he passed them and Rex, who had stopped at Catrin's side, raised his brows.

'Sit down, Rex,' James pushed a chair towards him. 'Like some wine?'

'I'd prefer a beer, but it can wait. I've come to see if Catrin would like to dance. How about it?' he asked, looking down at Davina's sister from his great height.

It was James who answered for her. 'Go on, Cat. Miranda's had her claws clipped for tonight. You're quite safe,' and flushing, Catrin got to her feet. Rex's gaze passed from James to Miranda and back before he turned and followed Catrin, but he asked no questions.

'No flies on him,' James remarked. 'I'll bet Rex has got the general picture.'

'About Miranda and Catrin, maybe. About you and me, I'm not so sure,' Davina said quietly.

By two a.m. most of the guests had left and Mrs Brehm, still looking as fresh as a daisy, suggested that they all had a hot drink before they broke up her birthday party. Davina, feeling unusually tired, was glad to sit down and swallow a cup of piping hot coffee, for her feet ached and she longed for the moment when she could slip away to bed. Rex Fitzpaine had not proffered a second invitation to dance, but surely this could not account for the depression which gripped her. No, it was his expression when he had caught James kissing her which stuck in her mind. Though he had apologised, something told her he had not been surprised. Surely he couldn't suspect her of carrying on an affair with her own cousin right under Grandmother's nose?

CHAPTER THREE

The feeling of deflation and anti-climax followed Davina upstairs to bed, for she had not found the lavish celebration party an unqualified success. She wouldn't admit to herself that this feeling was in part due to Rex's unspoken disapproval, and it did not salvage even a shred of self-confidence to find next morning he was leaving.

She came downstairs shortly before ten o'clock to find the big hire car at the door and Rex himself loading the boot. Davina stood at the open front door and watched as he stowed his luggage and locked up.

As he turned and saw her he said shortly, 'You're down at last. I was just off. I thought I'd have to leave a message with James.'

Davina thought it wiser to ignore the implication in this last remark. 'I didn't know you were going so soon,' she answered slowly.

Rex reached her side and halted long enough to say, 'While I have the car and a few days at my disposal it seemed stupid to miss the opportunity of seeing Italy. The rest of your family will be going back to London anyway tomorrow, I gather, and in any case, I'm sure your grandmother won't want me hanging around. I believe I've passed the test,' he gave her a slow meaningful smile and Davina flushed. 'Give me your telephone number again,' he finished, the tone an order, not a request.

Wishing she had the courage to tell him she'd changed her mind and that he could keep his job, Davina complied. She was letting his offhand manner get under her skin. Usually she took people as she found them, so what was so special about this tall, brown-faced man? she wondered as with a brief, 'So long. See you in London, then,' he strode on past her into the house, presumably to say his goodbyes to her grandmother.

During the days which followed, Davina made a determined effort to put Rex Fitzpaine to the back of her mind, but she could not fool herself into believing she was finding the beautiful Swiss mountain scenery and the cooking of Frau Wilhelm as enjoyable as on previous visits. In fact, she was quite relieved when it was time for her and Catrin to pack their bags in preparation for the long train journey home. She saw Catrin on to the train for Wales, then went slowly down the escalator to take the Tube to her digs in Harrow, relieved to find the first rush hour was over and the trains relatively empty.

For the first time since her grandmother's birthday, she felt a stab of excitement as she put her key in the door and spotted the letter awaiting her. The name of the magazine was stamped across the left-hand corner of the envelope and dropping her suitcase, Davina tore the letter open.

It was short and friendly but simply confirmed that they were awaiting her first two short stories, 'which if suitable will be published in our January editions.' Stopping only to tell Mrs Styles she was back, Davina went to her bedsitter and squatting on the bed, read through the letter again.

Would there be time to write one before Rex contacted her? It was over a week since she had seen him and apart from a 'thank you' letter to her grandmother, there had been no word. Perhaps he was still touring on the continent. She'd ring James to see if he'd heard anything at the office, Davina decided, as with a yawn she lay back, her mind switching to the embryo plot she was toying with as a possible for her first professional short story.

There had been no rest on the long overnight journey, and still clad in all her outdoor things, Davina shut her eyes and fell asleep right in the middle of her eighteen-year-old heroine's first encounter with the hero. When she awoke it was dark and someone was hammering on the door.

'You there, Miss Williams?' came Mrs Styles' voice. 'Telephone for you!'

Davina sat up with a jerk and an answering 'Coming!' She stumbled over to the light switch and saw by her watch that she had slept all day. All her clothes felt as if they were sticking to her as she hurried down to pick up the receiver.

'I was beginning to think the good lady had hung up on me,' came Rex Fitzpaine's voice. 'What took you so long?' Then immediately, 'Never mind explaining. Look, can you be ready to take off for the North tomorrow? I got back to find the lawyers had really got a move on and I'm told it's okay to take over the place any time I like.'

Davina was silent, alarmed by the feeling of excitement at hearing Rex's soft drawl once again. She had forgotten how pleasant his voice could sound and she shut her eyes

44

in sheer delight until he said, 'I hope you've not hung up. Are you there, Davina?'

'Yes, I'm here.' She took a firm hold on her emotions and trying to sound brisk said, 'I only got back this morning and was trying to remember if I've anything in the way of loose ends I ought to settle before I leave.'

'I should have thought you'd have done all that before you left for your grandmother's. You knew as soon as the sale was completed I'd be off. If you only got back this morning, I shouldn't think you've even unpacked. Look, I'll pick you up at nine tomorrow morning.'

This was certainly rushing things and Davina said contrarily, 'Now wait a minute. I haven't said I can be ready by then.'

If she thought Rex would offer to await her convenience she was mistaken. 'Then you'll have to come by train. But after your all-night journey, I should have imagined you'd have seen enough of trains for a while,' he ended slyly.

Davina let out a spurt of reluctant laughter. He had her there! She rubbed her back which still ached and capitulated. 'All right, tomorrow at nine. I think you have the address.'

'Yes—I'd mislaid it, but your cousin supplied it when the final negotiations were completed this afternoon. Don't keep me waiting in the morning,' and without so much as a goodbye Rex had rung off.

Davina stared at the telephone, then ran trembling fingers through her hair. She would have to hurry if she were to be ready in time and Rex did not strike her as being a patient man. The launderette kept open late tonight, thank heavens. She'd do her laundry and while it was drying off in front of the electric fire, she'd bath and shampoo her hair. What a mercy the trunk was ready! She ran upstairs two at a time to turn out her suitcase on to the bed.

Next morning she awoke early and after putting her clean laundry into the suitcase, she dressed in jeans, a clean blue shirt and a denim waistcoat, for despite the drizzle of rain the day was not cold. She had drunk a cup of coffee and eaten a slice of bread and butter when she heard the door bell, and a hasty glance at her watch showed her that the hands stood at a minute to nine.

Trust Rex to be punctual to the minute! she thought, running downstairs. Well, at least she was practically ready. There were only her toilet articles and cosmetics to slip into her capacious shoulder bag, and since Rex was sure to have bought a luxurious car, there was no need for more than a nylon raincoat should they stop for lunch.

But when she threw back the door, Davina saw with a feeling of dismay that instead of a comfortable saloon car, a serviceable Land Rover stood at the curb. Without waiting for an invitation, Rex walked past her into the narrow hall and when she turned to speak, Davina glimpsed a hint of impatience in the hard eyes.

'Where's your luggage? I'll get it loaded. And you'll need more than what you're wearing once we're moving. You'd better get a sweater or an anorak on.'

'But they're all packed in my trunk. I've got my raincoat—that's warm enough. And the trunk and my suitcase are in the room.'

As he followed her Rex said simply, 'Suit yourself, but don't complain if you feel cold later on.' It was not a good beginning and rather to her surprise Davina found herself making excuses.

'It simply never occurred to me that I might be cold on the journey,' she began, then angry with herself for apologising so meekly she added sharply, 'You didn't give me much notice, when all is said and done—and in any case, why didn't you warn me we'd be travelling in a utility vehicle?'

He grinned as if her acid protest amused him. 'I warned you the place was at the back of beyond, you can't deny that, so what did you expect? A Rolls? What use would an ordinary car be on a farm?'

He had her there, Davina had to admit. She simply hadn't given the matter serious thought. Perhaps at the back of her mind she had supposed Rex would have arranged to have two vehicles at his disposal, since if the farm was as remote as he suggested there would surely be occasions when she herself might require transport to shop in the nearest town. Apparently *her* convenience had simply never crossed his mind, so that if and when shopping had to be done, she was expected to wait until he saw fit to take her into town himself.

Ten minutes later, the trunk and suitcase loaded, her good-byes said to Mrs Styles, Davina found herself in the passenger seat as Rex manoeuvred the vehicle into a line of slow-moving traffic. Silence hung like a visible obstacle between them as they crept slowly out of the suburbs towards the north-bound motorway, for Davina felt obstinately reluctant to be the first to speak.

Her normal good-tempered nature was surprisingly ruffled by their initial altercation, yet she had to be honest with herself. She could as easily have asked Rex on the telephone last night whether to dress warmly as he to advise her to do so. Almost as if he read the thoughts jostling through her mind he said, his eyes on the road ahead, 'I guess you've never been a Girl Guide. Isn't their motto "Be prepared?"'

Davina smiled reluctantly, relieved to have the ice broken even if by doing so Rex aimed yet another dart of criticism. She leaned back in her corner, turned to smile at his profile and say, 'You must be already regretting your generosity in giving me a job, especially as you'd someone else in mind. I promise I'll try and do better.'

She turned away, so missed the curious twisted smile with which Rex responded to her last remark. After a few moments she turned to him again. 'You've never given me a hint of exactly where we're going. What sort of a farm is it you've brought?'

'It's in Cumbria—the other side of Alston. Do you know it?' When Davina shook her head Rex went on, 'It's a hill farm for running sheep. I'm giving myself a sort of sabbatical to try out a bit of experimental work. My ambition is to try and find a better breed to suit our needs.'

Davina's smooth brow wrinkled in puzzlement. 'But I've always been told Australian sheep are second to none.'

'Most of them are, I agree. But we could still use a breed more adaptable to our long droughts. Have you any idea how many acres are needed in some parts of Australia just to support one animal?'

'I don't know much about your country at all, and very little about sheep,' Davina admitted.

'You'll learn.' There was a grim note of amusement in Rex's soft voice, but as soon as she turned questioning eyes on his face he went on slowly, 'But I thought you'd been to Australia. I'm sure your aunt told me you'd been out there not too long ago.'

Davina laughed, real amusement in her voice as she replied. 'What Aunt Marjorie means is that I've seen Sydney and Adelaide. I don't call that the real Australia. I went there on a trip with them paid for by Grandmother and when I suggested we went to look at Alice Springs or the Barrier Reef, both Uncle Martin and Aunt Marjorie nearly had a fit. While Uncle Martin saw his business connections, Aunt and I like most visitors toured the cities. Very beautiful, I grant you, but a city's a city if you see what I mean. I'd have liked to see further afield. I'd always been told the outback is pretty inspiring. Maybe one day I'll get the opportunity to see, if not the whole of Australia, at least more than just two of its main cities.'

Rex gave a sort of grunt by the way of reply, then silence fell again as he put his foot down and drove as fast as was permitted along the six-lane motorway northwards. Davina was aware of feeling increasingly cold as the drizzle became a proper downpour and began to wish there'd been time to have more than a slice of bread and butter before setting out.

As she stirred restlessly, Rex glanced at his watch, then asked, 'Would you like to stop for something to eat? It's a bit early for lunch, but we could have sandwiches and coffee.'

'You must be a mind-reader. I'm simply ravenous!' Davina smiled, but it died out of her eyes as Rex cut her down to size. 'Nothing of the sort. I know women, though. Complete idiots when there isn't a man around to cook for,' he said briefly as he turned into the slip road leading to the transport café.

As she climbed out Davina shivered, as much from the intolerance of his remark as from the rain beating relentlessly on to her bare head. 'Well, go on, get in out of the rain. What are you waiting for?' Rex asked, and coming round the bonnet he took her arm and ran her into the shelter of the building.

There was an empty table beside the window, and with a

terse, 'Sit here,' Rex went over to collect a tray and walk along the serve-yourself counter, stopping several times to add another item to his tray. When he returned Davina gave a gasp and looked up to say, 'We'll never eat all that. There's enough food there to feed an army.'

A smile just touched Rex's firm lips. 'What's left is for later on. Just eat what you can, the rest we'll take with us. You'll see drinks too. Those are for the journey. The coffee's for now. Sugar?'

Davina shook her head and in silence opened one of the packets of sandwiches. The bread tasted as if it was made of a composition of felt and cardboard, but she was too oblivious to care. All her thoughts were taken up by Rex's uncompromising manner. Where were the beautiful manners now? Had they simply been put on for the purpose of impressing her family?

It was not until she was getting back into the passenger seat of the Land Rover that, turning to watch Rex stow the food and cans of Coke and beer, Davina noticed the portable Calor gas stove and the two camp beds. When Rex climbed in and put his key in the dashboard she asked, 'We are going to get there today, aren't we?'

Rex looked surprised. 'Of course. Why do you ask?'

Davina jerked a thumb over her shoulder. 'Why the camping gear, then?'

'Oh, that!' Rex smiled, though it wasn't a particularly reassuring smile. 'I don't intend to bed down on the roadside, if that's what you're wondering. Now I was a Boy Scout,' he turned his head and smiled ironically down into Davina's bewildered face. 'The farmhouse hasn't been lived in since the late owner died and I understand he wouldn't let anyone over the threshold to clean. As far as I can make out all the trustees of the estate have done is clear out the old man's papers and clothing, so it's possible the beds aren't fit to sleep in. I didn't want to be caught napping, hence the camp beds.'

As he drove out of the car park Davina digested this latest piece of information. It all sounded vaguely sinister—and come to that, wasn't Rex himself behaving in a very strange manner? He was treating her with what could be described as the minimum of courtesy and was making no effort at all to set her at ease by making friendly conversation. If Catrin were here, what would be her summing up now? Davina wondered.

She glanced sideways beneath her long lashes at the profile of the man behind the wheel. He was watching the road ahead, a slight furrow between his straight brows. Her eyes dropped to the shapely brown hands lightly holding the steering wheel. Had he got so used to having a large staff under his command that he had decided views on the way employees should be treated? If so, Davina thought grimly, Rex Fitzpaine was in for some surprises! A fair day's work for a fair day's pay he was entitled to, but he was not going to trample all over her as well.

Having reached a decision, Davina settled herself as comfortably as she could and gazed out of the nearside window, letting her thoughts dwell on plots for short stories and ignoring the remote attitude of the man at her side. Not that he was exactly easy to ignore, she realised, because he took up so much of the seat that his thigh touched her own every time he changed gear. It was a relief when eventually he pulled into a layby so they could stretch their legs and eat another snack meal before setting off once again on what Davina hoped was the last leg of the journey.

It was tea time when Rex turned off the motorway at Scotch Corner and headed in the direction of Barnard Castle. The rain had stopped, but the temperature had dropped steadily as they travelled north, and Davina would have given a great deal for a cup of hot tea. But Rex had said he didn't intend another break, so she tried desperately to hide the increasing discomfort she was beginning to feel, realising that in any case it was unlikely there was a café within twenty miles.

They were now travelling bleak mountain roads, unfenced apart from occasional dry-built stone walls or rows of fence posts set at intervals to guide travellers in snowbound weather. They had passed Alston and though it was much larger than her home town of Llantarwyn, Davina saw that it was no more than a market town of probably some two thousand souls.

As she tried to stifle a yawn Rex pointed ahead. 'There's Camshaw, our nearest village.'

Peering into the distance, she could just see a huddle of grey houses with the short square steeple of a church rising above the slate roofs. Five minutes later Rex drew to a standstill before a shop which from the variety of goods displayed in the window catered for the needs of everyone for miles around. It was also the village post office, for a red letter box was set in the shop wall.

With a brief 'Wait here' Rex got out and strode into the shop, and Davina was too tired to do anything but obey. She was thinking how cold, empty and unfriendly the place looked; even the door of the inn opposite was firmly shut. Rex returned carrying a large carton of groceries. He dumped it on to the luggage piled behind Davina's seat and with a, 'Hold on to that. It's our provisions for the next few days and I don't want to arrive with our eggs already scrambled,' he got quickly into his seat and restarted the engine.

He turned the Land Rover on to a road leading out of the village which was even narrower than the one they had travelled and for about a mile they passed only two cottages, both of which would have seemed deserted had it not been for the thin spirals of smoke coming from their chimneys. The moors stretched out in every direction, broken here and there by a gorse bush or a stubby tree bent by the wind into grotesque shape. A solitary house a little larger than the cottages loomed ahead, but Rex passed it by and at last, unable to keep quiet any longer, Davina burst out with, 'Where are we going? If I didn't know the earth was round I'd swear we'd be driving over the edge any minute!'

She was torn between amusement and disbelief as she gazed ahead, for there was no sign of another habitation. One corner of Rex's mouth curled, but it could hardly be called a smile and for the first time it occurred to Davina that he probably felt as tired as herself. When she thought he was going to ignore her remark he slowed down and slid to a halt before a gate bearing a weatherbeaten sign. 'The farm's in the hollow just over the rise,' and he pointed along the farm track.

The paint was peeling from the wood, but Davina could

just distinguish the words 'Nineveh Farm.' She turned to speak, but as her lips parted Rex broke in, a decidedly mocking note in his voice.

'Where I come from, it's usual for the passenger to get out and open gates.'

Davina stared into his impressive face for a moment before turning to climb out and push open the heavy iron gate. As Rex drove past and pulled up she slammed it shut, giving vent to the frustation building up inside. She hoped he had simply got out of bed the wrong side this morning and that he did not intend keeping up such a laconic manner towards her all the time. It came as a surprise therefore to hear him say mildly, 'Thank you' as she climbed back into her seat. At least life with him wouldn't be boring, Davina mused, for she never knew what he was going to do or say next.

As they crested the rise and the farmhouse came into view she saw it was larger than she had anticipated. Once through the last gate Rex drove round to the rear of the building and parked the Land Rover by a glassed-in porch.

Davina looked up at the grey stone, the unwinking windows like sightless eyes, and shivered, for it was rather like a scene out of *Wuthering Heights*. Rex had produced keys from his pocket and was unlocking the outer porch and inner doors and when both were open he stood aside to let her precede him into the house.

She walked into what was obviously the farmhouse kitchen, a huge room with a big black kitchen range at one end and furniture of equally large proportions. She stood looking around for a minute before expelling her breath in a long gasp. 'My goodness! How long did you say the owner had been dead?' she asked the silent man standing at her back.

'Several months, but I did mention he wouldn't allow anyone in to clean. That was years ago, apparently, after his wife died. They'd no children and it seems he had few friends. Maybe he just didn't care for appearances,' Rex concluded. 'Come along, let's take a look around.'

The kitchen with its filthy floor and table covered with old, yellowing newspapers should have prepared Davina for what was to come. But she stared in incredulous unbelief as they walked from room to room. The small room across the hall, judging by the single bed in one corner, had been in use as a bedroom, the two big rooms on either side of the massive front door were shuttered and musty and the upstairs rooms had seen neither duster nor brush for many a long day.

In the largest of the four first floor bedrooms Davina in an effort to get a closer view of the furnishings went over to pull aside the heavy curtains. As she did so they began to disintegrate, the shabby material tearing as soon as her hands touched it to hang in festoons along the floor. She brushed her hands together with an involuntary shudder of revulsion just as Rex remarked from the doorway in a wooden voice, 'A good bonfire would seem to be the order of the day.'

He turned to lead the way downstairs and Davina followed him. 'Just as well I bought those camp beds,' he remarked calmly, 'because we certainly can't use the ones up there. I'll sleep in the kitchen and you can bed down in one of the other rooms. At least we needn't worry about burglars,' he went on as they passed the front door. 'By the look of it that door's not been used for centuries.'

Davina followed him back to the kitchen without troubling to reply. At least someone had cleaned out the enormous grate, she saw with great relief. But whoever the solicitor had sent to clear up had done the bare minimum. Crockery was piled haphazardly on the dusty Welsh dresser and when Davina investigated the sink unit, the only concession to modern living in the room, packets of old detergent and cleaning utensils fell out, along with pans which looked as if their last scrub had been of the hit-or-miss variety.

She thrust them back and straightened to find Rex watching with an unfathomable expression in his hooded eyes which put her on her guard. Instead of the reproaches she had intended making to him for being persuaded to buy such a neglected property she asked simply, 'Wouldn't it be a good idea to unload the Land Rover before dark? If you'll show me how that portable stove of yours works I'll soon have a meal on the table. But perhaps you'd better turn on the electricity first. It must be off at the mains,' she added, flicking the switch up and down without results.

'We'll have to make do with candles and lamps until I can get the generator going,' came Rex's suspiciously innocent

53

reply, then as Davina's brown eyes widened in amazement he added, 'They aren't on the mains up here, I fear. They make their own electricity, but I shall have to fix the dynamo first.'

It was by now patently obvious to Davina that for reasons of his own Rex had deliberately kept her in ignorance of the true state of the farmhouse, but she determined to conceal the dismay beginning to creep over her. After all, it wasn't as if she had always been accustomed to every convenience. Until five years ago their cottage in Wales had sported a smaller edition of the monstrous range on the other side of the room. She smiled as she recalled her mother's endeavours to get it removed.

There was little chance of that happening here, Davina thought as Rex went away to begin unloading. She would just have to learn to live with it. A little more exploration revealed a big walk-in larder with a Calor gas refrigerator, and another door led into a bathroom.

At least there wasn't outdoor sanitation to add to the drawbacks facing her, she thought with relief as she stripped off her raincoat and gingerly hung it on a rusting hook behind the kitchen door. Removing the newspapers from the table she piled them into the empty grate and ten minutes later, sleeves rolled up, was busily scrubbing the kitchen table and the draining board.

The kettle was singing on the small portable Calor gas stove ready for rinsing, and its purchase had been no guard against a possible contingency. Before they started out, Rex must have been well aware of what awaited them at journey's end, for he had not needed to go and investigate to tell her about the electricity supply. Just what was he up to? Davina wondered, as she poured the boiling water into her bucket and began finishing off the table top.

A camp bed under each arm, Rex stopped beside her. 'Seeing you now, who would believe only a few days ago you were queening it in a mansion in Switzerland?' he remarked as she gave a last wipe to the table. She stared as he put down one bed and carried the other through to the hall, a frown between her clear eyes. So that was what he thought! That she liked pretending she had been born with a silver spoon in her mouth. There had been no mistaking the hint of malice in his deep drawl and she could not help wondering what she had done to incur such disapproval.

But there was no time to try and analyse Rex's strange behaviour if they were to eat this evening. The household pottery and pans were so obviously, in their present state, unfit for use, so Davina opened the trunk and got out her own.

That was one thing Rex had overlooked, she thought with satisfaction as she found a pretty tablecloth and set one end of the table with her rose-patterned crockery. She slapped lamb chops, sausages, tomatoes and mushrooms into her nonstick frying pan and set them to cook on the small portable stove. Uncovering a large crusty loaf, butter, cheese and a bag of apples in the carton of food Rex had collected at the village shop, she added them to the table. The room was soon filled by the appetising aroma coming from the frying pan, and after making a strong brew of tea, Davina went outside to tell Rex the meal was ready.

But if she expected some appreciation of the speed with which she had set to work then she was to be disappointed. He came into the kitchen carrying a portable lamp in one hand and a packet of candles in the other and began to wash his hands at the sink in silence.

As she placed a loaded plate at his place Davina's voice was acid. 'Do you think that will be enough?'

Rex sat down, took a look at his portion and replied, 'I could manage a couple of eggs as well,' as he cut into the loaf and began to eat.

Davina cracked eggs into the hot fat and bit back the words hovering on her lips. When they were cooked she walked over to slide them on to Rex's plate, then took her own place in silence. Rex apparently was not one to waste words and let food get cold, and until his plate was empty he did not speak.

During the meal it had darkened considerably and rain had begun to lash against the window. 'Good thing the unloading is finished,' he remarked, and got up to light the lamp and place it at the other end of the table. When he returned to his place, a huge shadow was cast on the wall behind him, and the thought it conjured up made Davina give an involuntary smile.

'What's so amusing?' Rex enquired as he helped himself to a large portion of cheese.

Davina flushed, for he would undoubtedly think her explanation ridiculous. 'This place for a start,' she gestured to the big shadowy room. Then as Rex waited, brows raised quizzically, she plunged impulsively on. 'When we arrived I thought the place looked like an illustration to *Wuthering Heights*, but it reminds me now of being taken by my father to see *Maria Marten*.'

'Who was she? Some relation?'

'No, the heroine in a Victorian melodrama. It was performed one Christmas by the Llantarwyn Amateur Dramatic Society back home. The villain, Sir Jasper, has the heroine in his power in a lonely barn.'

Rex helped himself to another piece of bread. 'And did he seduce her?'

Davina looked thoughtful. 'Do you know, I can't remember. Usually in those kind of plays the honest hero rides up at the eleventh hour and rescues the heroine.'

'But supposing he didn't arrive in time, or even if there was no hero at all?'

There was that odd note again, Davina noticed, and she looked curiously at the man sitting at the head of the table. Authors were supposed to have fertile imaginations, but the thrill of fear which coarsed through her was absurd. She said slowly, 'But he usually did—arrive in time,' then as something in Rex's smile stung she went on impulsively, 'and of course there's always a hero. What would be the point of a play without?'

'You have me there,' Rex said, then he changed the subject. 'You're not eating. Have some of this excellent cheese and another cup of tea. I'll join you,' he finished as picking up the teapot he refilled their cups.

It seemed less trouble to do as he said than to argue and she cut a minute corner of cheese and began to eat. Rex got out his makings and began to roll a cigarette, holding it up to ask, 'You don't object?'

'Not at all.' Davina laid down her knife with relief. The odd conversation had taken away her appetite and she had finished her meal with difficulty, glad when the plate was empty. While Rex smoked, she sat stirring her tea until he broke into her jumbled thoughts by stubbing out his cigarette and rising to push his chair under the table.

'While you wash and clear away, I'll run the Land Rover into the barn, then come and make up our bunks. I was going to suggest a walk before we turned in, but this rain's not going to stop before morning. We've both had a long day and as you've an early breakfast to prepare in the morning to which I'm sure you're not accustomed, I suggest we both turn in.'

It was a long time since Davina had been told in such uncompromising tones to go to bed that she began to feel the anger bubble inside as she mutinously got up to put water on to wash up. What right had Rex to order her about as if she were a child? She hadn't much cared for his last remark either. He sounded as if he thought her incapable of early rising. Well, she'd show him she wasn't prepared to knuckle under every time he acted like Captain Bligh of the *Bounty*.

But it was easier said than done. Since Rex was planning to sleep in the kitchen until the upper rooms were fit for occupation she could hardly insist on remaining in the room while he got ready for bed. She could of course say she wasn't sleepy, but he was capable of calling her bluff by the simple means of turning out the lamp or even removing her bodily to the dining room where he was busy erecting her camp bed.

She hid her resentment, however, behind a calm smile and when he returned to the kitchen and began on his own sleeping equipment, Davina with a 'goodnight, then' beat a retreat, hoping that her tone of voice did not reveal the inner anger at his peremptory orders. There was a soft sleeping bag on the camp bed with a spotless pillow at the head, and a lighted candle standing on a saucer together with matches on a small table.

He'd been thoughtful, Davina had to admit, but after she had undressed and blown out the light it was a long time before sleep claimed her. The mustiness of a long closed up room, the hardness of the unaccustomed bed together with her bewildered conjectures at Rex's strange manner, all combined to toss her restlessly from side to side. But youth and the conclusion that she would have to make the best of things finally calmed her and she fell asleep, stirring only when the alarm sounded in her ear.

CHAPTER FOUR

THOUGH she had set the alarm for six-fifteen and got up and dressed quickly, Davina found that Rex had beaten her to it. Dressed and freshly shaved, he had folded away his bedding and was on the point of making tea when she entered the kitchen.

'I've put a can of hot water in the bathroom. This will be ready by the time you're washed.'

No 'good morning.' No 'hope you slept well.' Catrin had certainly got it wrong, Davina decided as she went away to have a brief, hurried wash and brush her teeth. Of course, *she* should have been up to provide hot water and tea for Rex, not the other way around, she had to admit honestly. Swiftly she set about preparations for breakfast, cutting thick rashers off the quarter of bacon and setting the table. There was a hint of triumph in her voice when in a matter of minutes she was able to say, 'Your breakfast is ready,' as she put the heaped plate in front of Rex's place and slipped into a chair to sip her tea and butter a slice of bread.

His voice made her look up, a startled expression in her eyes. 'Is that,' a long forefinger pointed contemptuously at her plate, 'all you intend having?'

Davina's ready sense of humour bubbled to the surface at the disbelief in his voice. 'It's more than I usually have,' she answered provocatively, to which she got a swift reply.

'I think you'll find up here a bird's breakfast isn't going to carry you through the morning. You're let off today. I've an appointment with a sheep breeder the other side of Alston and neither time nor inclination for an argument. However, tomorrow you eat a proper breakfast, my girl. Don't let me see you making do with tea and bread and butter again,' and as if that settled the matter, Rex began to eat.

Not a good start, Davina thought as she reached for the

58

marmalade and peeped at him through her lashes. But he seemed quite insensible to her or the possibility of having bruised her feelings as he cleared his plate, and drained his cup.

As he held it out for replenishment he said slowly, 'I've no idea how long I'll be or when I'll get back, so don't wait lunch. That is if you intend having any,' he added sardonically.

'Oh, I always stop for a bite of something midday,' Davina answered airily, then added, 'Does that mean you won't have time to get the electricity going this morning?' hoping he did not discern dismay in her voice.

'Afraid not. The stock's more important. If I'm to have my ewes lambing by January, there's no time to be lost. We shall have to manage as best we can for the time being. I promise, though, I'll get down to looking into it the first free moment,' Rex ended, and encouraged by the kindlier note in his voice Davina asked,

'Well, please could you get a Calor gas cylinder for the fridge as you go through Alston. I would like to get that going for hygienic reasons. The larder's full of flies already.'

'Make a list. I'm sure you feel convinced there are several other indispensable items I've forgotten.' There was resignation in Rex's tone. Hiding a smile, Davina found pencil and paper. To the Calor gas she added a sizeable list of household materials as well as a new bucket and floorcloth. Might as well be hanged for a sheep as a lamb, she thought as she handed it over.

Rex had put on a jacket and as she handed him the paper he gave her a keen glance. Beyond a mocking smile as he saw the length of the list, however, he did nothing more than push it into his pocket and with a brief 'See you later, then,' opened the door leaving Davina listening to his departing footsteps.

When the engine of the Land Rover had died away, Davina poured herself another cup of tea and sat looking gloomily around the vast kitchen. No chance of getting down to her writing at least until this was more habitable. And for this hot water, and plenty of it, was a must. Suddenly coming to a decision, she got up, removed a couple of sheets of newspaper from the grate, and pushing them as far up the chimney as she could reach, set them alight.

They disappeared with a satisfying roar which told Davina that at least there were no birds' nests stuffed into the flue, and going outside she started exploring the possibility of getting a fire going. The first door she opened revealed a positive Aladdin's cave. Not only was there coal in plenty, but logs stacked in tidy rows and even a box of neatly chopped firewood stood against the wall. Filling a coal hod, Davina gathered up a bundle of kindling and made her way back to the farm kitchen.

Half an hour later the fire was well alight and she had the satisfaction of seeing the flames roaring under the back boiler. Changing into her oldest jeans, Davina tied a head scarf over her hair and started in on the mammoth task of removing the dirt of years from the old kitchen.

By five o'clock it was hardly recognisable as the unwelcoming room which had looked so depressing on their arrival. The kitchen range seemed almost to be smiling after a vigorous blackleading, because she had discovered that the old tins were not entirely unusable. The fire glowed cosily and from the oven appetising smells emerged as a casserole bubbled slowly for the evening meal. The dark Victorian furniture shone with polish and on the dresser, clean china twinkled, drawing the eye.

Glancing from the gleaming terracotta quarry-tiled floor to the clean curtains hanging at the window, Davina stretched wearily and gave a sigh of pleasure. As soon as the vegetables were ready and the table laid for supper, she reckoned she had earned a break. Fifteen minutes later, clad only in a dressing gown, she was running water into the bath and she relaxed in the perfumed water, suddenly aware of an ache in muscles she hadn't used so much for months.

Judging from the modern sanitary fittings, the bathroom had not long been installed. She had soaped, rinsed and dried when the sound of a vehicle approaching reached her ears. With her dressing gown firmly belted at the waist Davina emerged, hair in damp curls, just as Rex got the full impact of her day's work.

For a moment he was off guard. His usual inscrutable expression gave way to a look of astonishment as the transformation of the kitchen met his eyes. As he turned to speak, Davina with triumphant mischief in her smile asked, tongue in cheek, 'Like a bath before supper? There's tons of hot water if you do.'

But her own eyes were the first to drop. Why did he always get under her guard? With one glance he had made her aware that he knew she had nothing under the frilly dressing gown, and his, 'Thanks. That's just what I need,' as he ripped off his tie was done intentionally, Davina felt certain, to remind her that all his changes of clothes were in the suitcases beside the dresser.

She lost no time in escaping, but as she slowly dressed and made up her face she knew for a fact that Rex had not expected her to have achieved so much during his absence. When she heard water running in the bathroom she took the opportunity to return to the kitchen and put the vegetables on to boil before checking her list against the shopping Rex had piled on one end of the long table.

She was putting the last tidily away when he returned wearing a cream silk shirt and well tailored brown slacks and looking unbelievably handsome. Davina dragged her eyes away from the brown face and those all-seeing eyes as he asked, 'Is there time before supper for me to fix the fridge?' and at her nod pushed open the pantry door to say, 'I see no flies. Been having a blitz on them too?'

Feeling lightheaded, Davina laughed and said, 'As I think you say Down Under, too right. They're my pet aversion.'

'Really!' There was amused disbelief in his voice. 'An aversion, yes. Hardly your pet one.'

Outsmarted again, Davina thought, and bit her lip. Her face felt hot as she said airily, 'Well, I don't like them. The sooner they can't get at our fresh food the better. Is the fridge okay?'

Rex emerged wiping his hands. 'Working like a dream. I've put the bacon, butter, cheese and milk away. What's for supper? Something smells real dinkum,' then more slowly and with a smile curling his mouth he added, 'as we'd say Down Under.'

This time Davina's flush could not be concealed. It surged

61

from the low neck of her tee-shirt until it met her hairline, and the fact that Rex was watching with sardonic satisfaction did nothing to help her regain her usual equilibrium. As if he suddenly felt he had hassled her quite enough for one evening, Rex suddenly glanced round the room, returned his gaze to her face and said softly, 'You've not been letting the grass grow under your feet. The place looks great.'

'Thanks.' Davina's response came out jerkily as she turned to take out the casserole, glad to have an excuse to hide her face for a few moments.

'Can I help?' His question caused her to look up in surprise as she placed the dish on the table. He was smiling, for once without the unpleasant curl to his lips, and Davina, ever ready to meet an olive branch half way, smiled back shyly as she said, 'You could get the cheese while I drain the veg. I'm afraid I didn't have time to make a proper dessert.'

Rex turned on his heel to do her bidding, remarking as he put the cheese dish on to the table, 'It's something of a mystery how you contrived to prepare a hot meal and get all the cleaning done, so don't apologise. Fruit and cheese will do me. Now, don't you want to know how I spent my day?'

During supper he talked non-stop about the two rams which would be delivered the following day and about the different strains of ewes he had arranged to purchase for his breeding stock and which would be coming within a day or two. This was a different man from the silent, taciturn companion of yesterday and Davina had become her usual carefree self by the time the table was cleared and the teacups filled.

She watched his busy fingers rolling a cigarette, unaccountably relieved that the cold, unfriendly atmosphere was no more. Rex was as he had been when on his visit to her grandmother's house—friendly, casually relaxed in his manner towards her and, something she had not consciously comprehended in that busy household, abounding with a stark virility that made her suddenly aware of hidden needs. It accounted, Davina admitted to herself, for the feeling of emptiness when he had left for Italy so unexpectedly, and she stirred her tea telling herself not to be a romantic fool.

She grabbed at the first thing that came into her head to keep the conversation going. 'I know absolutely nothing about sheep. You'll have to educate me.'

Rex looked at her through the smoke from his cigarette and Davina saw a gleam of amusement come and go in the hard eyes watching her. 'What can they teach in English schools? Do you mean to tell me you've never heard of foot rot, liver fluke, flushing or twin lamb disease? Shame on you, but I daresay you're a quick learner.'

'I didn't realise I was expected to help with the sheep,' Davina began, then the blood came into her face yet again as Rex threw back his head and gave a great shout of laughter.

'Sorry, that wasn't fair,' he apologised, then promptly spoiled it by adding, 'but you rise beautifully. I simply couldn't resist the temptation. No, you'll have plenty to do keeping this place clean even if we leave some of the rooms closed. I've heard of a old shepherd who might be willing to come up part-time and give me a hand, so you won't have to play Bo-peep. Now, what about the dishes? You look tired, and no wonder, so I'll give you a hand with them.'

They cleared and washed up in a companionable silence and until bedtime played a hand or two of cards. After she had yawned twice in quick succession, Rex gathered up the pack and said, 'Off to bed. I must be up to get a couple of pens ready for the rams in the morning and you're half asleep already. I'll see to the fire,' and he pushed her out of the room as he spoke.

As her eyelids began to close, Davina promised herself that tomorrow she'd make a start on the neglected bedrooms. She was trying to remember which had looked the least forbidding when sleep claimed her, and tonight not even the whistle of the wind round the house nor the ghostly hoot of an owl disturbed her slumbers.

She was in the kitchen on the dot of six-thirty the following morning, but whistling from the bathroom and the neatly stacked bedding in one corner of the room informed her that once again Rex had beaten her. There were still some smouldering embers in the big fire grate and it took her only a few minutes to have the fire glowing again.

By the time Rex came out of the bathroom, the kettle was

whistling and an appetising smell of cooking bacon filled the room. 'By jove, that makes me feel hungry! I'll keep my eye on it for you if you'd like a wash.'

When Davina came back, Rex was putting rashers and eggs on to two plates and the teapot stood under a woollen cosy which she had unearthed the previous day. 'No argument, now. Sit down and tuck in. I daresay coffee and toast are a good enough breakfast if you're living in London where you're sitting most of the day, but you can't do a hard day's manual work on it. I'd bet my last dollar you didn't stop for much lunch yesterday either. I don't want to be accused by your family of letting you dwindle to a shadow, so get that eaten,' he ended as he sat down and began his own breakfast.

Davina wanted to tell him she had stopped for lunch the day before and he misjudged her, but a glance at his face made her hesitate. Meekly she picked up her knife and fork and began to eat, feeling slightly bemused by the thrill of pleasure his masterful attitude had given her. Through her lashes, she stole a glance at his intent face and instantly Rex turned his attention from his plate to her face.

'Well? Going to admit you're hungry after all and enjoying every mouthful? Or are you planning your revenge?'

'Yes, I'm enjoying it. I can't remember when I last ate a cooked breakfast, and this tastes really good.' She stopped for an instant before saying, 'May I ask you a question?'

Rex, who had resumed his meal, looked up and Davina noticed that his hair, still damp from his morning wash, curled over his ears and down the strong brown neck. 'Ask away. I don't promise to answer, however.'

Davina's face wore a suspiciously innocent expression. 'I merely wondered whether you'd have time this morning to get the electricity working,' then she laughed outright as Rex's face assumed a grim expression.

'Trust a woman! How right I was. You were planning your next line of attack.'

'You haven't a great respect for my sex, it seems to me,' Davina said thoughtfully as she scraped up the last bit of egg. Rex was buttering a slice of bread and as she waited for his reply, her eyes were drawn to the square capable hands.

As she automatically reached out and passed him the marmalade, Rex looked up to meet her eyes and ignoring her last remark drawled, 'By the way, I'll only be in the barn this morning, so if you'll give me a shout about eleven I'll come in for morning tea.'

So he wasn't to be drawn on the subject of women, Davina thought as she watched him finish his breakfast and roll a cigarette. Some girl must have caused this bitterness which peeped out now and then and revealed a distortion in his sense of proportion. Yet he had never turned the edge of his caustic tongue on Catrin, Davina recalled. Unlike her sister she obviously did not bring out the best in Rex Fitzpaine.

Perhaps it's simply that I'm not his type, she thought as she climbed the dusty staircase, then flushed as the thought, 'but he could be mine,' popped unbidden into her mind. She'd have to beware of losing *her* sense of proportion where this sometimes unapproachable Australian was concerned, not to mention her heart, she decided, as she firmly dismissed these uncomfortable thoughts and got on with the task in hand.

Three of the bedrooms on the upper floor were more or less the same size, but the fourth was decidedly smaller and judging by the furniture and oddments stacked haphazardly in it had simply been a lumber room. There would be more unwanted pieces to add, Davina thought grimly as she looked around the other three rooms. She ruled out the north-facing bedroom as being too dark and cold and concentrated her energies on the other two. One glance showed her the beds were useless. Stained mattresses, the flock escaping in places, lay over rusting springs. She removed them, together with the mats and rotting curtains, into the lumber room and by the time elevenses were coming up, the two rooms she had selected were as clean as soap, hot water and elbow grease could make them.

Neverthless, there was something like defeat on Davina's face as she went downstairs to put the kettle on. She found Rex hard at work in one of the barns and the disappointment vanished as she looked around with interest.

'I honestly believe the late owner of Nineveh looked after the outhouses better than he did the farmhouse itself,' Davina declared, having noticed recently whitewashed walls and no sign of the neglect so evident in the house.

'You're probably right,' Rex answered as with his hand at her elbow he walked back with her across the cobbled yard. 'I'm given to understand that after his wife's death, when not attending his sheep he was always in the saloon bar of the Shepherd and Crook in Camshaw.'

He accepted the cup of tea Davina poured and selected a biscuit. 'Poor man,' she said softly, then almost without a pause, 'Did you have time to look at the electricity generator?'

'Women never give up, do they?' Rex replied with grim resignation in his voice. 'I not only looked, I fixed. Try for yourself if you don't believe me,' and he nodded to the switch beside the doorway.

Davina flicked it down and instantly the bulb over the kitchen table lighted up. In impulsive gratitude she quite forgot that with this man it might be wiser to check her natural ebullience and giving him a swift hug said, 'Oh, you doll! Now I shan't have to crawl into bed tonight convinced there are all sorts of creepie-crawlies in that beastly dining room.'

As she sat down to take up her own teacup she was unaware of the gleam in Rex's eyes, but there was no mistaking the note of sardonic amusement as he asked, 'Are you always so lavish with thanks? If getting the electricity going winds you up, what will be my reward for ordering some items out of this catalogue?' and sauntering over to his bedding, he abstracted a bulky volume and laid it on the table.

Davina turned the pages slowly, looking with interest at coloured illustrations of all kinds of household articles. 'I could see those beds are unusable,' Rex said, and the devilry had vanished from his smooth voice, Davina was relieved to notice. 'We can't sleep on camp beds indefinitely, so pick out what you fancy and when the pens are finished I'll run down to the village and phone an order through to the shop— bedding and stuff as well. The rams aren't due to be delivered until this afternoon, so I'll have time.'

When he returned some time later, Davina had a list neatly filled out with sizes and colours. She had chosen autumn shades for Rex's bedroom, blue and green for her own. As he picked up the list and ran his eye down it she asked tentatively, 'Would you mind if I put a coat of paint on the bedrooms first? I've given them a good clean, but they're pretty dreary. I shouldn't think they've been redecorated for years.'

Rex's answer was to stride to the hall door and in a few minutes Davina could hear his footsteps overhead. He was soon back and she noticed once again the glint she had surprised in his eyes when he returned the evening before to find she had transformed the kitchen. It was not, however, apparent in his voice, which held only scepticism as he asked, 'Do you really want to tackle painting those rooms?' and at her nod he said slowly, 'I wouldn't have categorized you as the little homemaker, but if that's what you want, it's okay by me.'

There was so little encouragement in his voice that Davina held on to a rising temper with difficulty. Her voice was stiff as she said, 'Perhaps you feel for six months it's hardly worth going to so much expense. Forget I suggested it,' to which Rex said softly, 'Up on your high horse again? You surprise me. You don't give the impression of being thin-skinned,' which made Davina's eyes fly to his face.

It told her nothing, however, and she looked quickly away from that hard penetrating stare. 'If you're willing to do the work by all means let's cover that ghastly green paint and putty-coloured wallpaper. I think I saw the village shop sold paint. Any particular colours in mind?'

'No ... I thought ... could I come with you and see what they have?' Davina stammered out, surprised to notice an almost pleading note in her reply. Accustomed as she was to her fellow students' eagerness to offer assistance or simply do her bidding, she had seldom had to even ask a favour. But Rex was a different kettle of fish from Mike and her other friends. It would be difficult to imagine him going out of his way to do casual favours for any woman, an educated hunch which his answer endorsed.

'Come if you wish, but I've no time to hang around. Be ready by the time I've backed the old Land Rover out,' and picking up his jacket and the list Rex was gone.

Flying to the dining room, Davina dashed a comb through her hair and slipped into a thin waterproof which would, she hoped, hide the fact that her jeans and shirt bore evidence of her morning's work. She ran outside to find Rex at the wheel impatiently revving the engine, and he had the vehicle moving almost before her door was closed.

When they reached the first gate Davina was out and had it open before Rex could so much as turn his head, for his astringent remark on the duties of a passenger on their arrival here had flicked her on the raw. He stopped only to let her out at the village store when they reached Camshaw before driving on to pull up beside the telephone kiosk further along the village street.

There were several people in the large village shop when Davina pushed open the door and wandered to the corner where tins of paint jostled for space with detergents and toiletries. She hid a smile as she became aware of the curious glances being cast in her direction, for she was well used to the speculation any stranger aroused in a village community.

She waited for the first direct question, and it was not long in coming. Ignoring the prior claims of the other customers, the owner of the store appeared at her elbow, smiled and asked, 'Can I help? Is it paint you're wanting, Miss . . .' and he waited with unshakable confidence for Davina to fill the gap.

She gave an inward sigh of resignation and smiled back. 'Williams. And yes, I do want paint. Is this all you've got, Mr . . .'

For a moment the storekeeper looked taken aback, not used to having his own tactics turned against him. 'Berwick's the name, Miss Williams. Yes, I'm afraid we only keep the white, but I can order colours if you like. Take about a week to get here.'

Well aware that the other occupants of the shop were avidly listening to every word, Davina said, 'That's too long. I guess the white will have to do. Two large tins of the emulsion and one of gloss paint—oh, and a roller and some brushes, please.'

Her purchases were being carefully wrapped when Rex strode into the shop and joined her at the counter. 'Got what you want?' he asked as he took out his wallet.

The tying up of the parcel was halted for a moment as Mr

Berwick said, 'Morning, Mr Fitzpaine. I didn't know the young lady was with you.'

'We're going to do a bit of decorating at Nineveh,' Rex replied as he threw some notes on the counter. 'My sister felt she couldn't live with olive green paint. Oh, didn't she introduce herself?' he asked in apparent surprise as Mr Berwick looked too stunned to reply. 'This is my stepsister, Miss Williams. She's come to keep house for me for a while.'

All Davina's amusement at the unconcealed curiosity of the occupants of the store vanished as she listened to Rex's glib lie and she opened her mouth to refute his introduction just as a sharp pinch on her upper arm warned her to hold her tongue.

Her soft lips closed into a tight little line as Rex collected his change, picked up the parcel and led the way outside. As soon as they were seated in the Land Rover, however, she turned to her companion and demanded, 'What was the point of that whopping lie back there? I know you're a long way from home, but I'm not, and I haven't got a brother. Not even a stepbrother,' she finished, her eyes flashing fire.

'Cool down! I should have thought the object of the exercise was self-evident. Once it became known that you and I were not related, you know as well as I do what suspicious natures most country folk have, and they'd never have swallowed the housekeeper bit. No one would give a damn in Sydney or London what we were up to, but you tell me you come from a small village, and I know just what would be said over the galah session where I come from,' Rex's voice held amused irony. 'With a pretty little thing like you under my roof the neighbourhood tabbies would have the skin off my back before you could say Captain Cook.'

'Whose reputation were you protecting, then, yours or mine?' Davina enquired tartly.

'Both!' Rex's retort was brief and to the point. 'I could see everyone's ears flapping as soon as I put my foot inside the shop, and I'll wager anything you like by this time our supposed relationship is all round Camshaw.'

Remembering the gossip in her home village, Davina did not doubt his words for an instant. Just the same, the thought of sailing under false colours gave her an unpleasant feeling. She had always been a bad liar and she saw trouble ahead as a result of Rex's efforts to scotch a scandal. Despite her cousin's words of warning, the possible construction that people might put upon her keeping house for a man as attractive as Rex Fitzpaine had simply gone over her head. How short-sighted could a girl be, Davina thought, how dim-witted?

Either the lie he had been called upon to tell or her own reactions had sent Rex into another of his impenetrable moods. He drove in silence and at top speed back to the farm and as they got out, he handed Davina the parcel of paint and said stiffly, 'I'll be in for a meal in half an hour,' before striding off in the direction of the barn.

Davina burned with resentment, but she was wise enough to keep silent. Not that he had given her much chance to reply, she thought as swiftly she opened a tin of ham and prepared a salad. She had barely finished laying the table and making the inevitable tea when he came in, and taking her seat, she sat waiting for him to wash and join her at the table.

Picking up the carving knife and fork, he began to carve, asking in a perfectly affable voice, 'Hungry?'

No sense in letting him know how much his changeable moods chilled her, Davina thought, and looking up she smiled sweetly. 'Absolutely famished!'

Five minutes later, staring in something like dismay at her heaped plate, she wished she had been a little wiser, for Rex had served her as much as he had served himself. Wondering how she would get through it all, she noticed with resentment that Rex was tucking into his lunch with every evidence of enjoyment. Sleeves rolled above his elbows, he ate as if he hadn't a care in the world until, looking up, he caught her staring.

'Now what's biting you? You're looking at me as if it were feeding time in the zoo. Do none of your boy-friends have normal healthy appetites?'

Davina's long eyelashes flickered and she looked away, but Rex had no intention of letting her off without an answer.

'Cat got your tongue?'

Davina looked up, met the smile at the back of the hard eyes, and reluctantly smiled back. 'Sorry if I seemed rude. I was simply admiring your magnificent appetite.'

It was the best she could think of on the spur of the moment. Why did he always put her in the wrong so that she was forced to apologise?

'I've a big frame to fill, remember, and it needs stoking regularly from time to time. Tell me,' his voice dropped to a conspiratorial whisper as he leaned towards her, 'what's for supper?'

It was such a ludicrous remark from a man with a loaded plate in front of him that Davina let out an involuntary chuckle. She met the look in the hooded eyes and was unable to drag her own away. Something in his gaze made her stunningly aware of how breathtakingly attractive he was, from the top of his healthily shining hair down the strong brown throat to the powerful, muscular body.

She managed somehow to look away, for he had an uncanny habit of reading her thoughts. She could not have been quick enough, however, for as if conscious of the fact that she was with difficulty controlling an irresistible urge to touch him, Rex stretched out his long legs under the table until his feet encountered her own.

Quickly, Davina drew her feet back until they were under her chair, in no way reassured by Rex's soft laugh as he went on eating. She was gripped by a strange, hitherto unknown sensation of swimming in uncharted waters and for the remainder of the meal she did her best to keep her wayward thoughts under control and the conversation on strictly mundane lines.

There was wicked amusement plain to see on Rex's face as she asked about the rams which were to arrive that afternoon. Draining his tea, he pushed back his chair and got up.

'Why the sudden interest?' he asked as he took out his tobacco tin. He cocked a mocking eyebrow. 'I told you yesterday that wasn't going to be your province, that I'd a shepherd in mind. And here he is now,' he added as Davina heard a knock on the door.

Rex strode forward and threw it open to reveal an elderly man standing in the porch, a crossbred black and white dog

71

at his heels. He put a forefinger to his cap and said on a note of enquiry, 'Mr Fitzpaine?'

'Come in. You must be Mr Farr.' Rex stood back invitingly and with a 'stay' to his dog the stranger came in, smiling and removing his cap as he caught sight of Davina.

He could be anything between sixty-five and eighty, she decided, inviting him to have a cup of tea. His hair and beard quite white, he yet walked rigidly upright and his clear eyes and brown face revealed a life spent in the open air. Realising that the old shepherd and Rex would probably get on better without a third person, Davina collected the parcel of painting equipment and left them alone.

But once upstairs she did not start work immediately. The sensations she had experienced during lunch had to be taken out and examined. Nothing previously had prepared her for the upheaval she felt inside as a result of exposure to a man like Rex. If she were not to fall a victim to his dynamic and compelling masculinity, she would have to keep a strict watch on her emotions.

As she undid the parcel there was another facet of the whole business to be considered. She couldn't *afford* to get romantically involved at this stage in her career. It reminded her that so far she hadn't written one line since her arrival at Nineveh Farm, hadn't even unpacked her small portable typewriter from the depths of the trunk. There was a set determination on her face as she uncapped the paint and began putting a first coat of emulsion on the walls of what was to be Rex's bedroom.

Using a roller, it did not take long and she had just put the lid back on the tin when two vehicles pulled up in the yard below with a screech of brakes. Wiping her hands on a piece of rag, Davina ran down to see two bleating woolly shapes being firmly escorted into the barn by Mr Farr's black and white sheepdog, while Rex stroked the nose of a sturdy chestnut horse. Four men were busily unloading bales of hay and straw from the larger of the two lorries, and knowing Rex would expect her to have his favourite beverage on hand when the work was done, Davina turned back into the kitchen.

Only stopping to make sure the fire oven was hot enough,

72

she made a quick batch of scones and slid them in to cook while the kettle boiled. By the time Rex came in, the table held cups and saucers and·Davina was buttering the first of the hot scones, the tea brewing under a cosy.

'Clever girl!' Despite all her good intentions, these two simple words of praise made the colour run up under Davina's smooth skin and she was glad of the moments before the men trooped in to recover her composure. But the hand holding the teapot trembled slightly as she began to pour out, trying to conquer the indefinable weakness which came over her every time Rex smiled in precisely that intimate way.

It was almost as if he were determined to win her over, she thought as a steady tramp of feet announced the arrival of the men. In the flurry of finding out who took sugar and who didn't, Davina found the time to pull herself together and a compliment from the youngest man in the group on the lightness of the scones only made her smile cheekily at him and ask if 'they were as good as his mum made?'

By the time the teacups were emptied for the last time, not a crumb remained. With a, 'Thanks, miss,' they all trooped out, and as Davina cleared away she made up her mind that in future she was not going to let her susceptibility to Rex's undoubted magnetism get the better of her good sense. It wasn't the first time she'd met an attractive man. There had been one or two over the years to whom she had felt drawn, but never had she allowed her heart to rule her head. This time, she told herself, would be just like the others. She'd remain mistress of her fate, fancy free.

But as she was finishing the washing up, Rex returned to ask, 'Like to come and see the animals?' and she agreed without hesitation. In one of the big outbuildings, Rex had erected two adjoining pens for the stud rams and in a stall at the end stood the chestnut horse.

Davina could ride, but she wasn't particularly horse-minded and the rams were as yet an unknown quantity. One was black-faced with magnificent curling horns which he was tapping against the partition separating him from his companion. This one, hornless, with black and white face and legs, stood motionless on his freshly spread straw, a look of stolid resignation on his woolly face. Davina leaned over to tickle him between his ears, saying over her shoulder, 'It may be my imagination, but this one doesn't look too happy. I suppose that partition's safe?'

'Don't think much of my handiwork, then?' Rex asked mockingly, then as Davina glanced up, 'Of course it's safe. But if it were not, it wouldn't matter a cuss. Tapper here is merely trying to make friends.'

'Is that his name?'

'He hasn't got a name. Are you suggesting I christen them?' There was a note of wicked amusement in Rex's soft drawl and Davina straightened to meet his eyes.

'You're laughing at me,' she accused him sulkily, shaken by the look in his eyes as leaning nonchalantly on the top bar of the pen he gazed down at her from his impressive height.

'I was just imagining the look on my uncle's face if we attempted to put names to all our stock,' he said by way of explanation. 'But you're welcome to call these two what you like if that will make you happy.'

Feeling incredibly foolish, Davina attempted to dodge the issue, wishing that his nearness did not make her heartbeats quicken. 'Does your uncle live with you?'

'Rather say I live with him. He and my father were twins. When Dad died I was only ten and Uncle Lionel brought me up. Taught me all I know about running a station. I inherited Dad's share, so we're co-owners of the property and live in the one house.'

It was the nearest Rex had come to revealing anything about his family and it took Davina by surprise. Before she could reply, however, the sound of a car in the yard made Rex's head jerk up and with a 'Who the devil can this be?' he strode out of the barn.

Following on, Davina reached the door in time to see a figure emerge from the large, somewhat battered station wagon which stood in the cobbled yard. The man was about Rex's age or perhaps a little younger, Davina decided, as she caught sight of a thatch of silver-blond hair. He was wearing stained corduroy trousers, wellington boots and a torn cotton sweat shirt marked here and there with what looked remarkably like dried blood.

74

Advancing towards Rex, he held out his hand. 'Fitzpaine?' at Rex's nod he said, 'You left a message at my surgery. Name's Jim Thomas. What's the trouble?'

'None so far,' Rex answered, shaking the vet's hand. 'You must have received a wrong message. I simply left my name and said I'd like you to come and cast an eye over my ewes when they arrive on Monday. I'm afraid you've had a wasted journey.'

Jim Thomas's eyes were looking past Rex at Davina and he said slowly, 'I wouldn't say that. The village has been agog since we heard Nineveh had been sold at last. Do you and your sister know many people in the area?'

There was a very dry note in Rex's voice as he replied, 'No one, unless you count old Farr who will be shepherding for me,' and Davina felt a blush beginning as Jim Thomas walked over and shook her by the hand.

'Welcome to the district, then. We can do with a few new faces. And since you haven't friends in the district, how about coming over to my place Sunday evening? My sister is staying with me at the moment and I fear she finds the country a bit boring after London. Sunday I'm not on call, so I decided to throw a bit of a binge for her. The house is about a mile the other side of the village. You'll hear the dogs barking, so you can't miss it.'

Davina had got her feelings of guilt under control by the time he finished, but she gave Rex a reproachful glance. He'd started this 'sister' story and while it seemed he had done so with the best of intentions, she hated sailing under false colours. In any case, was it really necessary? People were so much more broadminded in this day and age.

But he obviously had no intention of setting the record straight. With a, 'Thanks, we'd like to,' he began to fix a time for the vet to call the following week and Davina, seeing they were for the moment too engrossed to notice, slipped away to get on with her household chores. During supper, she would have liked to challenge Rex's right to accept an invitation on her behalf without bothering to consult her wishes, but she had learned enough about him now to realise it would get her nowhere. He had an unhappy knack of getting the better of her in an argument.

After supper, she fetched her writing materials and putting them at the end of the long table began to draft out her ideas for a story. Rex had made himself comfortable in a chair beside the fire and was reading a farming journal—as if, Davina thought ruefully, they really were brother and sister. Or long-married husband and wife, her mind ran on, and the pen in her hand faltered. What could have put that idea in her head? He had, of course, she admitted to herself, and sighed for it had been unintentional. So far he had treated her with the utmost propriety. Not so much as the hint of a pass, she thought dolefully as she applied herself once more to the work in hand.

But as if he sensed her innermost thoughts, half an hour later Rex got to his feet and wandered round the table to look over her shoulder. When she turned her head, Davina found his eyes only inches away.

'You've done enough for one evening. Bed for you, my girl.' There was kindness in the softly drawled order and something more in the usually hard eyes. They were smiling beguilingly into her own and Davina drew in her breath as he straightened.

'I'll make the tea. Fancy a cup?'

Her hands trembling, Davina gathered her papers together, willing her voice to remain calm. 'Not tonight. See you in the morning,' and she made her escape. She was afraid to admit even to herself what was happening to her. Infuriating, arrogant, tyrannical even at times—yes, Rex Fitzpaine was all of those. He was also irresistibly attractive in large doses.

But the following morning when she asked innocently, 'What will you want with a horse?' Rex's voice held only impatience as he snapped, 'What most horsemen want—to ride, of course. I've never worked a dog, so I shall need a horse to muster. Or did you think I could drive the Land Rover over hill pastures if one of the flock goes missing?'

What was it with him? Davina wondered as she blinked in surprise. He could be all sweetness one minute, barely polite to her the next. She murmured a barely intelligible excuse which made Rex smile down at her grimly. 'I told you you'd a lot to learn,' was his parting shot as he departed, and ten minutes later Davina saw him ride up the track behind the farm where the ground rose steeply.

It was a warm day, and she left the doors open before she went upstairs to get on with the painting. When she came down again to prepare lunch a small black cat was curled up in front of the fire.

It rose and began to purr as she asked it, 'Now where have you come from?' Glass green eyes surveyed her approvingly as she informed it, 'Now I like cats and don't mind a bit that you've made yourself so much at home, but I doubt whether the lord and master will agree.'

Her supposition turned out to be only too correct. When Rex came in he spotted the intruder immediately and his order was terse and to the point—'Don't feed that thing, otherwise we'll be saddled with it for good,' as he went through to wash.

When the bathroom door closed behind him, Davina's eyes began to smoulder with anger. Insufferable man! If she had deliberately brought the cat in herself he couldn't have been more intolerant. She replied in monosyllables to his efforts at conversation during lunch until Rex in long-suffering tones asked, 'Now what's eating you?'

Davina's brown eyes flashed sparks. 'As if you didn't know! What harm can one small cat do to you?'

'None that I know of, but he must belong to someone and has probably been missed by now. As for doing me harm, the boot's rather on the other foot. Have you considered what will happen to the poor animal when we leave here?'

A conscience-stricken look replaced the anger in Davina's eyes. 'I never thought of that.' She glanced over to where the little cat was busily washing itself. 'Do you really think he belongs to someone and isn't just a stray?'

'Use your head. Does he look like a stray?' Rex asked sarcastically, and Davina had no answer—the sleek, well-fed look on the cat's face was answer enough. 'I shall be going down to the local this evening so I'll ask around,' Rex told her. 'Meantime, put him out. He might go home.'

The wind had freshened and the cat stood looking forlorn when Davina carried him outside with a, 'Well, I warned you, Puss. You'll have to go, I'm afraid.' Even the approving, 'I'm glad to see you took my advice,' from Rex did not entirely ease her conscience, for by supper time it had begun to rain. When he went out with a casual, 'Don't wait up,' thrown over his shoulder, Davina crept out and searched the yard, but the cat was nowhere to be seen. Pushing disappointment that Rex had not thought fit to ask her to join him to the back of her mind, she took the small portable typewriter out of her trunk and began a rough outline of her short story from last night's notes.

She worked doggedly on for more than three hours, then spun out more time by taking a leisurely bath. But she had been in bed some time before sounds in the kitchen warned her of Rex's return and she finally fell asleep wondering where he could have been until this late hour.

She got up next morning determined to ask no questions, thereby risking one of Rex's quelling replies. But her curiosity was to be satisfied none the less. She had finished decorating the bedrooms during the morning and had begun preparing the midday meal when she noticed the coal bucket was empty. Coming out of the shed into the yard, a loaded bucket in one hand and carrying an armful of logs, Davina was surprised to see a red two-seater sports car approaching at speed and stood rooted to the spot as it stopped with a shriek of brakes almost a yard away and a tall blonde stepped out from behind the wheel.

'Rex anywhere about?'

Davina, taking in the long curling hair, sea green eyes and superbly tailored slack suit, found her tongue curling into knots. There was more than a hint of impatience on the madonna-like features of the unexpected visitor as she said, 'I imagine you must be Davina. Rex spoke about you when Jim brought him up to the house last night. I'm Jim's sister, by the way, Adele Wickham.'

Supremely aware of looking like the poor relation in paint-stained jeans with hands covered in coal dust, Davina was about to reply when both girls heard the clip-clop of hooves, and Rex appeared on the moorland track. Adele, ignoring Davina, walked swiftly forward and was at his stirrup by the time the chestnut horse reached the farm yard.

Her greeting was very different from that which she had accorded Davina. A hand reached up to fondle his leg and, head tilted, the blonde girl invited, 'I'm at a loose end. Take me to lunch?'

Rex looked down, but his hooded lids hid from Davina what he was thinking. For a second he sat motionless, then leaning, he detached the hand caressing his knee, bowed to kiss it and as Adele's lips curled with satisfaction he was out of the saddle and tying the horse to the fence.

Davina's lips were also curling, but in derision as she watched the touching scene, and glancing across the yard, Rex caught the look of disgust she had no time to hide. He gave a small smile before turning to answer the blatant invitation.

'Sorry, I'm a working man. Simply can't spare the time during the day.' Then as Adele's lips parted he went on, 'I see you and Davina have got acquainted. Let me see, we're invited to a party in your honour on Sunday. Isn't that right?'

It was obvious that Adele Wickham was not used to having her invitations so summarily turned down. She said sulkily, 'Yes, Jim's got the idea that a country get-together is my idea of a good time. He forgets I'm used now to something more exciting than one of his housekeeper's hotpots washed down with red plonk. But I thought we'd get acquainted before then. Just you and I,' she added, giving Davina a disparaging glance. 'If I know Jim, he'll have invited all his old school chums and will expect me to do the pretty with all of them.'

Rex gave her one of his disarming smiles. 'I'm sure it won't be impossible to cut you out of the mob. After all, I'm used to that.' He took her arm and turned her towards the red sports car. 'Sunday will give me ...' he paused as if by accident ... 'us, something to look forward to.'

Adele was all smiles again. She slid into the driving seat and held out her hand again, giving a theatrical sigh. 'Sunday it is, then. Rex ...' she stopped and looked up seductively, 'it will seem a lifetime.'

Trying to hide her laughter, Davina turned and hurried indoors. As she made up the fire, the car started up and then she heard it disappearing into the distance. There was the sound of hooves as Rex took the horse back to its stall and then silence until he suddenly appeared in the kitchen doorway.

Davina looked up from the sink. 'Sorry nothing's ready, but I've been finishing the painting. I'll have your meal on the table in ten minutes.'

He pulled out a chair and began rolling a cigarette. 'I'm in no hurry,' and as Davina's eyes widened he seemed to guess where her mind had wandered, for with a smile curling up one corner of his firm lips he asked, 'What did you think of her?'

'I've rarely seen a lovelier girl, and her clothes...! I suspect Hardy Amies at least.'

'That wasn't what I asked you.' Rex put his cigarette into his mouth and applied a match.

'We only exchanged a couple of sentences before you arrived. It would be unfair to make a snap judgment,' Davina replied hastily, and went to fetch what she needed from the walk-in larder before her unruly tongue ran away with her.

Half way through their meal, she suddenly became aware that Rex was looking at her with undoubted amusement in his keen eyes and she gave him a questioning glance.

'Is it the latest fashion to go around with white spots all over your face,' he asked, 'or merely just your personal preference?'

Davina put a hand up and felt the rough places where paint must have splashed down when she was painting the bedroom ceilings. 'Oh, bother! I never thought to look in a mirror.' Her eyes widened in horror. 'What must that girl-friend of yours have thought?'

'The description doesn't fit. I only met her for the first time last night,' Rex drawled, then his eyes fastened on her face as Davina muttered unwisely, 'You could have fooled me!'

'So you did make a snap judgment after all.' His words bit as they were intended to do and Davina flushed vividly, wishing this man was not so quick off the trigger. He was always needling her into losing her cool, and the fact that she knew she was looking the complete opposite of the elegant girl who had called at the farm did nothing to bolster her self-confidence.

Reluctantly she admitted the indictment. 'Of course I did. She's an out-and-out man-eater. Who would believe she could be related to that nice young man who called yesterday? They're as different as chalk from cheese.'

There was now an undoubted twinkle lurking at the back of the hard eyes. 'Another snap judgment! You'd do well, my girl, to think before you speak. One of these days your impulsiveness will get you into trouble.'

'Exactly what James said. He warned me that it was risky taking a job with you,' Davina said before she could stop herself.

'Did he now?' Rex's drawl was softer than usual. 'But you didn't take his advice, I notice.'

Faint pink stained Davina's clear skin. 'No! Well—if I followed all the advice my family hand out, I'd never go anywhere or do anything,' she offered by way of explanation. Then in an attempt to turn Rex's thoughts she asked quickly, 'When do you think they'll deliver the furniture? The bedrooms have had two coats of paint each and I must say I'm looking forward to sleeping in a proper bed again.'

Rex's quizzical look left her in no doubt that he was well aware of the smoke screen, but he answered her perfectly politely and the rest of the meal passed off without a further clash between them. Davina had a bath as soon as he had gone out and when she had changed into clean things, she spent the rest of the afternoon writing long-overdue letters to her immediate family.

In her letters to her mother and grandmother, she was careful to restrict her comments on her new environment to descriptions of the wild beauty of the district without mentioning the isolation of Nineveh Farm or the deplorable state of the farmhouse. But in a letter to Catrin she let all her vexation at Rex's high-handed manner and the neglected dwelling in which he was expecting her to live flow from the end of her pen.

'Don't tell Mum or Grandmother, they'd only worry,' she ended. 'But honestly, Cat, you should see this place! Cold Comfort Farm is what it should be called. I've scrubbed and polished until I've no nails left to speak of. Still, I'm licking things slowly into shape. The house, I mean. I wish I could say the same for his lordship. He must be the most exasperating man ever born.'

CHAPTER FIVE

She was licking the flap on Catrin's letter when Rex walked into the kitchen. 'Can't do any more today. What do you say to a meal out?'

Surprise flashed into Davina's clear eyes and Rex's brows rose.

'No need to look so stunned. I just thought you might like a meal cooked by someone else as a change. And don't think this invitation is a criticism of your culinary abilities,' Rex went on as Davina opened her mouth to speak. 'You've turned out to be quite a passable cook.'

'I suppose coming from you that's tantamount to being proclaimed Cook of the Year,' Davina retorted. 'Mother insisted that both Catrin and I do our share of the housework you know. Contrary to what you may imagine, neither of us was born with a silver spoon in her mouth,' she finished acidly.

One corner of Rex's mouth twitched, but he said quite soberly, 'Does that mean you think my idea's a good one?' and when Davina said grudgingly, 'Oh, I suppose so,' he replied dryly, 'It's nice to have one's invitations so charmingly accepted,' which caused her to give a reluctant smile at his deadpan expression.

She dimpled apologetically as his face did not relax. 'Sorry if I sounded particularly rude, but you must admit it comes as a bit of a surprise—wanting to have a meal out to save *me* trouble. I seem to remember you saying you "didn't keep dogs and bark yourself." You can hardly blame me if my immediate thought was that you fancied a decent meal for a change.'

'Well, for once you maligned me. And thank you for the apology. It's accepted, qualified though it was.'

Davina got up from the table, giving an appreciative chuckle. 'Game and set to you, Rex. Where are you taking me? I'd better go and get into something more feminine,' she added, glancing down at her denim trousers.

The restaurant Rex had chosen turned out to be in a converted country mansion some thirty miles distant, and as they entered the thickly carpeted foyer, Davina was glad she had put on a floor-length dress. Rex himself was in a lightweight suit with a brown silk shirt and tie, and several female heads turned as he ushered Davina towards the door leading to the dining room.

They were met by the head waiter, who greeted Rex by name. 'My apologies, Mr Fitzpaine. Your table will not be ready for five minutes. Perhaps a drink in the bar . . .' and he smiled ingratiatingly.

Davina was shaken by silent laughter as Rex turned to lead her to the cocktail lounge. He looked down, eyebrows raised. She lifted smiling eyes and said, 'You fraud! Much good it would have done had I refused, since you'd evidently booked a table before you suggested we eat out. How did you come to hear of the place anyway?'

'Stayed here when I was looking round the district,' Rex explained. 'Do you like it?'

'The décor's pleasant,' Davina commented, looking round the tastefully furnished bar. 'But I'll be able to give you a better idea when I've tasted the food.'

'Then you'll like it. They have a French chef and the food is excellent.'

'My goodness! This is indeed an honour,' Davina commented outrageously and, tongue in cheek, Rex caught her up.

'Nothing's too good for the ladies I entertain.'

'Does that include stepsisters?' Davina came back, and could have sworn he was genuinely amused as he said firmly, 'Especially stepsisters,' though his face remained serious.

The head waiter came to summon them a few minutes later and himself took their order. As a waiter changed the cutlery on the snowy linen tablecloth Davina grinned.

'Now what atrocious thought is going through that curly head?' Rex enquired, just as the wine waiter bowed himself away.

'I was simply wondering how much all this red carpet treatment must be going to cost you,' Davina admitted, and Rex's mouth twitched.

What he might have been going to say had to be postponed, because at that moment a trolley covered with a lush assortment of hors d'oeuvres was wheeled to the table and the subject was forgotten in the business of selecting their personal choice. The big room was more than three quarters full and at one end a few square feet of floor had been cleared for dancing to the tunes being softly and discreetly played by a trio of musicians.

They were at the coffee stage before Rex said, 'Your foot's been tapping for the last five minutes. Want to dance?'

Davina's answer was guarded. 'Only if you do. There isn't much room.'

Rex pushed out his chair and rose. 'A perfect excuse, then, if we want to dance cheek to cheek,' he said, and took her elbow.

But he'd have to lean a long way down, Davina thought, had he really wanted to carry out his threat, for her cheek came just up to the lapel of his dark brown lounge suit. She repressed a shiver as his long arm held her firmly pressed to his strong, lean body and closed her eyes as they circled the tiny dance floor.

'Do you habitually close your eyes when you dance, or does it make it easier that way to forget who your partner is?' a voice above her head enquired in casual tones.

Davina's eyes flashed open and she leaned back against the encircling arm so she could see Rex's face. His lips were curled in a mockingly unkind smile and his eyes held an expression she was at a loss to interpret.

'You're so tall, I didn't think you'd notice,' she answered lamely, then froze as a hand with long lacquered nails caught at Rex's arm.

Adele Wickham, looking enchanting in a black chiffon dress, diamonds winking at her ears and on her fingers, was devouring Rex with her eyes, apparently quite impervious to the feelings of her partner. 'Why didn't you tell me you were coming here?' She stopped to throw Davina a careless glance. 'We could have made a foursome.'

Rex moved just far enough away to cause Adele to release her hold on his arm as he replied suavely, 'We decided to come on the spur of the moment,' and Davina bit back a smile as his fingers pressed hers warningly.

'No reason why we can't join up now, though,' Adele

persisted. Then as no one answered she went on, a note of irritation creeping into the sugary tones she had been using, 'This is Roy—Roy Comstone.'

The tall, rangy man with whom she was dancing followed the murmurs of 'hello' and 'how do you do' from Rex and Davina by nodding to them, then saying sardonically, 'I wondered, Adele my sweet, when you were going to remember your manners. And since this is my party, couldn't you have at least consulted me before you added to it?'

There was a slur to the stinging remark which showed that the man, if not drunk, had certainly had a good deal to drink. A quick glance showed Davina that Roy Comstone, though he was holding himself well, was more than a little inebriated, and instinctively her fingers clung to Rex's big hand.

His remark was addressed to Adele Wickham's partner and not to her. 'We've no intention of butting in, however welcome, because we're on the point of leaving. I've a dawn appointment with my stock,' Rex finished, stretching the truth a little.

To Davina's relief, the musicians picked that moment to take a break and five minutes later they were in the Land Rover heading towards the farm. But the uncomfortable scene on the dance floor was still on her mind.

'Where's Mr Wickham?' she asked.

For a moment she thought Rex was not going to reply. He was driving fast and although the road was clear of traffic its winding course needed a good deal of concentration. Then he replied in a noncommittal voice:

'Her brother tells me she's on the point of divorcing her husband—or maybe it's the other way around. I rather gathered her absence from the scene was advised and as she and Jim have no relations to speak of she's come to stay with him until the scandal blows over.'

Davina was silent for a moment. 'I'd have thought she'd have taken refuge in a more salubrious place. The country obviously bores her to death and I'd have thought she'd have been more at home in one of the fashionable spots like St Tropez or Sardinia.'

Rex threw her a sideways glance. 'Places like that take money,' he replied cynically.

'I know that,' Davina replied impatiently, 'but judging by Adele's clothes and jewellery, that shouldn't bother her.'

'Perhaps she's no money of her own. Jim Thomas has a good veterinary practice around here, but he's not wealthy by any means. My guess is that until the divorce solicitors on either side have sorted things out, Adele will not have a lot of pin money.'

'That's a nice old-fashioned expression,' Davina said, forgetting for the moment her curiosity about Adele. 'I wonder if I put it in a story the teenagers would know what it meant.'

'It's one we often use in Australia,' said Rex. Then he added thoughtfully, 'Pity, isn't it, that Adele's manners are not as beautiful as her looks? She's certainly an eyeful.'

Putting a hand instinctively to her dark curls, Davina was swept by a wave of depression. In the darkness, however, Rex did not notice the look of chagrin which swept across her face as she said lightly, 'You're right, and of course all gentlemen prefer . . . or so I'm given to understand.'

To her surprise a hand left the wheel and covered the two clasped together on her lap. 'Brunettes are lovely too,' there was a caress in Rex's voice as he went on, 'And didn't Shakespeare feature a Dark Lady in his Sonnets?'

Astonishment kept Davina silent all the way back to the farm, for Rex did not take his hand away from hers for several moments and when the gate hove in sight he said, 'Stay where you are. Exceptions are made for high heels and long skirts,' before he slid out to open the gate himself. Back at the farmhouse door he came round to help her alight and with a brief, 'Put the kettle on while I garage this,' he left her to make her own way inside.

Davina had the kettle on and was adding a log to the smouldering embers when he came in. She looked up and his aura of strength under complete control caught her breath yet again. She straightened up, glad that the business of getting out cups and saucers offered an opportunity to turn her back, for Rex had accurately interpreted her moods before now. It would spoil everything were he to guess that she found him at times almost irresistably attractive.

When Davina opened her eyes the following morning, the hands of the small alarm clock stood at ten minutes past eight and she was out of the sleeping bag and dressing in seconds. Somehow or other she must have forgotten to set the alarm to 'on' the previous night, and what Rex would have to say didn't bear thinking about.

But when she hurried into the kitchen the fire had been lit and used dishes on the draining board told their own story. There was a note propped against the cooling teapot. 'Shall not be back until tea-time. It seemed a pity to wake a sleeping beauty. R.'

Davina stood looking down at the firm, clear handwriting. The sting in the tail of the message made her flush, for it was an embarrassing thought to have been caught napping in the literal sense. Had he merely looked in, or had he stood beside the cot bed while he made up his mind to let her have a lie-in? Either alternative gave Davina a sick feeling in her stomach and she could have kicked herself for not setting the alarm.

But she had hardly finished clearing away and tidying the kitchen when a large furniture van came swaying dangerously down the track from the main road. As well as the beds and the bedding, Rex had added to the bare essentials Davina had listed. The carriers made several journeys from the van to the first floor, and when they finally left, she went to invesigate.

Polythene wrappings flew here and there as her scissors went to work disclosing woollen rugs for each bedside, a dozen fleecy towels and curtains not only to match the bed coverings in each bedroom but replacements for the bathroom and kitchen. Stopping only for a cheese sandwich and a mug of coffee at midday, Davina made up the beds, hung curtains and trailed up and down the stairs with clothing. The big old-fashioned wardrobe in the room she had picked out for Rex was soon filled with the contents of his suitcases, and feeling smugly pleased with her choice of colour schemes, she went downstairs to burn the packings and give the kitchen a final spit and polish before preparing tea.

She was making up the fire when Rex's footsteps sounded in the porch and he came in, his eyes flying to the flame-coloured velvet curtains at the window. Looking up, Davina saw a spark of amusement in his eyes as he asked in an expressionless tone, 'You like them, then?'

Davina's face lit up. 'Of course I do. They cheer up the place no end. I'd washed the old ones, but they'd faded badly. I've made up the rooms, so we'll be able to go to bed tonight in a civilised manner,' she finished in a rush of excitement.

Rex gave a reluctant laugh but merely replied mildly, 'I hadn't realised we'd been going to bed in an *uncivilised* manner,' which made Davina's face flush delicately at the implication behind the words. He saw the blush and took pity on her by adding, 'I hadn't realised the housewifely instinct lying dormant either. Do all women go starry-eyed over a couple of beds and some new curtains?'

Davina gave an embarrassed laugh and peeped at him through her eyelashes as she said demurely, her tone suspiciously innocent, 'I couldn't give a generalisation, but then not all women are unfortunate enough to be brought to a house in this condition.'

Rex's firm mouth twitched as he hung up his jacket. 'Touché! But I thought the few extras would redeem my character. In fact you can do over the whole house if that's your ambition.'

'It's not, and in any case it would be a wicked extravagance just for six months.'

'We might do the small room across the hall, though,' Rex remarked, sitting down and beginning to roll a cigarette. 'We shan't want to sit in here every evening all through the winter. However, first things first. It can wait until later,' and with his cigarette alight he reached for the teapot which Davina had just put down on the table.

She was getting into the brand new bed, feeling the spring interior mattress sink luxuriously beneath her weight, when she recalled that she had not apologised for oversleeping, nor had Rex taken the opportunity to give her one of his sly digs about her failure to be up on time. She lay staring into the darkness turning over this unexpected forbearance and decided at last that the longer she knew Rex, the less she understood his sudden swing of mood. Had someone, somehow, given him a poor opinion of womankind in general? Yet it seemed ridiculous to imagine him as crossed in love.

What girl could fail to respond if a man of Rex's undeniable attractiveness were to make himself agreeable? He would simply sweep her off her feet.

During breakfast the following morning when with a decided twinkle in his eye Rex asked Davina if she had slept well, she remembered her speculations of the night before. He was obviously in a teasing mood again and she had difficulty in giving him a cool smile of acknowledgement as she endeavoured to turn the tables by saying, 'Marvellously. Did you?'

He let her off the hook by lowering his eyes to his plate and saying simply, 'Yes, I always do,' then after a brief pause, 'You haven't forgotten we're invited round to supper at the vet's house this evening?'

'I had forgotten, yes,' Davina replied slowly, wishing there was some way of avoiding another confrontation with Adele Wickham. She glanced up to intercept a keen-eyed look as Rex said with a drawl, 'Never mind. You'll have me to see you don't get swallowed up.'

He got up with the words, leaving Davina staring at his broad back. Now what had he meant? she wondered, a frown between her brows. It seemed as if once again he had read the thought behind her too expressive face.

Since she had no means of knowing what the other guests would be wearing, she decided on a velvet trouser and waistcoat suit, teamed with a toning silk blouse of the same pinky lilac shade, and laying them out along with clean undies, she went downstairs to have a bath. She had turned on both taps and undressed when an ominous rustling accompanied by a series of soft squeaks made her pick up a towel and wrap it around herself before cautiously backing towards the door.

There was nothing to be seen, but all her thoughts were bent on arming herself with the kitchen poker without delay. She opened the bathroom door and backed out, to give a gasp of fright as two long arms engulfed her from behind.

She had walked straight into Rex and found herself a prisoner against his broad chest. But she was blind to the possibilities of the situation as she whispered over a bare shoulder, 'Something's in there. I was going for the poker.'

He bent his head and whispered in her ear, 'What is it? A king-sized jabberwock?'

Davina turned a reproachful look and he released her to say, a note of amusement in his smooth drawl, 'I'll see to it, I expect it's only a rat,' which caused her a shudder of revulsion as he walked past her.

She waited in breathless silence listening to Rex moving about inside the bathroom. Suddenly the door swung wide as he came out, his face perfectly solemn.

'What was it? Have you killed it?' Davina demanded, and for answer Rex brought one big hand from behind his back and held his fist on a level with her eyes.

'See for yourself!' Slowly he unclenched his hand. 'Here's your jabberwock,' he said, and Davina found herself being surveyed by two bright eyes in a tiny face about the size of her thumbnail.

'Why, it's only a fieldmouse!' She looked up slowly to meet Rex's eyes. 'How could such a tiny thing make so much noise?' She stopped abruptly and before he could reply demanded, 'You're not going to kill it?'

Rex walked past her. 'Of course not.' She heard him open the porch door. He returned to say, 'I expect it got up one of the outlet pipes and was simply more scared than you were.'

Davina was still standing, her bare feet curling on the polished tiles, clutching the towel around her like a sarong. Rex stopped in front of her and ran a careless forefinger from her ear and down neck and shoulder, to stop at the towel top.

'You look delightful, but the bath water must be getting cold,' he drawled, and as if released from a spell, Davina blinked and darting back inside the bathroom, shut and bolted the door, feeling oddly breathless.

But when she stepped into the bath she lay quite motionless for some minutes before she began to wash. Her reaction to Rex's casual caress had come as something of a surprise, and squinting down, she almost expected to see a mark where he had trailed his finger.

Product of her age, it wasn't by any means the first time Davina had been the target of wandering masculine hands, for modern bikinis were an invitation in themselves. It was, however, the first time she felt as if she'd been touched with a live wire. She suddenly recalled the warm safety of his arms when she had cannoned into him, and a shiver ran through her despite the warmth of the water.

It was therefore with a feeling of unusual shyness that she came down later ready to set out for Jim Thomas's party, but Rex's mood of intimacy had vanished as he asked indifferently, his eyes running over the outfit she was wearing, 'Going to be warm enough without a coat?'

'I've got a shawl,' Davina replied nervously, holding it up, and with a, 'Come on then,' Rex led the way outside.

There was no difficulty in finding the house. Apart from a number of cars parked in the driveway, lights shone from every window and the sound of music could be heard. Davina got out before Rex could come round to help, determined to keep out of his reach for the rest of the evening. In this she had help from both Adele and Jim, for they were no sooner inside the house than Adele, looking like an advertisement from *Vogue* in a turquoise blue figure-hugging evening gown, swooped upon Rex and carried him off to the far end of the long drawing room.

Davina was left smiling a 'hello' at Jim. Tonight he was tidily dressed in well cut slacks and a turtleneck matching sweater, with his silver-blond hair neatly combed. 'You didn't recognise me? Admit it!' he said, and smiled into her eyes. 'Wouldn't do to wear anything decent when you've just delivered a calf, though,' he went on. 'What would you like to drink? Everyone else is about three ahead of you.'

Davina let him lead her to where a table covered with bottles and glasses stood inviting the guests to help themselves. Most had done so pretty liberally, she decided, as a redhead, her make-up smudged, tilted the glass she was holding and only Jim's quick hand saved both of them being doused with gin.

'Sorry about that,' he said as he poured a sherry for Davina. 'I think a spot of food as blotting paper is indicated. Come along to the kitchen and meet my Mrs Hepburn. We can help her dish out the grub. That's if you don't mind,' he finished apologetically.

'Of course not,' Davina assured him, secretly glad to get

away from the crowd of noisy strangers. There was a mouth-watering smell coming from the big electric oven. A trolley with a hot plate stood ready, loaded on its lower shelves with plates and cutlery, and the big casseroles, their contents topped with crisply browned potatoes, were soon added and Jim wheeled it carefully down the hall.

While Davina and Mrs Hepburn served, Jim carried plates round to the guests who were soon sitting on the floor or a convenient chair to sample the housekeeper's cooking. Davina was surprised to see Rex appear beside her and there was a note of dry amusement as he said, 'I saw Jim had you safely in tow, but it's a bit of a busman's night out to expect you to do this,' and he waved his hand at the steaming dishes.

Davina gave him her dimpling smile just as Adele came up. 'Why, how sweet you are to help out,' she said patronisingly, then to Rex, 'Grab a couple of plates, darling. We can sit on the stairs and get away from this mob for a bit,' and picking up some cutlery, she sailed away in a cloud of expensive perfume.

Rex seemed about to make some comment, but as Jim Thomas came back for more plates, whatever he might have said remained a mystery. With a whimsical expression of resignation, he picked up two portions of hotpot and turned to follow Adele.

When everyone was served, Jim and Davina sat down on the floor to eat their own supper. 'I'm glad you could come. When the food's cleared away, I'll introduce you to some of the gang.' He put a finger on Davina's arm and pointed. 'That's our local doctor. He and I went to school together. He's always had a crush on Adele. I hope he doesn't build up false hopes now she's back.'

'For good?'

Jim shrugged. 'You can't tell with Adele. I thought when she married Reggie Wickham we'd got a bit of peace at last. Mother died when we were both small, unfortunately, and Adele could twist my father round her little finger. Thank goodness he's not still alive to see her making such a mess of things.'

Davina gave him a searching look but said nothing. She suspected a scandal of mammoth proportions might account for Adele Wickham burying herself in this remote spot, but it was really none of her business to probe. Jim, however, needed no prodding, for he went on gloomily, 'I only realised tonight that the story of Reggie coming back unexpectedly from a business trip and finding my sister practically *in flagrante delicto* would reach Camshaw, but apparently it has. Oliver Matthews who is vicar here and another old friend refused to come this evening, and as for the Comstones—well, the Squire cut Adele dead in the middle of Alston yesterday, which makes it a bit tricky. I see to all his cattle as a rule.'

'But surely your clients don't hold you responsible for the behaviour of your sister?' Davina asked, then her brows drew together. 'Comstone—that name rings a bell. I think the man giving your sister dinner the other evening was called Comstone.'

'Yes, Roy. I went to school with him too,' Jim said with his lopsided grin. Then his face became serious again. 'Roy's here tonight somewhere,' and he looked around the room, but in the smoky atmosphere it was difficult to pick out individuals and Jim gave up to look down into Davina's face. 'No good judging the feelings of the Comstones by Roy. He's the black sheep of the family and practically disowned by the old man. The Squire was in the Navy before he retired to farm, and between you and me, he and Mrs C. were born about fifty years too late. Couple of real old Victorians. If I so much as say damn, the Commander makes me feel as if I've spat on his quarterdeck!'

Davina's gurgle of laughter made several people near by turn their heads and she and Jim were invited to share the joke. But getting to his feet, Jim Thomas fobbed off questions by saying it was a private conversation and Davina was left to mull over the confidences which had been poured into her ears.

But not for long. Jim returned with a dark, curly-headed man whom he introduced as 'our local quack. Tom Mulholland.' The young doctor held on to Davina's hand and pulled her to her feet, taking her arm when she was standing and dismissing his host with a, 'You've monopolised her long enough. Go away and entertain your other guests,' and

Jim, with a monkey-like grin of distaste, obeyed.

The young doctor took her over and introduced her to a circle of his particular cronies and Davina forced herself to join in the conversation without looking around for Rex. For all she knew he could be in the room, but there was such a crush of people she could not be sure.

Some time later Jim Thomas returned to whisper, 'Care to come and help me make some coffee? I've sent Mrs Hepburn to bed.'

Davina gave the stairs a glance as they went down the hall, but though several people were using them as a sitting out spot, Rex was not one of them. She gave a yawn as they went into the deserted kitchen, cleared now except for a tray laden with cups on the big formica-topped table.

But when Jim had switched on the big electric percolator, he seemed in no hurry to serve his guests. He walked over to where Davina was leaning against one of the working surfaces, stifling yet another yawn, and asked gently, 'Tired?'

'A bit. I was up at six-thirty,' Davina apologised, and Jim leaned an elbow on the cupboard behind her and propped his head on his fist as he leaned down to tuck a curl behind one of her ears. 'I shall be up at Nineveh tomorrow afternoon. Will you be glad to see me?' he asked.

Davina's heart sank. Surely he wasn't going to be difficult? She had had enough of the party and felt in no mood to stave off an amorous host. She smiled brightly, put up a hand to hold Jim's which was now caressing the lobe of her ear and said sweetly, 'Of course. Rex and I are always pleased to see visitors. I'll even give you a cup of tea and a scone when you and Rex have finished your business.'

'But if I don't take Davina home now, she'll be in no state to bake in the morning,' a drawling voice said from the doorway, and Davina let go of Jim's hand as if she had been stung. Two bright spots of colour stained her cheeks as Rex strolled into the room, a knowing smile on his lips which made her long to hit him.

The drive home was made in silence. Davina knew once again that she was being made to feel in the wrong, despite the fact that he and Adele Wickham must have spent the entire evening together. And Adele was not the kind to let things stay on a strictly platonic level for long, Davina thought spitefully, and suddenly realised that her reactions were remarkably like jealousy—and heaven knew, she had no right to feel that way. If Rex had a mind to encourage Adele, it was none of her business.

When they reached the farmhouse, Davina would have gone straight to bed, but Rex said, more in the tone of an employer than a friend, 'Put the kettle on. I feel like a cup of strong tea after a party like that.'

With a glance of surprise, Davina did as she was told, but she could not help herself saying impulsively, 'I thought you were having a good time being lionised by the fair Adele.'

'What about you and the fair Adele's brother? I fancy I came in just in time to prevent your being thoroughly kissed,' Rex retaliated, and Davina was left with nothing to say. She had been holding Jim's hand and it would be well nigh impossible to convince Rex that she had been on the point of repelling Jim's intentions on her own account. Coming in, it had probably looked the exact opposite.

They drank their tea in silence far from companionable. In fact it fairly bristled with things left unsaid. As Rex stubbed out his cigarette and picked up his teacup, Davina rose, saying, 'Well, I'm for bed.'

Rex drained his cup and stood. 'Leave these. They can wait until the morning.' Once more it was in the nature of a command and Davina's back was stiff as she led the way upstairs. She was about to throw a casual 'goodnight' over her shoulder when a long arm shot out and closed on the nape of her neck, turning her gently round.

'I suppose now all the local wolves have had a look at you, I'll be holding them off in droves,' Rex drawled, and Davina looked up to meet his eyes.

'You flatter me.' She was too taken aback to say more.

'Do I? I'd lay a small bet that Jim Thomas's scalp will soon be hanging at that trim little waist,' said Rex, and put his other arm out as he spoke. Too surprised to resist, Davina let herself be drawn close and felt his lips on her forehead. He drew back his head and she looked up into the hooded eyes to have the landing light blotted out as he lowered his head and swiftly kissed her parted lips.

It all happened so quickly that Davina blinked with shock as Rex kissed and released her all in one quick movement. One minute she had been lying against a broad chest, the next he was holding her bedroom door open and saying with the sardonic note uppermost in his voice, 'Off you go, and don't forget to set your alarm.' He closed it quietly behind her and Davina leaned against the door and listened to his retreating footsteps and the sound of the other bedroom door snapping shut.

She didn't know about Jim Thomas's scalp. But there was no doubt her own had been neatly collected by that big man in there. If she'd really been in any doubt about her feelings, that unexpected kiss had settled them. For good or evil, she had fallen head over heels in love, really in love, for the first time in her life.

CHAPTER SIX

IF only, Davina thought wistfully at seven-thirty next morning, Rex had felt the same magic, but when he came in for his breakfast, his manner could not have been more casual or matter-of-fact. They were only half way through the meal when the old shepherd arrived, and seeing him look longingly at Rex's plate, Davina put more bacon on to cook.

Rex and Mr Farr thereafter talked sheep exclusively. Davina could follow foot rot treatment, for as a child she had watched the Welsh farmers put their flocks through foot baths, but drenching and raddling had her stumped.

Finally, she stopped listening to the men's talk and had just begun to clear away when noises on the track caused her to turn and say, 'I think the animals are here.' Soon the yard was full of bleating sheep and when Davina opened the kitchen door to shake the crumbs from the tablecloth, the little black cat darted between her legs and took up its place at the fireside.

'You know you'll get me into trouble,' she told it, but the cat only blinked golden eyes and purred contentedly. Unwilling to put it out into the crowded farmyard, Davina left it where it was as she got on with the housework.

It was fast asleep when Rex brought Mr Farr in for their midday break. The trucks had gone but the bleating from outside showed the ewes were still uneasy. 'I thought I told you to get rid of that cat,' Rex began harshly as the old man broke in.

'Well, bless me! Fancy the old cat coming back. She belonged to Nineveh, but after the old man's death, young Peter McKay came up and took her home. I'll call in and tell the boy where she is. He'll be right bothered that she's missing.'

'If you know where it lives we can drop it off when I take you home,' Rex said. Then turning to Davina he added mockingly, 'Didn't I tell you it looked too well fed to be a stray?'

So they were back to square one, Davina thought, because there was certainly nothing loverlike about Rex this morning. It was a sop to her wounded pride therefore when Jim Thomas arriving to check the ewes made no secret of his delight at seeing her and she found herself responding to his wink and whispered 'See you over tea' with an encouraging nod, despite the grim smile she glimpsed on Rex's lips.

That evening she managed to finish the second short story and sat up later than usual to type it out for despatch to the magazine office in London. As they had their last cup of tea before going to bed she asked, 'Would there be any objection to my borrowing the Land Rover tomorrow to drive into Alston?'

'Ever driven one?'

'No, but I've had a driving licence for three years. We need stores and I'd like to take the bulky washing to a launderette.'

'I'll see how you shape up. If I think you're competent, I shall not be using it during the morning.'

He was as good as his word. As soon as breakfast was over he got up and beckoned Davina to the doorway. 'Five minutes to show me how good or bad a driver you are,' Rex said shortly, and led the way outside.

When Davina had driven down the track, reversed, driven into the shed where the Land Rover was housed, backed out again and parked it neatly, he declared himself satisfied.

'Leave the keys in the ignition, you can go whenever you're ready,' he said, then stopped and drew a roll of notes out of his pocket.

'You'll need money for food and bring a couple of spare canisters of Calor gas. I think I owe you some wages too,' he added, eyeing her flushed face with a quizzical gaze. 'Even I have to admit you've more than earned it,' he added, and watched with an unnerving look in his deep-set eyes as Davina's flush deepened, this time with annoyance.

She turned on her heel and went inside to fly through the morning chores and then collect the washing in a plastic bag. With a handbag and her precious envelope clutched under one arm she hurried aboard.

But when she pressed the starter button, nothing happened. She made sure the ignition was turned on and tried again, but there was not so much as a sound from under the bonnet. Uttering an exclamation of annoyance, she got down to search for Rex, but he was nowhere to be found and frustration at the wrecking of her plans made her kick the fence with childish disappointment.

It was a beautiful morning, though the breeze off the moors was fresh and Davina was glad of the chunky wool jacket she had slipped over her shirt and jeans. She had not had a chance to really explore the track behind the farm and maybe she would find Rex up there.

But when she paused some half hour later to get her breath and take in the view, she could see no sign of another human being as far as her eye could see. The moorland stretched in every direction, purple now with heather and broken by the occasional furze bush. Drystone walls lined the rough track up which she had come and in the distance she could just see a faint haze of smoke which she took to be Camshaw. The sun was warm, and Davina sat down to rest, taking off her head scarf to let the breeze play through her curly hair.

She had been up late finishing her typescript last night and late the previous one. The sun, the peace and a convenient root of bracken did the rest. When Davina next opened her eyes, she saw with dismay that the hands of her watch stood at one o'clock, and getting to her feet she ran nearly all the way back to the farm.

Long before she reached the cobbled yard she had seen and recognised Rex's large unmistakable figure with the much smaller one of the old shepherd standing beside him. When Davina arrived panting he had turned to watch her precipitate arrival and the look on his face was far from reassuring.

'Where have you been? You asked if you could use the Land Rover, but as far as I can see it's never been out of the shed since breakfast time.' He glanced meaningly at his watch. 'Do you realise what time it is?'

'Yes—and do you know the Land Rover won't start?' Davina ripped back at him, furious that Rex should reprimand her in front of an audience. 'I decided to go for a walk instead.'

'Without troubling to leave a note of your change of plan. Didn't it occur to you that seeing the Land Rover here, I'd expect to find you around?'

'Since I'm free and over twenty-one—no, it didn't,' Davina retorted acidly, trying to ignore the old shepherd listening to the argument with bright eyes alight with amusement.

'Over twenty-one you may be,' Rex said harshly, 'free you're not. I expect you here at meal times, so don't forget in future.'

Tears of rage were ready to spurt out of Davina's eyes as she turned her back and made for the kitchen door, determined not to give Rex the satisfaction of seeing her cry. In the pantry, she blew her nose before selecting a couple of tins and carrying them out started preparing the meal. But when she turned from washing her hands, the men had not waited to be called to table, and though they talked farming while she worked, Davina was only too aware of the two pairs of eyes watching her every movement.

In other circumstances the hawk-eyed gaze of the man sitting at the head of the table might have made her fumble nervously, but an ice cold rage steadied her as nothing else could. Smouldering at what she considered to be treatment verging on the inhuman, she picked at her ham and mushroom omelette, all gentler thoughts forgotten until Mr Farr put down his knife and fork and remarked, 'That were a treat, missie.' Then turning to Rex he added with a twinkle, 'Kissing don't last. Cooking do,' as he searched in the pockets of his ancient tweed jacket for his pipe and tobacco pouch.

Across the table Davina's eyes met a gleam of devilry in Rex's and her anger vanished. He spared her blushes, however, by saying, 'You couldn't be more right. If I take Davina into Alston do you think you could finish the drenching on your own?' and at the old man's nod, he said to Davina, 'I'll get the Rover going. Leave the dishes and powder your nose. Five minutes—and no more, mind,' and he followed the old shepherd outside.

Since he was perfectly capable of making her go as she was with windblown hair, Davina didn't waste a minute and she was ready and outside when the Land Rover rolled out of its shed. 'What was wrong?' she asked, but Rex ignored her question and said, 'He doesn't miss much, does he?'

'Who doesn't miss much? I don't know what you're talking about,' Davina said crossly, for the Land Rover was going like a bird and half her mind was still occupied with why it hadn't started for her.

'Farr, of course. Surely you guessed his remark after lunch was directly at us?'

Davina began to feel hot. 'But he thinks like the rest of Camshaw that you're my stepbrother. And in any case,' she added, his words reminding her of the raking down Rex had given her before the old man, 'if he didn't, he can hardly have thought you nurtured any tender thoughts for me after your ticking off this morning.'

'The gate needs opening,' Rex replied blandly, and turned amused eyes on her flushed face; with a sniff, Davina got down to open it.

There was silence until they were nearly in Alston when Rex broke it by asking, 'Still sulking?'

Davina, who had been studiously observing the scenery on her side of the road, turned to glance at his profile, noticing with renewed anger that amusement curled one corner of his mouth.

'No, I simply had nothing to say,' she said quietly, then added, 'Do you mind if I ask you something?'

'Depends what it is,' Rex replied cautiously.

'I wondered if you behaved like this at home. Do your mother and your uncle get the rough edge of your tongue if they step out of line?'

Rex laughed as if he was genuinely amused 'Trying to worm my family history out of me now, eh?' to which Davina replied stiffly, 'Far from it. I simply wondered if you were only gratuitously rude to relations and employees.'

If she had hoped by her words to annoy Rex, she was in for a disappointment. 'Do you know,' he said in confidential tones, 'when we were in Switzerland I'd never have tagged you as a thin-skinned girl, unable to face a bit of bluntness. You struck me there as a "couldn't care less" type of female. I'm sorry if I was rough with you. I couldn't imagine where you'd got to, and you could get lost pretty easily on the moor, you know?'

From Rex this speech was tantamount to an apology and Davina's rage melted away. The precious document was posted, the stores purchased and while Rex went to the hardware shop, she took their washing into a convenient launderette.

He came back to pick her up just as she was folding the last garment into the plastic carrier. 'There's a café right next door. Care for a cup of tea before we start for Camshaw?'

Davina nodded and they were soon sharing a small table in the window drinking cups of what Rex described as 'hot sheep-dip'.

Davina's chuckle made him look up from his disgusted examination of the contents of his teacup. His hooded eyes held a gleam as he said, 'And that's mild to what my uncle would call it.'

'I expect your mother is a super cook so he's been spoiled. Has he never been married?'

'Never.' The note of amusement had left Rex's soft voice, Davina noticed. 'Mother cured him of wanting to tie himself up,' he added, noticing the question in Davina's clear eyes. He sighed. 'She was Dad's one and only mistake. Met him in Sydney and it was a case for them both of marrying in haste and repenting at leisure. Mother hated the country. She stuck it until Dad was killed, then six months later she took off on what was supposed to be a month's holiday. She never came back.'

'You mean she deserted you?' Davina asked in disbelieving tones.

'Well, it wasn't quite like leaving me in a basket on the

steps of an orphanage,' came the dry reply. 'She couldn't have taken me had she wanted. Dad left me in the guardianship of Uncle Lionel and his half share in the property.'

'Cutting your mother off with the proverbial shilling?'

Rex looked up and smiled as he glimpsed the contempt on Davina's face. 'Not all men are vindictive. He arranged a generous allowance as long as she remained unmarried.'

'And you don't call that vindictive?'

'No, do you?' There was genuine astonishment in Rex's voice. 'Spare your pity for someone who really needs it.' There was bitterness now in the deep, soft drawl. 'Before that month was up she had met and married a wealthy barrister and I don't believe she ever really gave me another serious thought.'

'Hence your acquiring a real stepsister,' Davina said lightly. 'But did you never see your mother again?'

'Frequently. Uncle Lionel is a stickler. Every holiday, I was sent to stay with Mother in Sydney. And hated every moment,' he ended. Then abruptly, 'But I'm talking too much. Come along,' and getting up he put a helping hand under Davina's elbow.

They arrived back to find an ill-assorted couple sharing the farmhouse kitchen. Sitting beside the fire placidly smoking sat Mr Farr while on the far side of the table, swinging a shapely leg, sat Adele Wickham.

She was the first to speak. 'Couldn't you at least get a telephone put in this godforsaken place?' she asked petulantly as Rex stepped over the threshold carrying a carton of groceries.

He smiled with real amusement. 'Now, Adele, you didn't come here simply to complain about the lack of amenities.'

He put down the carton and Adele got up to come and stand beside him. 'But I wanted to speak to you, darling. And you not having a phone has meant I've had to drive up your atrocious lane. I'm sure my car's damaged.'

'And I'm certain it isn't—unless, that is, you drove like a bat out of hell. Come on, I'll take a look at it before you go home,' and he pushed Adele out of the house, leaving Davina and the old shepherd to try and break an embarrassed silence.

Davina was the first to speak. 'We're having an early supper. I bought a spit-roasted chicken and there are potatoes baking in their jackets in the oven. Would that suit?'

'Thank you kindly, miss. Since my Martha died, I've missed a bit of good home cooking. But are you sure Gaffer won't mind?'

At that moment the door opened and Davina and the old man saw Adele drive off in a cloud of dust. As if he had been present when Davina offered supper to the old man Rex said forthrightly, 'You'll stay for a meal, of course, then I'll take you home. Or if you'd prefer it a pint at the Shepherd and Crook?' he ended, one eyebrow lifted.

The old shepherd smiled and nodded. He and Rex discussed the next day's plan of action when the ewes should all have been treated for worms, and Davina repressed a shudder of revulsion as she laid the table. Her expression of disgust was not lost on at least one of the men present. 'You'll have to cultivate a stronger stomach than that,' Rex commented dryly as she passed his chair. 'This is a mild discussion to some you may overhear about sheep rearing!'

Davina pulled a face at him, but under the bright gaze of the old shepherd bit back the retort hovering on her lips. He seemed unusually interested in her skirmishes with Rex, and the knowing light in the keen eyes beneath the snow-white brows made her feel vaguely uneasy.

Supper over, they left her to clear away and wash up. Davina had put the last plate away and was washing her hands in scented soap when she heard a car approaching. It certainly was not the Land Rover and in any case, if Rex was treating Mr Farr to a drink at the local, it was much too early for his return. Peeping through the kitchen window, she was just in time to see Jim Thomas step out of his battered station wagon.

After a perfunctory knock he walked straight in. 'Adele's expecting company and I've been made to understand I'll be very much in the way if I stay in this evening. My calls are being taken by my colleague Petworth in Alston, so how about coming out for a drink?'

Pleasurably surprised by this invitation, Davina nodded acceptance. She had been piqued that Rex had not thought fit to take her along when he left with Farr—a sociable drink would have rounded off a busy day very nicely.

'Thanks, I'd like that,' she smiled at Jim. 'Give me five minutes to change and leave Rex a note and I'll be with you,' and serve him right, Davina thought as she went upstairs. It will do Rex good to come back and find me out.

But when Jim brought her home, the house was in darkness and her note still propped on the table where she had left it. Jim's voice held a note which made Davina frown as he picked up the scrap of paper and said slowly, 'Now I wonder . . .'

As he stopped, Davina snapped, 'Wonder what?' though her quick brain had already followed his line of thinking.

'Whether Rex was the reason Adele wanted the house to herself tonight?' Jim replied, and he sighed. 'She'll never learn that playing with fire always burns in the end.'

'Well, from what you told me the other evening, it won't be long before she's free to please herself with whom she plays around,' Davina said shortly as she made coffee and brought it to the table. 'Though Rex told me he was taking Mr Farr to the Shepherd and Crook. However, if he and Adele made a date this afternoon, surely that's their affair?'

'So that's where she was,' Jim said softly. 'Her solicitor rang to say he wanted to discuss something and of course she didn't get back until it was too late to ring him back. That didn't improve Adele's temper. As a matter of fact I was quite glad of an excuse to get out of the house,' he finished with brotherly candour.

'Oh, thanks!' Davina said sarcastically, but she laughed as Jim began to look guilty. She leaned forward and patted his hand. 'No, I know you didn't ask me out simply because Adele was difficult. I was only teasing.'

Jim turned his hand over and grasped hers. 'What a sweet thing you are,' he said warmly, and Rex chose that moment to walk into the kitchen.

As Davina snatched her hand away he said flatly, 'So you're back at last,' as he turned to fill the kettle.

'I didn't hear the Land Rover,' Davina stammered out the words and immediately wished them back, for Rex's face adopted the old sardonic smile as he asked, 'Then you didn't notice it was in the shed on your return?' and as she shook her head he said softly, 'Other things to think of, I daresay.'

Jim seemed unmoved by this interchange and he simply winked as Davina turned pleading eyes in his direction. 'I've that special dip you wanted in the car,' he said to Rex. 'When you've had your tea, I'll get it out. No need for me to tell *you* how to use it,' he added.

Rex simply grunted as he made tea, then sitting down he began to roll a cigarette. Inevitably, the two men started talking sheep, and when at last they went outside together, Davina stacked the used cups in the sink and went up to get ready for bed.

If Rex had been back before them, it was likely their conjectures about him and Adele had been way off the mark. Just the same, she had no wish for another passage of arms today. He had certainly not been pleased to come in and find her to all intents and purposes holding hands across the kitchen table with the young vet.

But he was affable to the point of absurdity the following morning until after breakfast, as he opened the outer door, the little black cat ran in before he could swoop and stop it. 'Blast the thing!' he burst out. 'I can't keep taking it back home. I suppose you've been encouraging it?' he accused Davina, who had dissolved into giggles at the sight of the cat so easily getting the better of such a huge man.

'Honestly, Rex. I haven't,' she replied at last, and tried unsuccessfully to stifle her laughter as she saw his grimly smiling expression. 'As soon as I've cleared, I'll walk down to Camshaw myself with it.'

Rex's face softened. 'No, don't do that. I'd like you to make a start on the room across the hall if you will. Throw out the bed and all those musty books and give the place a good clean. Then we'll decide what to do. I can use it as an office as well as a sitting room. Once the ewes are mated I'll have to keep records.'

The problem of the errant cat was solved in a way neither Rex nor Davina had anticipated. Coming into the kitchen to start the men's meal with a bucket of dirty water in her hand, Davina discovered a small boy crouching on the fireside rug, the cat leaning on his knee.

'Hello! She seems to know you,' said Davina, emptying the bucket and washing the grime off her hands. 'What's your name?'

'Peter, and she ought to. Lives with us, her does. Mr Farr said she'd come back up here t'other day, so when she didn't come home last night, I came to find her.'

'I'm sorry, but Mr Fitzpaine was going to bring her back later.'

'He's the gaffer here, isn't he?' There was an excited light in the boy's eyes. 'Can I go and look at his 'orse?'

'Not without Mr Fitzpaine's permission,' Davina said firmly, and added, 'Surely you ought to be at school?'

The boy eyed her with patent disapproval. 'Sent home at twelve, we were. Teacher took sick, and Mam said I could come up for Tibby. You can ask her if you don't believe me. Look, she gave me some sandwiches, so I needn't go back for me dinner,' and out of his trouser pocket, Peter produced a squashed paper bag.

'I think you'd better eat with us,' Davina told him, laying another place at the table. 'Then when Mr Fitzpaine comes in you can ask him to show you his horse.'

Apparently this met with the lad's approval, though his voice was still sullen as he asked, 'Suppose you'll want me to wash me hands, then?'

Davina bent and turned one of his small hands palm upwards. It was so grimy she had difficulty in holding back a chuckle as she answered poker-faced, 'It might be an idea. There's a scrubbing brush and soap at the sink.'

He was half way through the reluctant ablutions when Rex and the old man came in. Rex's eyebrows lifted. 'I see we've a visitor.'

'This is Peter,' Davina explained hastily. 'He came for his cat. There's no school this afternoon, so I've invited him to stay for lunch.'

'And see your horse,' the boy broke in. 'Can I ride it?'

'No, you may not,' Rex told him decidedly. 'You can come and look at him by all means and I'll show you how I groom him.' He paused, then asked the boy, 'How old are you?'

'Going on twelve. Thanks, Gaffer,' and he literally fell on

to the portion of hot meat pie Davina had at that moment placed before him. Rex seemed amused as he accepted his own plate and looked up to say softly as Davina leaned down to put his cup of tea conveniently to hand, 'Our circle of acquaintances grows every day.'

'Want to learn to ride,' Peter informed Rex, his mouth full.

'Do you?' Rex replied. 'Well, you have to learn how to care for horses first. You're lucky we've been busy with the sheep, because I intend to give George his brush down as soon as I've had this break.'

After this promise, the boy gobbled down his food and then wriggled impatiently on his seat as he waited for Rex to finish his meal. As soon as he saw him drain his second cup of tea, the boy shot to his feet. 'Ready, Gaffer?' and Rex looked for once genuinely amused as he said resignedly, 'I suppose I'll get no peace until I am. Come on,' and he got to his feet, laying a hand on the old man's shoulder as he did so.

'No need for you to come. Stay and have a smoke,' he ordered before following the boy outside.

There was silence for a space of a minute until looking up Davina saw the old shepherd had somehow divined her surprise at Rex's tolerant acceptance of the boy. When he spoke, however, he simply said, 'I'm right glad that boy came up for his cat. If I'm not mistaken, Gaffer will give him the run of the place if he behaves. His mam has her hands full, her being in the family way most of the time. I dunno how many bairns her's lost since Peter was born.'

'What about the father?'

'Village layabout, if you ask me. You'll find him most evenings in the Shepherd and Crook.'

'Oh, I see,' Davina said slowly, and was surprised when the old man put his pipe back in his mouth and said, 'Thought you might, missie. I'd better be getting back to work,' he added with a twinkle. 'No good came of calling other folks layabouts when you're sitting about doing nothing yourself.'

After supper, Davina brought her writing materials into the kitchen, for if the first two short stories were approved, she had contracted to write a series. But somehow tonight she could not concentrate on teenage love and she began to doodle on the paper. She had always been good at art and the rough sketch of a fairy sitting on a mushroom which grew under her fingers turned out with a face remarkably like Peter McKay's.

It reminded her of the stories she had told Catrin as children when her sister had gone through a phase of being afraid of the dark. Thinking back, Davina found she could remember one almost word for word, and she began to write. It had been about an elf, eager to win a medal for helping humans to gain their heart's desire, who had invariably made a mess of his do-gooding, leaving nothing but chaos in his wake.

As her pen flew over the paper, Davina could almost hear Catrin's youthful giggles as she had told her the ridiculous tale. She was so absorbed she did not notice Rex watching from the other end of the table and, as she finished, she glanced up to meet a look she could not fathom in the keen eyes.

He rose slowly and stretched. As he walked towards her he said, 'The story must be an absorbing one. Has boy met girl and they're about to live happily ever after?'

Rex knew she had been commissioned to write teenage love stories, but trust him to make it sound all a bit frivolous and beneath contempt! As he towered over her, Davina had a sudden urge to cover her fairy story from his sight, but he had already bent, placed a hand on the table either side, and was reading page 1.

Davina made herself as small as she could, for she was within the circle of his arms with Rex's profile only inches away. Although he shaved every morning, by now his chin was beginning to darken and she experienced an urge to run a finger along the line of his jaw which she was forced to crush down.

As he read on silently to the bottom of the first page she wondered if he had been Adele's secret guest the evening before. But she had no means of knowing how long he had been back at the farm before she and Jim returned. It could have been two hours before or only five minutes.

Suddenly he turned his head and met her eyes. 'I don't know much about children's stories, but you write well. Why didn't you think of making a career with this sort of thing instead of writing for a magazine?' Before she could answer he looked back at the sheet of paper. 'You draw well too. You've caught the boy's expression exactly.' He stood up. 'Will you let me have this?' and he nodded down at the pages on the table.

Once again he had taken her by surprise. Davina shuffled the sheets together and handed them over. 'What do you want with a fairy story?' She made no attempt to hide her astonishment.

'I've a friend who runs a publishing house in Sydney. He might be interested, though I can't guarantee anything. Now come along. It's a beautiful evening. We'll walk up the rise before bed.'

As if he took her consent for granted, Rex pulled Davina to her feet. 'Better wear this,' he draped an anorak over her shoulders, and going to the door pulled it open.

Full moonlight greeted them as they stepped into the yard, silvering the outbuildings, and Davina paused to look up into a cloudless sky aglitter with stars. Rex stopped in his tracks, came back and took her hand, saying gently, 'Come along, just up the hill. The stars will look even better from there.'

She tried to pull her fingers free as they walked up the stony track, but Rex held fast, murmuring something about her catching her foot in a rabbit hole if he let her go. When at last they stood hand in hand at the top of the hill beyond the first pasture, the grey farmhouse looked mysterious, even mellow in the gentle light, while grazing sheep looked like so many bundles of cotton wool.

Davina gave an unconscious sigh and sensed rather than saw Rex turn his head. She turned to smile at him. 'Wonderful, isn't it? Seen like this?' He did not answer, so she went on thoughtfully, 'Grey slate roofs aren't homey like thatched ones, but parts of Wales are bleak-looking too. It can be pretty intimidating—all that wildly beautiful country, I mean. My father used to say it made for humility.'

Rex squeezed the slim fingers lying in his hand. 'Not a

common reaction where you're concerned,' he remarked cruelly, and as Davina stared at him with bewilderment in her eyes at this unexpected attack he went on, 'I'd judge in the main you're rarely humble enough to forget all your good points.'

Davina stood, her small hand still lost in his larger one, and stared, feeling sick at heart. The soft, deadly voice went on, 'Be honest for once. You have beautiful hair, a complexion many a film star would give her right arm to possess, a figure that goes in and out in all the best places and the intelligence to make full use of them. You can't tell me you look in a mirror every day without being conscious of how Providence has smiled on you.'

Determined to control her voice, Davina managed to say evenly, 'You make me sound a complete . . .' The derogatory slang died on her lips. Her mouth felt dry as she tried again. 'You sound as if you hate me.'

'Hate you? When I've got the perfect housekeeper and a pretty one at that?' Rex's back was to the light, but imagining the expression in those hooded eyes Davina tried once again to free herself.

It was a mistake. With a jerk on her hand, Rex pulled her against him until her nose was almost touching his pullover, then with her firm little chin in his free hand he tipped her face up.

'As I've said before—too thin-skinned by half.' He bent and pressed a hard kiss on her lips. 'Come along. Moonlight becomes you, but we've both got a busy day ahead.'

It took a good deal of self-control to walk back to the farmhouse at Rex's side apparently quite at her ease, but Davina congratulated herself that he did not guess how much his changeable moods and cruelly placed barbs could hurt. Standing in her bedroom some half hour later, she looked out on the moonlit scene and tried to unravel the enigma of her unpredictable employer. Was he taking out on her his innermost frustration, perhaps over Adele? Or was he becoming angry at finding himself falling in love? And if so, with whom?

Davina's lips twisted in a humourless smile as this thought came and went. Oh, he'd kissed her right enough, but might it not have simply been a ploy to divert her mind from his compliments which had been no compliment? He'd listed her physical attributes as if he resented the fact that nature had been kind.

She frowned at a niggling unease which would not be pushed to the back of her mind. Try as she would it was impossible to dismiss the conviction that Rex actually enjoyed undermining her self-confidence. Maybe he had an understanding with some girl back home in Australia and disliked finding his heart pulled in two different direction. If he had a heart, that was, Davina thought as she slowly undressed. Well, whatever the cause of Rex's strange behaviour, it was up to her to keep their association strictly platonic for the future.

But that was going to be a difficult task, she discovered, for when Rex came in from his pre-breakfast chores, he seemed to bring a little of the autumnal sunshine with him. He was agreeably good-humoured and when he set out to be charming, Davina guessed he must have few equals. Within minutes last night's resolution was forgotten as she found herself responding to what, in another man, she would have interpreted as an attempt to flirt. But Rex quizzed rather than flirted and when the meal was over he leaned down, kissed her unresisting lips as if he had every right, and said before she could utter a word, 'I'll be in the first pasture when Jim Thomas arrives,' leaving Davina feeling dizzy with an unexpected joy.

Several times during the morning she stopped work to put up a hand to her mouth. Light as Rex's casual goodbye kiss had been she found herself reliving the moment. Why couldn't he always be in such a charitable frame of mind? she thought as she automatically got on with her work. Whatever his intentions, she knew she was falling more and more under Rex's spell.

It was nearly lunchtime when Jim Thomas drove into the farmyard looking even more disreputable than ever in a faded tartan shirt, muddy wellington boots and stained jeans. His eyes twinkled as Davina's expressive face revealed her thoughts and as he got out his equipment he asked, 'Thinking of entering me for the Best Dressed Man of the Year contest?'

Davina giggled. 'I must say your sartorial elegance always

knocks me for six. Rex is up in the first pasture, by the way.'

'Right!' Jim paused as he glanced at his watch. He said diffidently, 'I suppose I couldn't stay for a sandwich when I've had a look at this ewe? It's Mrs Hepburn's day off.'

'What about your sister? Not that you wouldn't be welcome,' Davina added swiftly as Jim's usually pleasant face stiffened.

'Adele's gone in to Carlisle,' he replied abruptly. 'Thanks. I'll see you later,' and he was off.

Davina watched his retreating figure thoughtfully. What was Adele Wickham up to now? Whatever it was, it found no favour with the brother on whom she'd planted herself while her divorce went through, she decided as she went indoors.

If Rex was put out to find Jim Thomas was staying to share the cold meat and salad, the huge apple pie and cream, followed by Rex's inevitable pot of strong tea, he gave no sign. The meal passed off well, for Jim had them infectiously laughing at his encounter that morning with an unco-operative pig. 'I got the better of it in the end, but not before it did its best to land both the farmer and myself on our backsides,' he ended, which made even Mr Farr's eyes twinkle with amusement. Then turning to Davina, Jim added, 'Which makes me feel I'm entitled to a bit of light relief tonight. How about coming out and having a drink?'

There was a moment's hesitation before Rex, a steely light in his eyes, answered for her. 'Sorry, old chap, but we're going to try and get a coat of paint on the study this evening. Your date will have to wait,' and he turned his head to look at Davina, as if challenging her to deny his story.

She wet her lips. 'Ask me another evening,' she said, to try and soften Rex's uncompromising refusal, but Jim Thomas, glancing from her face to Rex's, answered, 'Yes, I'll certainly do that,' and got up to leave, his blue eyes unusually serious as he thanked them for their hospitality.

The post arrived shortly after he left and a letter bearing Catrin's handwriting made Davina hurry over the washing up so she could sit down and read it at her leisure. There were several sheets covered in her sister's scrawl, but it was the last paragraph which had Davina sitting upright, something approaching horror on her face.

'You'll never believe it,' Catrin wrote, 'but in his last letter David asked when my next leave was due. If it coincides with his, he wants me to visit his home and meet his parents. But this is the amazing coincidence. They live in Camshaw. Have you met them yet? I think I told you his father was in the Navy too before he retired, and David has one brother, Roy.'

Davina racked her brains, but she had no recollection of Catrin telling her any such thing. And she had never once mentioned David's surname. What a disastrous coincidence that out of all the places in Britain, Catrin's boy-friend had to come from Camshaw! And be the son of parents noted for their strict code of behaviour. Davina could imagine the kind of reception her sister would receive once she admitted to having a sister in the district, one living under the roof of a man as handsome and attractive as Rex.

Which brought to mind the lies Rex had told about their supposed relationship. What a fool she had been to go along with the story! Even if the Comstones were the sort to give her the benefit of the doubt once they heard she and Rex had pretended to be related, they would imagine the worst. And then a further complication occurred to Davina. If Rex was supposed to be *her* stepbrother then he must also be Catrin's, and by this time David had no doubt written to his parents giving them a run-down on Catrin's background. No way around the problem that way. It was a tangled web indeed.

Davina glanced at her watch, re-read the part in the letter where Catrin had described her off-duty times, then collecting a purse and a cardigan, she set off for the village. It was a long walk, but she had no time to waste if she was to tip Catrin off before she replied to David's letter. Reaching the telephone kiosk, Davina made sure she had plenty of change, then dialled the number of Catrin's hospital.

Several minutes later, her sister's voice came clearly over the line. 'Nothing wrong, is there, Dav?'

'Yes and no. I've just got your letter—about David's parents, I mean,' Davina answered. 'Have you written to him yet telling him I'm up here?'

'No, I was hoping to get the time to write tonight. But what's the problem? You sound in a regular tizzy.'

'I am,' Davina said in a tight voice. 'Rex, to save our good names, thought fit to put it around that we were stepbrother and sister. And your David's folk are apparently not the sort to swallow a tale like that once they know it's a cock and bull story. I have it on very good authority that they're old-fashioned to the point of absurdity. From the horse's mouth —Roy Comstone.'

'Oh, you've met Roy. What's he like?'

'Difficult to say. He was described to me as the black sheep of the family, and the first time I met him he had about half a bottle of gin inside him.'

Catrin giggled. David did tell me his brother doesn't live at home any more. Do you suppose his father threw him out?'

'No idea, but it's possible, if Squire Comstone is as anti-quated in his ideas as everyone says. Are you really serious about David, Cat? Because if you are I see trouble ahead.'

'Don't worry,' Catrin's voice was full of youthful confidence, 'I bet I could twist the old man round my finger within ten minutes of meeting him. But that may not be for some time, so keep your hair on. I know I'm not getting Christmas off this year and David is due to do a spell of duty in the Far East some time soon, so the chances of my getting up to Cumbria before you leave are pretty remote. I shall tell David, of course, but not in a letter. He'll fall about laughing when I tell him what's happened.'

Davina smiled wryly. 'Trust you to think it's all a huge laugh,' she protested. Then as Catrin asked, 'How is my . . . my stepbrother, by the way?' Davina replied, 'That's quite enough of that. I just wish I'd listened to James and stayed in London. Got to go,' as the pips began, and the last thing she heard was a burst of laughter from Catrin before the line went dead.

She trudged back to the farm to find the horse tethered to the fence with Rex showing an eager boy how to brush it down. He turned as Davina reached them to say, 'Where the devil did you get to this time?' but his voice was soft and in-dulgent.

'I had to telephone Catrin in a hurry,' Davina admitted, and then as Rex cocked an enquiring eyebrow she went on rather reluctantly, 'It transpires her special boy-friend is the younger son of the Comstones, so you'll appreciate my difficulty,' and was astonished to hear Rex give a shout of laughter.

It was the first time she had heard him laugh so heartily and she looked at him with puzzlement in her clear eyes. As he met the reproachful glance Rex tried to control his mirth and put out a hand to take hers, kiss the pink palm and say contritely, 'Sorry, but you must admit there's a certain irony about the whole thing. I concoct a story to protect our reputations from the local gossips, only to find your kid sister has become almost engaged to the son of the most distinguished family for miles around. Who says it's a very small world?'

'Catrin's as amused as you appear to be,' Davina said gloomily, 'but what are we to do? I think I'd better throw up my independence and go and stay with Grandmother just until I'm earning enough to pay my way.'

'Shame on you!' Rex still held her by the hand. 'Would you really sink your pride and go cap in hand to Mrs Brehm? I take it you've warned Catrin about the Comstones' antiquated outlook, so where's the need to run away? In any case,' his thumb rubbed back and forth across her fingers as he spoke, 'what about me?'

Davina raised startled eyes as Rex said very softly, 'Do you really want to go and leave me to try and cope all alone?'

There was more in his soft drawl than in the actual words, which made Davina's heart beat quicker, then as she noticed Peter eyeing them both with evident curiosity, she pulled her fingers free. 'I suppose I'm panicking for nothing,' she admitted. 'Chances are the Comstones don't even know of our existence. Just the same I wouldn't like to spoil anything for Catrin,' she ended, and smiled shyly.

'Forget about it,' Rex advised. 'By the way, supper early this evening. Remember you said you'd give me a hand painting.'

She'd done no such thing, Davina thought as she went into the house. It had been Rex's excuse to Jim Thomas for refusing his invitation. She was surprised to find that the study had been prepared for the redecoration, for the furniture she had cleaned and polished was under covers and the fireplace blocked off.

'Who did this?' she asked Rex as he joined her, paint and brushes in his hands, and he raised his eyebrows.

'I did. Measured the wood I'd need and knocked it up out in the barn. Incidentally, I've ordered three portable gas heaters for here and the bedrooms. And some furniture. The desk and bookcase are quite good, but the rest is only fit for a bonfire.'

As they worked, the problem of Catrin and the Comstones returned to bring a furrow back to Davina's smooth forehead. She was unaware of Rex's attention as she mulled the matter over again and again until he suddenly said harshly, 'Go to bed, you're flaked out. Things won't look so bad in the morning—and no lying awake worrying, mind. Now off you go.'

Davina obeyed without argument, glad to get away from the hard eyes from which all the sympathy had fled. Rather to her suprise, she fell asleep as soon as her head touched the pillow, and did not awake until the alarm sounded the following morning.

Peeping into the study as she passed, she saw that Rex must have stayed up late, for the ceiling looked as if it had received two coats of white paint, while the drab walls now glowed with a pearly sheen like the inside of a shell. Despite this, he was already up and had gone out, presumably to feed the stock, because Davina was just in time to see him riding into the yard, leading a protesting ewe at the end of a rope.

She walked outside to greet him. As he dismounted he said grimly, 'Can you hold breakfast over? I must pen this old lady well away from the others. Jim gave her an injection yesterday, but it hasn't done the trick and Farr will have to put her down.'

Davina gave the ewe a sympathetic glance, for it looked as despondent as she herself felt. She looked up to find that Rex had lifted the saddle from the horse's back and was standing with it in his hands watching her face.

'I'll be as quick as I can,' he said, and nodded behind her.

'Here comes the old man now,' and Davina turned to see the shepherd coming down the lane.

Somehow the ewe's death sentence was the final straw. Though she tried to keep up a pretence of eating, every morsel stuck in Davina's mouth. As soon as the meal was over Rex said, 'Leave Farr some sandwiches for his lunch. You and I are going for a picnic this afternoon.' And when Davina raised her face, surprise in her eyes, Rex said, 'I want to take a look at Hadrian's Wall and there's nothing urgent that can't wait until tomorrow.'

An hour later they were in the Land Rover, a hamper containing a picnic lunch behind Davina's seat. Rex drove fast and to her surprise seemed to know just where he was going. 'Only parts of the Wall are left standing now, and not all are accessible,' Davina warned him as a signpost for Hexham flashed past.

'I looked out a route before I came up here and showed it to the old man. He agreed this is the best way, so stop worrying and just enjoy the scenery.'

'What an amazing man you are,' Davina murmured thoughtfully.

Rex turned his head to meet her eyes. 'I learned at an early age to plan beforehand,' he said as his gaze returned to the road ahead. 'It's not much use leaving things to chance, though Lady Luck does play into one's hands unexpectedly from time to time.'

Davina waited for him to elaborate on this cryptic statement, but Rex had obviously no intention of satisfying her curiosity. She turned to admire the wild beauty of the countryside and they did not speak again until Rex pulled up in a car park and said, 'I guess we have to walk from here.'

Davina gave an involuntary shiver as the cold wind cut through even the thick woollie she had put on over her cotton shirt and Rex said dryly, 'Trust a woman to come ill prepared! Here—put this on,' and he thrust a tweed jacket into her arms.

Slipping her arms into the sleeves, she hid a smile. Rex took her arm and they stepped on to a footpath which led across the close-cropped turf to where other sightseers were brushing up on their Roman history. When they stood at last on the section of the old wall built so long ago as a defence against the warlike Scots, Davina drew a deep breath of the keen air blowing from the north. 'Strange to think people lived and worked here nearly two thousand years ago,' she said absently, and Rex at her side topped her remark by, 'You ought to see some parts of Australia if you think this awe-inspiring. Not man-made monuments of the past, mark you, but none the less impressive for that.'

Davina looked up and he pulled her against him. 'You're still cold even with that jacket. Stupid! Why didn't you wrap up? Come along, we'll find a warm hollow somewhere and have lunch. What you need is a hot drink. I hope you've packed a flask of tea.'

'Two actually,' Davina said demurely, then laughed outright as Rex gave her one of his keen glances. 'I've learned your capacity, you see,' she ended as he gave her a reluctant smile.

The bracken was beginning to brown already up here where the winds blew keenly from the north, but Rex found a sheltered spot where two drystone walls met and spread out the rug. They were neither much inclined to break the silence until their appetites had been satisfied, when Rex sank back, head on folded arms.

He closed his eyes as Davina began to fold away the wrapping papers and uneaten food into the picnic basket. She knew Rex was not asleep as she asked, 'What made you suddenly decide to take an afternoon off?'

Eyes closed, one mobile eyebrow rose higher than the other as Rex replied, 'Do I have to have a specific reason for everything?'

Davina looked away, a stem of grass between her lips. She said thoughtfully, 'I must say I'm a little curious.' Her eyes returned to his face. 'Somehow it seemed out of character.'

'Meaning that I'm a bit of a slavedriver?' Rex asked, and opened his eyes to meet hers.

Daringly Davina nodded. A small hint of that dimple at the corner of her mouth came and went as she added, 'I'd like to think it was because you felt sorry for me, but sometimes I get a feeling you don't give a damn about women, either individually or as a whole.'

'Trust a woman to get hold of a stick by the wrong end,' Rex responded, and when Davina promptly tickled his chin with the end of the long stalk of grass in her hand and said, 'That's exactly what I mean,' he sat up suddenly and grasped her upper arms.

Davina expected a hard kiss as punishment for her audacity, but Rex had frozen, his hands grasping her rigidly upright. 'Keep quite still,' he ordered through lips only open sufficiently to whisper the three curt words, and as one hand left her arm to reach for the thermos flask standing on the rug, she noticed his eyes were fixed on a spot behind her.

Suddenly she was flung to one side and Rex was on his feet, hitting at some object on the ground near where she had been sitting. Feeling decidedly shaken, Davina got to her feet as he flung down the broken flask.

She walked to his side. 'Why, it's an adder,' she said slowly, and gave an uncontrollable shudder.

'Are they poisonous?'

'Yes, but there's an antidote. I haven't seen one since our minister's wife was bitten when we were on a Sunday School picnic years ago. She was in hospital for over a week.'

'Good thing I saw it was about to strike. We must have disturbed it,' Rex said casually, then as Davina continued to gaze down at the dead reptile he turned her to face him.

'Not going to have hysterics now it's all over, are you?' he asked roughly, and she threw herself against him and hid her face in the thick wool of his sweater. As his arms closed as if instinctively around her she said in a muffled voice, 'No, I'm not, but thanks.'

Rex felt for her face and turned it up. 'I've never seen anyone react so quickly,' she added hastily, her heart beginning to beat in thick uneven strokes at something deep in the hooded eyes looking into her own.

'Put it down to my early training,' Rex said lightly, and flicked the end of her nose with a careless forefinger. 'My father taught me how to take care of myself as soon as I was old enough to understand. He didn't believe in feather-bedding, and you need all your wits about you back home.'

Looking up to meet that enigmatical smile, Davina decided Australia was not the only place one needed to keep

all one's wits about one as the sky was blotted out as Rex
bent and claimed her lips. But the sensation as if solid ground
had fallen away beneath her feet was not so silly as it seemed.
When the world tilted back to normal and she opened her
eyes her feet really were off the ground, for Rex had lifted
her and she was lying against a hard, muscular body.

'Hadn't we better be getting home?' he cocked an im-
pertinent eyebrow. 'Farr will be wondering what's happened
to us and I promised the boy his first riding lesson before
supper.'

Nettled, Davina said sharply, 'I might agree if you'd just
put me down,' when to her annoyance Rex gave her another
light kiss and a taunting,

'You're so small, I could simply pop you in my pocket,'
before lowering her to the ground.

He'd had the last word again!

CHAPTER SEVEN

THE following morning Davina awoke with a sore throat and
the beginnings of a headache, which by lunchtime had become the forerunner of a really heavy head cold. Rex, coming
in to wash, caught her sneezing and stopped to say, his keen
eyes missing nothing of the shivering, the heavy eyes and red
nose, 'I told you you should have worn something sensible
yesterday. You've got a chill. Go on up to bed and don't come
down again until I say you may.'

When Rex was in this mood, argument was useless, but
Davina had no wish to argue. Bed seemed at that moment
greatly to be desired and she wasted no time in undressing
and laying her aching head on the cool pillow. She must have
drifted into an uneasy sleep, for when she opened her eyes
she found a hot water bottle had been slipped under the bedclothes and she felt warm and comfortable. As she stirred,
the bedroom door opened and Rex entered.

'I didn't think you'd want anything to eat, and in any case
you were fast asleep when I last looked in. Farr's gone and

I packed the boy back home so his chatter wouldn't wake you. Come on, sit up and drink this while it's hot.'

'This' proved to be hot lemon liberally laced with whisky. Leaning on an elbow, Davina grimaced as she sipped it and swallowed the aspirin on Rex's palm.

'Haven't you anything more substantial to wear than that flimsy thing?' he barked, and Davina nearly dropped the beaker as she saw his eyes were fixed on the thin cotton nightie, with its shoestring straps and ribboned neckline.

Her eyes flew to his face as hastily she drained the hot toddy, handed it back and pulled the covers up to her chin. 'I never wear anything else,' and her face flushed as Rex uttered an exasperated sound. He strode out, to return a few minutes later with a pyjama jacket, and with a sharp, 'Sit up,' he bundled her into the jacket, buttoning it across her chest and turning up the sleeves up nearly to her elbows.

If Davina had not felt so ill she might have laughed, because she had a pretty fair notion of how she must look in the top of a suit of pyjamas made to fit a man of Rex Fitzpaine's stature. He gave her no time to comment even if she wanted to, for with a peremptory, 'Lie down and get some sleep,' he picked up the beaker and went away again.

But Davina was far too wide awake now to doze off again and she lay listening to the sounds from downstairs. Even with the bedroom door closed, she could imagine Rex's movements, as the kitchen lay beneath. She hugged the hot water bottle and heard the preparation of the meal, a silence while he ate, then the clatter as the dishes were put into the sink. Minutes later the outer door opened and closed, and she heard his footsteps cross the yard.

She was watching the last light fade when the sounds of cars approaching reached her ears. The first was being driven at speed and pulled up beneath her window with a crashing of gears and a screech of brakes which she easily identified as typical of Adele Wickham's usual method of driving. The second car approached and stopped a good deal more sedately, and as car doors banged Davina heard Rex's voice.

The words were few and too quietly spoken for her to over-hear, but Adele's reply was clear. 'Don't be ridiculous, darling. We've not come all this way to be turned away without so much as a drink. Come on, where do you keep it?' and the kitchen door crashed open.

The next sound to reach Davina's ears over the murmur of voices and the sound of an argument taking place was the clink of glasses. So Adele had got her way! Davina could imagine how she would have smiled as she coaxed Rex into giving way, her golden hair glinting and her seductively willowy figure no doubt clad in some eye-catching and very expensive creation.

But footsteps were coming up the stairs and across the upper hall. The door opened to reveal Rex with the young doctor at his elbow.

'I've brought Doc Mulholland to have a look at you.'

Forgetting the borrowed jacket, Davina shot up in bed. 'I don't need a doctor,' she protested as Tom Mulholland, eyes twinkling, unscrewed the cap off his thermometer.

'No harm in my running the rule over you, since I'm here,' he said, and popped the slim glass tube between Davina's lips before she could utter a word of protest. He took up her wrist and as he checked the pulse rate asked over his shoulder, 'How long's she been like this?'

Ignoring the spark of anger in Davina's eyes, Rex replied as if she were part of the furniture, 'Only today. The silly girl went out without a coat yesterday afternoon.'

As Tom removed the thermometer, Davina said angrily, 'I don't usually catch anything. And anyway, I hadn't realised how sharp the wind was going to be,' she ended lamely, aware of the derision in Rex's eyes.

'Well, you've certainly got a fever,' Tom Mulholland said, 'though I think it's simply a chill,' he went on, feeling the glands in Davina's neck. 'Stay in bed for the next twenty-four hours. Lots of fluid and aspirin, of course. I'll leave Rex something, so you'll be sure of a good night. It's marvellous what a good sleep will do. Incidentally,' he went on, and the twinkle had returned to his eyes, 'I like the nightwear. Very fetching!'

Rex looked even more than usually sardonic as he said, 'I told you she was a silly girl. Even when she's ill she hasn't the sense to wrap up.' Abruptly his expression changed as Tom Mulholland asked,

'Like me to get rid of that crowd down there? I recommend an early night for this young lady here.'

'Can you? They look dug in to me,' Rex answered.

'Don't you believe it,' Tom Mulholland answered cheerfully. 'Come and watch while I say Davina's infectious. You won't be able to see how quickly they'll remember pressing appointments elsewhere,' and Rex gave a smile of grim satisfaction as with a 'goodnight' from Tom, the two men went away.

Not five minutes later, the sound of departures came clearly to Davina's ears and when Rex strolled into the room to draw the curtains she asked, 'What did he say I'd got? Cholera?' and Rex smiled faintly.

'Nothing quite so drastic, but it served the purpose. Give me your hot water bottle and I'll refill it while you clean your teeth. Five minutes, mind, then you're to be back in bed.'

Davina had no wish to extend the time limit, for she found herself to be strangely unsteady on her trip to the bathroom and returned to creep thankfully back to bed. Rex, coming in with the hot water bottle, was also carrying a cup of tea, some hot buttered toast and a sleeping pill. Davina eyed it with disfavour. 'Do I have to take that?'

'You do,' came the remorseless reply, and when she said in a small voice, 'But, Rex, I'm not used to taking sleeping pills,' he answered, 'There's a first time for everything. You may have to get used to doing a lot of things you're not used to doing one of these days. In any case,' he finished unkindly, 'it will obviate me being called up during the night if you've had a knock-out drop.'

'You're a beast,' Davina announced, but her voice was mild. She was suddenly aware that the chill was indeed her own fault and that Rex, though he had censured her for her stupidity, had been remarkably kind. His sick-nursing might be rough and ready, but it was nevertheless efficient and he had taken the trouble to find out that it was no worse than he suspected. Another man might not even have noticed she was off colour, let alone sent her off to bed.

She swallowed the pill and began to sip at the tea, quite unaware that her face was mirroring these thoughts. Rex sat on the end of the bed watching her finish the meagre supper and when the last crumb of toast had vanished he asked, 'More tea?'

Davina shook her head and yawned. The drug was already beginning to take effect as she smiled dreamily, slithered down and said sleepily, 'No, thanks. See you in the morning, Rex,' as she felt a hand tuck in the covers.

But it was past midday when her eyes opened again and she blinked and rubbed her eyes. She picked up the little bedside clock to give it a shake, thinking it had stopped, but the steady tick told her she really had slept all morning. She lay back again, glad that her sore throat felt better and the pain in her head reduced to a faint twinge only when she turned it from side to side.

She was considering getting up when she heard Rex coming upstairs. He opened the bedroom door quietly, then seeing she was awake, came right into the room. 'Well, Sleeping Beauty! Feeling better?'

Davina smiled sleepily as he walked forward and sat down on the bed. He laid one hand, large, brown and infinitely gentle, against her forehead and said, 'Cool as a cucumber,' before she could frame a reply.

As she reached up and took his hand between her own, she smiled again. 'I don't know what Tom gave me last night, but I feel well enough to get up. I'm sure you're fed up having to be cook and nursemaid, especially as it was entirely my own fault.'

'Glad you admit it,' Rex raised a quizzical eyebrow. 'However, there's no sense in rushing things. Stay where you are until this afternoon. I've some soup on the go. Fancy a drop?'

'Please.' Davina, suddenly conscious she was still holding Rex's hand, let go and struggled to a sitting position, aware that there was amusement and instant awareness in the hard eyes watching. However, Rex had apparently no intention of making the most of the situation, for with a casual, 'I'll be back with your lunch in ten minutes,' he strolled out of the room.

Even when she heard Rex and Mr Farr return to the barn, Davina still stayed where she was. The day in bed or the after-effects of the sleeping pill had left her feeling extraordinarily lazy and it was some time before she summoned up the energy to collect clean clothes and go down to the bathroom.

She washed her hair as well when she discovered there was plenty of hot water and rubbed it almost dry before coaxing it into neat curls and waves. Feeling a good deal more lively now she was up and dressed, she went to the kitchen, stopping on the threshold as she saw it was as neat as a pin.

She had expected a sink piled with dirty dishes awaiting her and food left around, but the room was as orderly as when she was in charge. Going into the pantry, Davina discovered that Rex must have stocked up, probably this morning while she slept, and feeling a twinge of dejection, she carried a leg of lamb into the kitchen and began preparations for the evening meal.

She was thinking that Rex Fitzpaine was a man of many talents, one who could cope perfectly well without a woman's help, when Jim Thomas drove into the yard.

He came into the kitchen carrying an armful of red roses and stopped in his tracks when he saw Davina standing at the sink peeling potatoes.

'My goodness, that was a quick recovery! I got the impression you were on the verge of pneumonia last night and came along expecting to hold the invalid's hand,' he teased.

Davina dried her hands. 'I caught a chill braving your winds inadequately clad. Are those for me, Jim? They're lovely,' she added as Jim pushed the roses into her arms. 'But two dozen! What an extravagance!'

Jim pulled out a chair and sat down. 'I felt like throwing myself in the River Eden this morning, then I saw these in a shop in Carlisle and thought you might like them,' he announced gloomily, and as Davina, a questioning look in her eyes, continued to stand eyeing him over the fragrant armful of flowers, he took a letter from his pocket and flung it on the table.

'This arrived in the morning's mail.'

Davina put the roses down and reached for the letter. 'Read it,' Jim suggested, and dug pipe and tobacco pouch out of his other pocket.

'Sure you want me to?' Davina sat down opposite him and at his nod reluctantly withdrew the letter. It was brief and to the point. Mr Jonathan Comstone presented his compliments to Mr James Thomas, and wished to inform him that his professional services were no longer required by the Camshaw Hall Estate.

'You don't mean to say this is because . . .' Davina stammered to a halt in her astonishment.

'I told you it was a possibility. I went up to ask for an explanation first thing after my morning surgery. The Squire kept me waiting twenty minutes before he saw me, then told me to my face that he couldn't do business with anyone who condoned adultery. Condoned adultery!' Jim repeated. 'I ask you, Dav—In this day and age when the divorce rate is so high. And did he expect me to turn my own sister from my door as if she were some kind of leper? The trouble is, Jonathan Comstone is a pretty influential man in the county. I'm bound to lose other clients when this gets around.'

'Oh, Jim, I am sorry!' Davina reached over and put a hand over one of his. But she was aware of concern on her own account as well as his as he laid down his pipe and took her hand between his own.

Jim looked grateful for the instant sympathy as he said, 'Thanks I had to talk to someone and I could hardly tell Adele.'

Adele again, Davina thought, and tried to withdraw her hand, but Jim had a tight grasp on it. He seemed unaware of having said the wrong thing, for he said thoughtfully, 'Perhaps when all the bother and publicity is over the Squire will change his mind. As soon as her finances are settled, I daresay Adele will want to be off.'

But divorce settlements sometimes took months, Davina thought to herself, and wished Catrin had fallen in love with anyone other than David Comstone. How fate could twist and complicate things, she was thinking as the door swung open and Rex came in.

Lost in unhappy speculation, Davina had not heard his approach and she snatched her hand from Jim's as she saw Rex note their clasped hands and the old ironic gleam appear in his eyes.

'I came to say I'm just going to run Farr and the boy down to the village,' he drawled, and his eyes moved to the roses. Davina felt a flush colouring her cheeks as he went on suavely, 'The old chap's having tea with his sister-in-law and Peter has got choir practice, so they won't be here for supper.'

'I'll take them. I'm just going,' Jim said, getting to his feet. 'Save you a journey. I only came up to see how Dav was getting on.'

'Up and about again, as you see,' Rex answered. 'Thanks, I'd be glad if you'd take them down,' and he followed Jim outside.

He returned again five minutes later and one glance at his face told Davina she was not to escape this time. 'You do realise the poor chap's well on the way to falling in love with you?' he began, and when Davina opened her mouth to protest he held up a hand to silence her.

Picking up the roses, Rex looked at them in silent appraisal while she watched his face. Suddenly he looked up and met her anxious eyes. 'No one buys two dozen long-stemmed red roses if their intentions are purely platonic. But then I think you know that. The scene I interrupted ten minutes ago was anything but platonic.' Rex's tones bit, making an involuntary shiver run down Davina's spine.

'I was only trying to comfort him. Things are far from easy for Jim, so it was sweet of him to come up to enquire how I was.'

Rex had a distinctly sceptical gleam in his eyes as he retorted, 'No need to let him think his advances would be welcome, though, is there? And what, may I ask, is he finding far from easy?'

Davina hesitated, unsure whether Jim would wish her to pass on his confidences. When Rex said harshly, 'Don't try and tell me you're a soft touch for a hard luck story,' however, Davina forgot caution and replied hotly, 'It wasn't a hard luck story. He's had his contract with Camshaw Hall terminated because of Adele's divorce.'

As soon as the words were out, Davina regretted them, for laying the roses down Rex turned to face her and there was undisguised amusement in his face. 'No doubt that the Squire believes in practising what he preaches! Any chance of Catrin's infatuation fading?'

Davina turned away, chilled by Rex's hard, implacable tones. 'Not as far as I know. She thinks it would be an easy matter to get David's father softened up.'

Rex did not reply and Davina looked over her shoulder to find he had become lost in thought. Becoming aware of her questioning glance, he seemed to pull his thoughts back to the present as he said, 'Since Jim's taken over as chauffeur, I'll be in the barn until supper's ready,' and he went out, leaving Davina's mind in a turmoil as she got on with the cooking.

He had not returned when the roast was ready, and Davina went out to look for him. Sounds coming from the barn led her in that direction and she found Rex, sleeves rolled up, mixing a concoction in a large tin. It smelled strongly and Davina's nose wrinkled in disapproval. 'Whatever is it?'

'Linseed oil and distemper. Very good for the sinuses,' Rex explained patiently. 'Red for the Welsh ram, black for the other,' and he pointed to another tin nearby. 'We're raddling tomorrow as the ewes have been fed enough for mating.'

Seeing Davina's continuing perplexity he went on, his soft drawl now holding a note of mild amusement at her ignorance, 'It's necessary to know how many marriages have been properly consummated once the rams are put with their flocks. Hence the dyes.'

Enlightenment dawned and Davina laughed. 'Of course, how stupid of me. Supper's ready. Will you be long.'

'Coming right now. This is ready.' Rex straightened. 'I've got something to show you after supper.'

As he wiped his hands on a piece of rag Davina asked, a ripple of excitement in her voice, 'What is it?'

'Wait and see,' Rex ordered, and putting away the things he had been using he walked her back to the house.

No one could have eaten in a more leisurely fashion, Davina decided a hour later as, his appetite satisfied at last, Rex got out his makings and began his rolling of the inevitable after-supper cigarette. He looked faintly amused when Davina, her patience exhausted, said, 'Well! What was it you wanted me to see?'

'All in good time. It will keep. I'll help with the dishes.' Rex seemed bent on being provoking as he chatted casually while helping her clear away. But as soon as she had laid the tea tray, he seemed to relent, as with a, 'Don't put the kettle on yet. I won't keep you in suspense any longer,' and taking her by one hand, he led her across the hall into the study.

Davina let out a gasp of surprise. 'Why, it's all finished! And furnished. When did you do it?' she asked, but her eyes were on the softly glowing walls, the colourful Turkish carpet and the two new armchairs and matching curtains, picking out the predominant colour in the carpet. The desk was obviously already in use, for books and papers lay in neat piles, and in the fireplace stood a brand new portable heater.

'The furniture arrived today while you were still asleep,' Rex said, then, 'Try one of the chairs. I'll bring the tea.'

He came back to find Davina curled like a kitten in one of the huge armchairs. 'They're super,' she announced as he put the tea tray down. 'But why did you buy such big chairs?'

He stood, hands on hips, looking down at her. 'Do you see me really relaxing in something of smaller dimensions?' he asked in a challenging voice, then added wickedly, 'In any case, I'd another possibility in view when I picked them out.'

Davina fell right into the trap. 'Another possibility?' she queried innocently, then gasped as two long arms swept her out of the chair and Rex sat down with her cradled in his lap. 'Precisely!' a soft voice whispered. 'I thought they'd hold two perfectly. Tell me—are you well enough to be kissed?'

Davina looked up, met his eyes and was lost. Almost of their own free will her arms twined themselves round his neck and she said shyly, 'I think so,' and hid her face against his collar.

'Well, we'll never find out while you continue to bury your face in my shirt,' a mocking voice said, and a firm hand felt and found her chin, turning her face up again.

For ten minutes all coherent conversation ceased until Davina began to feel as if her whole body was on fire. A hypnotic feeling of inertia seemed to have taken possession of her as caressing hands and warm lips expertly roused her sleeping desires. Before she became quite incapable of resisting the urge to give in to Rex's increasing demands she dragged herself ruthlessly down to earth and tried to struggle upright.

With a fiery gleam in his eyes Rex said thickly, 'I'd say

you were *quite* recovered—but why the halt to such pleasant proceedings?'

Davina captured a wandering hand. 'You must know the answer to that. We're not children. Anyway,' she went on, clutching at straws, 'the tea must be getting cold.'

Rex began to look amused. 'Good try! It must have been too cold to drink some little time ago. Let's forget the tea. You're an extremely attractive female and I imagine you know I'm no plaster saint. Neither are you, come to that. I've seen you kissing your cousin James in a most uncousinly fashion, and heaven knows what would have happened this afternoon if I hadn't interrupted the touching scene taking place right here in the kitchen.'

Davina unlocked her hands and hid her face in them, partly to cover up her flushed cheeks, partly to conceal the hurt expression in her eyes. Rex seemed to believe she met every man more than half way! She looked up bravely and wet her lips. 'I seem to have somehow given you the impression that I habitually indulge in ...' She stopped, at a loss for the right words.

'... indiscriminate lovemaking?' Rex supplied as she hesitated, and there was mockery in his glance. Davina swallowed a hard lump in her throat as she met that sardonic look, deciding that to dispel the hateful cynicism nothing but the truth would do.

'I happen to have fallen in love with you. That's the only reason for this,' and with trembling fingers she rebuttoned her shirt. 'Don't ask me how or when it happened, because I don't know,' she went on as he did not speak. 'When we first met, it simply never occurred to me that we'd ever be likely to form any kind of a relationship, because you seemed a bit distant. Almost as if you didn't care for the cut of my jib,' she added with a rueful smile.

'And now?' Rex pulled her back into his arms and kissed her breathless.

Her face was pink when he finally let her up for air, but her flush was no longer due to embarrassment. 'Oh, Rex! Do you feel as I do? You can't imagine how happy that makes me,' she added before he had time to answer. 'But what are we going to do? Everyone thinks we're brother and sister.'

'Stepbrother and sister,' Rex corrected her, then to Davina's surprise he got up and deposited her in the chair. 'Don't worry, I'll think of something. Meanwhile—tea,' and picking up the teapot he strolled out.

Davina snuggled into the chair still warm from his body, but there was a puzzled frown between her brows. It was beginning to dawn on her that there had been something not quite right about his response to her admission of love. For the first time in her life she had committed herself frankly and fully, but would it have been wiser to have waited, played hard to get? Perhaps, their mutual attraction having been established beyond doubt, Rex felt it unnecessary to put his feelings into words. It would have been nice if he'd been more forthcoming, Davina thought, then sighed. On occasion he could be a man of few words. A pity this was one of them, she mused, as he returned with the tea.

The first frost of the coming winter lay over the gardens and fields, Davina discovered when she got out of bed next morning, but it could not chill the warmth inside her as she remembered Rex's passionate goodnight kiss before he had pushed her almost roughly inside her bedroom and closed the door between them last night. Wings seemed to have been fitted to her feet as she sped downstairs and prepared breakfast, but when Rex came in there was no smile in the hooded eyes as he said, 'I'm going to Barnard Castle right after breakfast. Tell Farr when he arrives that the rams are out. I don't know what time I'll be back, so keep an eye on the boy. He thinks because I've let him get his leg astride the horse a couple of times he knows how to ride. I don't want to be accused of letting him break his neck.'

His whole manner was so prosaic and matter-of-fact that Davina stared, unable to believe her ears. Impossible to convince herself that this was the same man who had kissed her into submission, for the romantic lover of yesterday had vanished as if he had never existed. Perhaps this morning he was regretting letting passion off a tightly held rein, triggering as it had her rash admission of love.

Too late for recriminations now, Davina thought, when with a casual, 'See you later,' Rex had gone. Suddenly she saw the bracken was turning brown on the hills, the heather blossom already dead. She was relieved to have the day broken into by the old shepherd coming up to the house at midday for a hot meal. The housework was all done and she had no heart today for writing a love story.

'How are you settling down in our north country?' the old man asked when, the meal over, he reached for his pipe. 'Missing the city life, I dare say?'

'Not really,' Davina smiled as she met the shepherd's kindly eyes. 'I was brought up in the country, though not so wild as up here. I expect you get a lot of snow in winter?'

'We're certainly in for it this year,' he nodded. 'I know the signs and it's my guess the first snow will be early. You'll need something warmer than those cotton pants, missie, in a week or two.'

Davina glanced down at her jeans. 'I've got waterproof trousers to put over them and a winter-weight anorak, so I should be all right. I've done a fair bit of hill walking since my teens, and it doesn't do to be caught out in a winter storm.'

'Nor in a stiff wind either,' the old man ribbed her. 'Gaffer was fair kicking himself for letting you catch a cold t'other day. Though as I told him, he's not used to our climate either.'

So Rex had been anxious and blamed himself for her brief indisposition, despite his words of condemnation as to the proper attire for a windy day, Davina thought, and her heart lightened. But when he returned in the late afternoon he did not so much as come near the house, for a few minutes after the engine stopped, she caught a glimpse of him striding up the track towards the pastures where the sheep had been put out to graze.

When he finally came in, supper was almost ready. 'I feel like a bath and a stiff whisky. Have I got time?' he greeted Davina after a swift glance at the places set at the table.

At her silent nod, he simply said, 'Good,' then as he reached the door into the hall, 'Farr is staying to supper. I take it Peter didn't turn up?'

Davina managed a 'no' as the door closed behind him. Tears were almost choking her as she laid another place at the table, for there was no doubt now that last night was over and forgotten as far as Rex was concerned. How vexing he must have found her unsolicited declaration of undying love!

'I may be late,' he told her baldly as he and the shepherd got up to leave. 'Mr Farr's playing in a darts match at the pub, so I shall stay and cheer him on.'

Davina fancied there was pity in the old man's eyes as he thanked her for the meal, but in trying to hold back the tears, she could not be sure. As soon as the Land Rover could no longer be heard they overflowed and Davina, her head on folded arms, wept until she could weep no more. She eventually pulled herself together, blew her nose and faced up to the unpalatable fact that Rex's lovemaking must simply have been a spur-of-the-moment affair, without depth or sincerity.

But a bruised heart, not to mention a feeling of sick self-loathing for being so naïve, does not disappear simply by facing facts squarely, and Davina gave a sigh of relief when the clock on the kitchen mantelpiece chimed ten. But when she dragged herself upstairs and crept into bed sleep eluded her as she lay staring like a lost child into the darkness.

Long after Rex returned and she heard the slam of his bedroom door she lay wide awake, wishing with all her heart that she had never gone to have supper with James that fateful evening. Life would have been more tolerable had she never been introduced to the heartless man in the room across the landing.

CHAPTER EIGHT

A PROLONGED bout of weeping followed by only four hours' sleep do nothing for a girl's looks, and Davina gave a gasp of dismay when she caught sight of her face in the mirror the following morning. Before she started on the day's work she made up carefully, and only went down when she felt certain all trace of last night's orgy of self-pity had been hidden.

But she had underestimated Rex's powers of observation.

As she put breakfast in front of him he said idly, 'You're not looking your usual bonny self this morning. Had a bad night?'

Davina's glance across the table showed her there was not a vestige of sympathy in the ruthless eyes of the man opposite, and suddenly her mouth felt dry. She who was usually ready with a witty reply, a quick jokey remark, could think of nothing to say.

But Rex did not seem surprised at receiving no answer. His hard eyes took in the complicated make-up which Davina had hoped would deceive him. 'Expecting someone? Or is the warpaint for my benefit? Sorry, but Farr and I have a busy morning ahead. Perhaps this evening, eh? It's surprising how a comfortable room, a good meal after the day's work is done and a willing female can turn a man on. And you, sweetie, are attractive enough to bring out the old Adam in any man—even without the perfume and eye-shadow.'

Davina felt as if she had been slapped. With a muffled gulp she got up, dragged a quilted jacket from a hook behind the door and ran outside. She did not pause until the house was out of sight when, winded, she stopped to catch her breath.

She found she had run up the track and over the rise and glanced nervously over her shoulder, but there was no sign of pursuit. Either Rex was giving her time to cool down or he simply did not care how his words had hurt. She walked slowly on, hands in her pockets, until groups of sheep came in sight. Sitting down on the drystone wall, she watched them moodily, wondering what to do next.

This problem was solved by Rex himself some half hour later, for he came cantering gently along the track to pull the horse to a standstill at her back.

He sounded quite unconcerned as he drawled, 'So this is where you've got to,' as if they had met by accident in the middle of Piccadilly. 'We've got an early visitor—our minister, no less. I've left him sharing a pot of tea with Farr. Come on, up you get!' and the next moment Davina felt herself hoisted off the wall and dumped, none too gently, in front of Rex.

'Good thing you're only pint-sized,' he told the back of

her head. 'I daresay the poor beast finds my weight quite enough. However, it's not so far and he should manage to carry us both without buckling at the knees.'

Davina sat as stiffly as she could and did not reply. She was determined not to unbend, but she had reckoned without the devastating effect to her overwrought nerves of a ride clasped against Rex's broad chest. He guided the horse with one hand, holding her firmly against his body with the other, and even through the anorak she could feel her whole body responding to that masculine warmth.

Clinging tightly to her last shreds of self-control, Davina gave a tiny sigh of relief as George's hooves clattered into the yard and escape lay ahead—but Rex hadn't finished with her yet. Before she could get her leg over and slide to the ground he dismounted and turned to put his two hands at her waist and lift her off the horse as if she were no bigger than a doll.

For several seconds he held her hard against him, her feet just off the ground, and smiled maliciously down into her wide eyes. Then as electricity sparked between them, he suddenly set her gently down and turned to pick up the reins. 'Tell Farr to come to the barn if he's finished his tea,' he ordered casually as he led the horse away.

Davina watched him for a moment or two, anger beginning to smoulder in her breast before she turned to walk into the farmhouse. The two men at the table got up and when she smiled at them, the old man said 'This is our rector, miss—Mr Matthews. Gaffer wanting me, is he?'

Davina nodded before she turned to shake hands with the tall, ungainly young man in the clerical collar. He looked faintly anxious as he said, 'Sorry my first call on you had to be this early. Mrs McKay lost the baby yesterday and Mother insisted that as she herself is laid up with a sprained ankle it was my duty to visit her.'

Davina gave him a sympathetic glance. 'A bit of an ordeal, I imagine. Peter comes up here pretty often. Is there anything we can do?'

They both sat down and the young minister smiled ruefully. 'I'm not married, so Mother usually deputises for me in cases like that. It's not the first time, you know.'

Remembering something Mr Farr had said, Davina nodded. 'So I've heard. Isn't Peter's father . . .' She hesitated.

'Yes, the black sheep of my flock.' Mr Matthews' eyes were full of amusement. 'However, he's the best tenor in the choir—which brings me to one of the reasons for my visit. Would you be willing to take part in the Nativity play this year? We're very short of angels.'

Davina gave an astonished laugh. 'But Christmas is weeks away. You don't mean they're starting rehearsing already?'

'Mother believes in leaving nothing to the last minute,' came the reply, 'and as soon as I knew I was coming out this way she insisted that it was a good moment to approach you. Can I tell her you'll be along at the Rectory on Wednesday week? We're meeting there at seven-thirty for a first reading.'

Davina could see the young rector's mother was obviously a force to be reckoned with, perhaps the mainstay of the parish. She answered slowly, 'May I let you know?' and at Mr Matthews' nod added, 'and if Peter's mother needs any help I hope you'll call on me to give a hand.'

She ought perhaps to have apologised for not attending his church, she thought as she watched her visitor drive away in his ancient Mini. Once a regular churchgoer, since her father's death she had been a bit of a backslider. A frown marred her smooth forehead as she got on with the morning's work, for a part in the Nativity play committed her to staying on here and after Rex's thinly veiled insults of this morning she was not sure of her future plans any more. He had always been unpredictable, and she was far too much in love with him to simply stay and be a conveniently available female when he felt in an affectionate mood. Sooner than lose every vestige of self-respect she'd go back to London, take a full-time job and try to do her writing in the evenings.

Which would be a most unsatisfactory arrangement, she was thinking when he came in for lunch. Bringing a smell of tobacco and sheep disinfectant into the room he washed before sitting down to cut himself a slice of bread as Davine ladled thick vegetable broth into two soup bowls.

'I suppose I can make an educated guess as to why young Matthews came up to see us? He wants to know why we haven't joined his congregation.'

'No, he didn't mention that at all,' Davina replied. 'He came to ask if I'd take part in his mother's Nativity play. Apparently she produces it every year and they're short of angels.'

In the act of picking up his soup spoon, Rex laughed. It was anything but a pleasant sound and Davina's nerves tightened as she recognised the contempt in his response to her remark. 'You! An angel! There would be a nice piece of miscasting if you like,' he said in harsh tones. 'Now if they'd wanted a king they'd have come to the right place, since King is my name.'

Scarlet stained Davina's cheeks at the humiliating tones of his voice. Under his watchful eyes she gathered every scrap of pride and ignoring the first part of his reply asked, 'King and Rex meaning the same, I suppose you mean that qualifies you for the role?'

'No, I mean precisely what I said. I told you to call me Rex, but in fact my name is Kingbury—King for short. My mother suffered from a weakness for grand-sounding christian names. My brother's is nearly as bad.'

Davina felt as if the room was spinning round her as she repeated tonelessly, 'Kingbury.' She looked up, feeling sick with despair, to meet a tigerish gleam in the eyes watching her. 'Then you're . . .'

'Got it at last, haven't you? Yes, I'm Barton's brother. I'm sorry we didn't met during that remarkably short engagement, but Mother only gets in touch with me when she wants something.'

As Davina's lips parted Rex held up his hand and silenced the words about to pour out. 'Spare me the excuses. No matter how convincing the lies you could undoubtedly think up, I wouldn't believe them if you stood on a stack of bibles. Though Barr is a good deal younger than me and we've not been allowed to see one another as much as we'd have liked, it might surprise you to know I'm fond of him—sorry for him too, for between Mother and you, he very nearly died. When he discovered you had no intention of marrying him it was the final straw. He tried to kill himself.'

'You can't be serious!' The four words were jerked out of Davina with something approaching horror in her voice.

'It's hardly the kind of thing I'd joke about. Mother was

prevented by my father's will from keeping me and living the kind of life she craved, and I think that made her determined nothing should take Barr out of her custody. My stepfather died when my half-brother was sixteen, and thereafter Mother forced Barr to dance to her piping. She insisted he study law and become a lawyer like his father, when all he wanted was to be a farmer. You can imagine Mother's reaction to that ambition!' Rex's voice was hard and cynical. 'She heard of a job in a law firm in San Francisco and was so sure Barr would get it that she'd even begun her arrangements to sell up and move to America with him. Barr knew how angry she'd be when he told her he'd not got the job.'

'You make him sound like a jellyfish,' Davina interrupted hotly.

Rex eyed her thoughtfully before he continued. 'You've obviously no idea of constant pressure on a sensitive young man. I suppose you were so busy flaunting your undoubted attractions for his benefit on the boat that you never noticed how depressed he was?'

As Davina tried to interrupt and tell Rex that this was precisely why she had sought out Barton Patterson, Rex waved her words aside. 'What for you was simply a shipboard romance to while away the journey no doubt must have seemed to Barr the answer to all his problems. He thought you were an heiress, you were patently interested in him, and to arrive back with such an advantageous marriage in the offing would more than pacify Mother, it would reconcile her to his failure to get the job in the States. Added to which of course he'd fallen for you hook, line and sinker. It didn't need much persuasion from Mother that you'd be delighted to see the announcement of your engagement in the Sydney newspapers.'

'She got Barr to insert it? I thought he was as surprised as me,' Davina said, then shuddered as she recalled the interview with Mrs Patterson when she had told her it was all a mistake.

Rex saw the shudder, but he misinterpreted it. 'I don't suppose it ever crossed your mind that you'd have to pay for what you did. How do you feel? I hope you meant that very rash declaration the other evening, because it will teach you a lesson to have a little of your own medicine. As soon as Barr was on the road to recovery, I took him home with me. Once he'd learned to walk again I left him in Uncle Lionel's care and set out to trace the girl responsible.'

Davina's mouth had gone dry. 'You said he tried to commit suicide.'

'So you've enough heart to be curious at least,' Rex remarked cruelly. 'Barr simply went swimming when the shark nets were down and lost a foot before the beach guards could get him out of the water.'

'He couldn't possibly have done it on purpose,' Davina was almost pleading. 'He couldn't have noticed the warning flags.'

'Oh, don't delude yourself. Barr knew all right. With sharks a constant danger we Australians are taught the risks as soon as we're old enough to so much as paddle in the sea. What beats me is how he got past the guards.'

Davina closed her eyes as a too vivid imagination got to work. She felt sick, but this was no time to lose her head. She swallowed, lifted her chin and faced Rex bravely. 'As soon as I've cleared away, I'll pack. I suppose you won't refuse to run me to the station?'

'You're staying right here. You surely don't think I've come half across the world just to give you a reprimand? I laid my plans carefully, so don't imagine I've any intention of simply letting you walk away.'

'You don't mean that all this,' Davina gesticulated around her, 'was only arranged with some mad kind of revenge in mind? It must have cost you a small fortune!'

'You overrate your importance, but it's worth every penny just to sit here and tell you at last precisely why I brought you up here. And now you know why the Land Rover wouldn't start the other day. I'd no intention of letting you jazz all over the countryside without myself to keep an eye on you. You can go on the farm where you please, but off it, you ask me first. Understand?'

Davina got up so hastily she overturned her chair. 'You must be crazy if you think I'd really do as you say! If you won't take me to Carlisle or Newcastle I'll get someone who will. Or crawl on all fours sooner than stay another minute,' she ended with a faint hint of defiance, and made to walk round the table.

Rex stopped her progress by the simple expedient of putting out a hand and closing it over her upper arm. 'Before you go, I think I should remind you of something you appear to have forgotten.' Stopped in her tracks, Davina stared down into remorseless eyes with a kind of panic in her own. She made no attempt to escape from his hold as he added softly, 'Catrin and the Comstones.'

She let out a shuddering sigh and her shoulders drooped. Rex released her to start rolling a cigarette. 'I think I told you when we went on that picnic that Lady Luck can sometimes come up trumps. I'd been wondering what kind of lever would keep you here, and the perfect weapon was handed to me on a plate. I was introduced to your sister's prospective father-in-law yesterday. He's all that's said of him, and more —old-fashioned, bigoted, prejudiced. And I have it on good authority that his wife is as bad.'

'And if I don't do as you say, you'll see to it that the Comstones find out who I am, with no doubt a highly coloured story about our relationship in an isolated farmhouse?' Davina accused him bitterly.

'It shouldn't be too difficult to set tongues wagging,' Rex replied mockingly. 'But you won't let it come to that, will you? Somehow I don't believe even you would be prepared to jeopardise your sister's future.'

Davina took a deep breath. 'You're utterly despicable! Do you know that? I believe I hate you.'

On the point of going outside, Rex looked over his shoulder. 'I doubt that. I doubt it very much. But hate away if it makes you feel better, so long as you don't imagine it bothers me one way or another,' and the door closed behind him.

Tears welled into Davina's eyes, but she dashed them away. They served no purpose except to reduce her to a state of exhaustion. As she began clearing away the lunch, it suddenly occurred to her that her soup, now cold, had not so much as been touched. She poured it away and putting on the kettle again, made a fresh pot of tea.

As she sipped a cup of the hot, refreshing liquid she went

over the conversation with Rex and the truth which had emerged of his real identity and purpose. She tried to remember what Barr had told her about his elder brother, but apart from the fact of his unusual christian name and that they had had different fathers, there was little she could recall. She faced the fact that if Rex did indeed intend to keep her virtually a prisoner it was going to take all her courage and resilience to stand up to the ordeal of daily contact with a man who hated her. Pointless too to try and get him to see her side of the story. Rex had already as good as called her a liar.

The next weeks were going to be a test of her endurance, but just how big a test, even Davina could hardly have guessed. Once he had revealed his true reason for coming to England, Rex gave up all pretence at friendliness, and the erstwhile easy companionship, those moments when he had excited her by his lovemaking, vanished overnight.

Davina discovered him to have a hitherto unsuspected talent for killing any attempt at conversation stone dead with one well-chosen monosyllable. Once or twice during the days that followed Davina, glancing at him, could hardly credit that the stern-faced man sitting at the table was capable of taking a girl into his arms and kissing her with tempestuous passion. That he felt no qualms of conscience at his treatment of the girl he blamed for his brother's unhappiness and near tragedy was confirmed by his hearty appetite. While Davina, sick at heart, picked at her meals, Rex invariably had a second helping of the excellent food as if he had not a care in the world.

What a fool she'd been to walk so guilelessly into the net he'd spread for her unsuspecting feet, she thought one evening as he cleared his plate—but Kingbury Fitzpaine had been an artful spider. She had not for one moment suspected that an ulterior motive lay behind his intention of setting up this experimental sheep farm and like the fly in the nursery rhyme she had walked into the trap. She still didn't know if he intended to let her take part in the Nativity play; come to that, she didn't know what to call him, Rex or King. A month, even a week ago, she knew she would have laughed if anyone had told her she could so easily be cowed into unresisting submission, but this man had undermined her defences before he had struck.

The only time Rex let down his guard and threw her a friendly word was when Peter McKay or the old shepherd were about, and Davina found herself deliberately encouraging them to drop in for a chat or stay for a meal. If Rex noticed this manoeuvre he kept it to himself, though on one occasion when Peter had been in and out for most of the day he said with raised brows, 'Isn't it time you were on your way home, young man? Your mother will be wondering where you've got to.'

Mr Farr answered, 'Don't think so, seeing as she knows he's safe up at Nineveh along of us, Gaffer. Her's not properly over losing her baby—and then there's that husband of hers,' and behind Peter's back the old man went through the motions of lifting a glass to his lips.

Davina saw Rex's hard eyes soften as he glanced down at the boy, until as he saw she was watching him, the usual expressionless mask fell once more over his face as he said carelessly, 'In that case, Davina can feed you both before you go. I shan't be here, but I know I can rely on you to see the lad gets home.'

As she heard Mr Farr's, 'Right-ho,' anger welled inside Davina, for Rex had given her no indication that he wouldn't be eating with them as usual and she had made special efforts with the evening meal. By the time it was on the table, he had bathed and changed into a well cut lounge suit with a silk shirt and matching tie.

She could hardly bear to look at him, overwhelmed by an almost irresistable urge to touch this gian-sized, alluring man. But her response to his magnetism was nipped in the bud by the sound of a car careering up to the house in Adele Wickham's unmistakable style, informing everyone of the identity of Rex's dinner companion.

As he threw her a malicious smile of farewell, Davina was aware of an uncharitable hope that news of Adele's latest flirtation would reach Camshaw Hall and the Squire's ears. If Rex allowed himself the indulgence of escorting a girl as beautiful as Adele, gossip about herself would inevitably soon be dismissed as nonsense. But as she watched the car disappear, she knew it would be about a million to one chance if the Comstones so much as listened when Adele's name was mentioned. By this time, the whole neighbourhood must know that both she and her brother were no longer welcome at the Hall.

Still, one never knew. If Rex could spread scandalous gossip, so could she! But for this she had to have opportunity, and tonight was the first time since the disclosure of his true identity that Rex had left her to her own devices.

It was getting dark by the time the meal ended, the old man went out for one last look at the animals and Peter to bid the horse a loving farewell. Seeing the keys for the Land Rover lying on the dresser, Davina decided to see if she could start it and run them home. In case Rex had once again removed the rotor arm she said nothing before going out to the open barn where the vehicle was parked.

Taped to the steering wheel was a note. 'I don't doubt you'll try and give Farr and the boy a ride home, but in case you're thinking of taking advantage of my absence, I've made a note of the mileage. Straight to the village and straight back.'

There was no signature. There was no need of one. Davina's soft lips tightened as she snatched at the note, screwed it into a ball and threw it furiously on to the ground. Was there no getting the better of her gaoler? It seemed he was prepared for every move she might make.

When she had dropped off her passengers she drove half way back to the farm before pulling off the road and dimming the headlights. She wished she had the courage to call Rex's bluff, but she was too afraid of the consequences to risk an act of open defiance. Rex wasn't the kind to issue idle threats and she knew him to be a force to be reckoned with, one who had never come her way before.

His manner towards her these last few days convinced her he had no intention of forgoing his plan of revenge and that he really had gone to the trouble of tracing her whereabouts and travelling thousands of miles simply to make her pay for what Rex considered had been criminal disregard for the feelings of his younger brother. If Davina thought there was the remotest chance of convincing him, she would have tried to make Rex see she had merely taken pity on Barr, seeing how lonely and out of things he had looked amidst that throng of seagoing merrymakers.

But she shied away from even the attempt, imagining the look of contempt which would cross his face, the blighting sentence with which he would dismiss her explanation. She was contemplating yet another humiliating confrontation with her relentless employer when Jim Thomas appeared beside the Land Rover saying, 'You were miles away. I honked twice before I pulled up behind you. What are you doing all alone here this time of night. Broken down?'

Davina summoned a smile. 'No, just wishing I was dressing up to go to a theatre.' It was the first thing which popped into her head as an explanation for lacklustre eyes and a drooping curve to her lips.

'Oh, if that's all that's troubling you we can soon put it right. Not tonight—I'm on call. But tomorrow put on your glad rags and I'll take you into Carlisle to sample a bit of North Country night life. See you around seven. Be ready!' and with a pat on her arm, Jim turned and went back to his car.

As soon as he had driven away with a wave of his hand, Davina started the engine and made her way back to Nineveh. To be able to escape the atmosphere of animosity even for one evening would be a relief. Jim's cheerful, uncomplicated manner was exactly the tonic she needed, and by bedtime she had finished a neat short story about a nineteen-year-old girl who cleverly turned the tables on the sophisticated man of the world who had planned her downfall.

But despite preparing for bed with the satisfaction of knowing she had written a clever story, as soon as the light was out, her imagination set to work. Regardless of good intentions, her thoughts kept returning to Rex and Adele. Where were they now? Was Rex holding that sinuous body in his long arms, rousing Adele with the same expertise he had used on herself? Two big tears formed in her eyes and rolled down her cheeks as she remembered how incredibly gentle those large brown hands could be, how her body had responded. Her whole inside ached as pulling the bedclothes right over her head, she curled up, one huge ball of misery.

There were violet shadows under her dark eyes when she went down next morning to prepare the breakfast, and Rex coming in from outdoors to sit and attack a huge plate of bacon, sausages and eggs as if he hadn't a care in the world did nothing to raise her sinking spirits. They were halfway through their now customary silent mealtime when he suddenly took a long envelope out of his pocket and threw it down on the table.

'That came for you yesterday. Sorry, but I forgot to give it to you.'

He didn't sound sorry, and as Davina picked up the envelope and saw the typewritten address she intercepted the unpleasant smile Rex was slanting in her direction.

'Not bad news, I hope,' he said suavely as she took out the contents of the envelope and a brief businesslike letter from the publisher informed her that the two pilot short stories had been satisfactory.

'Much you'd care if it were,' Davina answered tartly before she could check her unruly tongue, and Rex's instant soft, 'Oh, getting our second wind, are we?' made her bite her lip for giving him an opening.

She fixed her eyes on her plate, for his nearness, the soft beguiling tone of his last remark were having their inevitable effect. Despite her conviction that he had probably made mad, passionate love to Adele Wickham only hours ago, all she desired was to wrap her arms around this man, lay her cheek against the V of sun-browned skin revealed by the unbuttoned shirt and feel his arms close round her slim body.

What had happened to turn her into such a spineless girl, ready to tumble headlong into his arms at the drop of a hat? Peeping at Rex as he poured himself a third cup of strong, black tea, Davina had difficulty in remembering he was nothing more than a heartless monster. She would have given ten dates with Jim Thomas for just one genuinely kind word from the man sitting two feet away and calmly rolling himself his after-breakfast cigarette.

All she got, however, as he rose and pushed in his chair, was an aloof command, 'Have a decent hot meal ready for one o'clock. The wind is really icy this morning, but the old man insists on coming along to show me how they make the winter sheep shelters up here. I intend to see he has a good feed and knocks off early,' and he was gone.

Why couldn't he extend a little of this thoughtfulness towards her? Davina thought savagely, but at least a proper midday meal meant a light supper which would give her the opportunity to bath and change at her leisure before her date this evening. Cold meat there was in plenty, she saw when she went to check the contents of the larder. She smiled as she imagined Rex's surprise that evening when he saw the table only laid for one.

But when she emerged from the bathroom later that evening, her freshly washed hair bundled up into a towel, she walked straight into Rex and there was a distinctly uncompromising slant to his stern mouth.

He pulled her towards the kitchen table and gestured to the cold buffet she had prepared. 'I've had a long day and expect a decent meal when I come in—not this!'

Rather to her own astonishment, Davina found herself stammering excuses. 'You had an enormous three-course meal at lunchtime. Surely cold meat, salad and pickles are sufficient? I'm going into Carlisle for the evening with Jim Thomas.'

Silence followed her words as, hands on his hips, Rex surveyed her slowly from her face down to her feet and back again. It was an insolent, unreassuring look and Davina felt a throb of fear. However, his voice was quite expressionless as he said, 'Sorry to disappoint you, but I want something hot. Chops with a couple of eggs will do. I'll let you off a dessert. Cheese and biscuits will suffice.'

Davina counted silently to ten, took a deep breath, said, 'Very well,' and turned to go and dress.

Rex, she discovered, was between her and the door. 'Now,' he replied implacably.

Looking up in astonishment to meet his eyes, she gestured towards her dressing gown. 'Like this?'

'Why not? I daresay it's not the first time you've prepared a meal for a man clad only in your dressing gown.'

The implication was outrageous and Davina's face slowly flushed as the calculated insult hit home. Turning, she stalked, back ramrod-stiff, towards the pantry and in complete silence began to arrange chops in the frying pan. She was aware that Rex watched her every move as she took away the cold food, made the inevitable tea and turned the sizzling chops. Anger stiffened her resolve to give him no hint of her embarrassment as the dressing gown loosened with every move she made.

She had just placed the plate before him on the table when the distinctive sound of Jim's station wagon negotiating the farm lane reached her ears. Davina gave a gasp and said quickly, 'Keep Jim talking while I dress. I'll be down in ten minutes.'

Rex grinned unkindly. 'Take your time. There's no need to hurry, I can assure you.'

No hurry! Davina thought furiously as she scrambled into clean undies and laddered two pairs of tights in her haste. When she unwrapped the towel from her hair, she stared aghast—for tonight, of all nights, her usually manageable hair was sticking out in all directions. Rex's fault, for normally she combed her curls into place while they were still wet. Tonight, still in the turban, they had dried as she cooked.

She was trying to make the last curl do her bidding with an extra application of hair lacquer when she heard Jim's car start up, and abandoning any further attempt to improve her appearance, she picked up her coat and handbag and hurried downstairs.

Rex was still sitting over the remains of his meal, but he was alone. Something about his mocking smile as he looked up rang a warning bell in Davina's head as she asked, 'Has Jim really gone?' and at Rex's nod added bluntly, 'Why?'

'Perhaps because I told him you'd gone to bed with a migraine,' Rex replied unhesitatingly. 'I did tell you several days ago that you were not free to go anywhere without my say-so. What gave you the idea I'm not a man of my word?'

He got up with the words and his calm air of authority was the last straw. Losing her last shreds of self-control, Davina hurled herself at him, pummelling his broad chest with ineffectual fists until one large hand came up and imprisoned them. Holding her firmly at arm's length while she still struggled impotently, Rex said tauntingly, 'What's happened to that British stiff upper lip we Australians are always hearing about?' and goaded beyond endurance, Davina burst into a storm of weeping.

Immediately he pulled out a chair and thrust her into it. A large white handkerchief, smelling faintly of tobacco, was pushed into her hands and he ordered, not unkindly, 'Mop up. If I know women, this time tomorrow you'll be downright ashamed of letting yourself go so thoroughly. What you need is a good cup of tea,' and while Davina struggled for self-control he filled the kettle.

She wiped streaming eyes, blew her nose defiantly, then spoiled the whole effect by emitting a hiccoughing sob. To her surprise, this seemed to melt Rex a little, because he asked quite kindly as the kettle started to sing, 'Fancy some buttered toast with your tea?'

She shook her head as he placed a clean cup and saucer at her elbow. 'Just a drink, thank you,' she said in a low voice, and looked up to meet his eyes. It was impossible to gauge his mood, but she was dismally conscious of tear-blotched cheeks and dishevelled hair. How immature she must appear compared with Adele's sophistication and 'woman of the world' manner! She buried her nose in her teacup and wondered what Rex would say next.

But having poured himself a cup of the fresh tea he was stirring it in silence, his face more granite-like than usual. It came as something of an anticlimax, therefore, when he put his cup down and said, 'I'm going to put in a couple of hours getting my paper work up to date. Get an early night,' before the door to the study closed behind him.

CHAPTER NINE

SINCE Rex had given a fictitious migraine as the excuse for dismissing Jim Thomas the evening before, it was rather ironical that Davina awoke the following morning with a genuine headache. Even aspirin failed to relieve the sensation of ten little men with hammers busily at work inside her head, and she was not too surprised therefore when Rex suddenly remarked, 'What's the matter? You're as pale as suet pudding this morning.'

She grimaced inwardly. Rex certainly did not believe in flattery! 'Just a headache,' she answered.

'You don't get enough fresh air. As soon as you've cleared up here bring a flask of tea to the far pasture. Farr's not coming up today, so we can lunch off that cold stuff you were so keen for me to finish up.'

Davina looked away, for she could imagine the expression on his face, but at least this was better than being ignored. As soon as he had left the house she tidied the kitchen, made the beds and put all the laundry in the dirty linen basket, then pulling on her thickest trousers, she added a high-necked matching jumper and her hooded anorak.

The wind was blowing strongly from the east, but it was good to be out. Davina had put some scones in a plastic bag along with the thermos of tea and as she topped the rise and met the full force of the wild moorland breeze she hitched the bag higher on her shoulder and turned up the collar on the anorak. Far away in the distance she could just make out Rex as he moved among the sheep, a tiny dot for all his size. He must have eyes like a hawk, she thought, for suddenly she saw him raise a hand and wave in her direction.

She waved back before setting off to cover the distance between them. She was out of breath by the time she joined him beside the erection of corrugated iron and straw bales intended as a wind-break for the sheep when the winter really arrived.

'Will this really be sufficient to protect the ewes in bad weather?' she asked.

'So Farr says, and he should know. They'll all be built to protect the animals from the prevailing wind and they're stronger than they look. Here, sit down and tell me if you don't find it cosy,' and Rex picked up his jacket from the top of one of the bales and threw it down for her to sit.

She slid to the ground and found immediate warmth now the wind was not playing on her face. She looked up, unconsciously giving Rex one of her dimpling smiles as she said, 'The old boy certainly knows his business. It makes a tre-

149

mendous difference. But are the sheep sensible enough to make use of them?'

A glint appeared for a moment in Rex's hard eyes, but he said mildly enough in answer to her question, 'Most animals have an enormous sense of self-preservation, an instinct if you like.' He leaned to take the shoulder bag and pour out their tea as he spoke.

Handing a cup to Davina, he went on, 'This is only the first. We'll be building others. I think they're all in lamb and I don't want to lose any mums-to-be.'

'You sound almost as if you care for them as individuals,' Davina replied. 'I would have thought after a lifetime of sheep rearing they'd just be so many pounds of wool or so many pounds of meat to you.'

Immediately the heavy lids closed to slits and the mouth of the man facing her thinned to a stern line. Davina's hand clenched hard on the plastic cup as she saw her careless comment had dissipated all hint of the softer mood she had sensed during breakfast. Falling in love seemed to have robbed her of all her usual tact and charm. Or was it simply that Rex undermined her self-confidence?

Whatever the reason, her tactless remark had made him withdraw behind an icy barrier once more, and with an indifferent, 'Thanks for the tea. I must get on now,' he wandered away from the sheep shelter, examining a ewe here and there at random. Feeling as if her spirits had reached rock bottom, Davina sat huddled miserably against the straw until a shout brought her upright to see Peter McKay waving excitedly as he cantered George along the track.

By the time she was on her feet, Rex was striding rapidly back and he exclaimed angrily when he came within earshot, 'What's got into the boy? I've told him repeatedly not to canter over those loose stones.'

'It looks as if he's the bearer of tidings,' Davina answered pedantically, but she was secretly glad that the youngster had broken the ice. Her guess proved to be correct, for as soon as they reached the field gate Peter scrambled to the ground and said, 'You've got visitors, Gaffer. I was saddling old George here, so I said I'd come and tell you.'

Rex looked amused, Davina noticed as he took the reins

out of the boy's hand. 'I'd forgotten it was Saturday. Who's visiting this time of day?'

'Mr Thomas and his sister. They said they'd wait.'

Rex was in the saddle and lengthening the stirrups almost before the boy had finished speaking. 'Right, I'll ride on. You walk Miss Davina back—and mind you shut the gate,' he ordered over Peter's head to a silent Davina.

Davina went back to fetch the tea things and noticed that in his eagerness to see Adele, Rex had forgotten he was only in shirt sleeves. She picked up the jacket and went back to where Peter was waiting for her by the field gate. He chattered happily all the way back to the house, leaving Davina to follow slowly. She was not looking forward to inventing more lies about last night to appease Jim and even less to having to sit and watch Adele playing off her tricks for Rex's benefit.

For this reason she pressed the boy to come in for a sandwich and some lemonade, knowing it was an inducement he would be unable to resist. As she had anticipated, Adele Wickham looked very much at ease sitting beside Rex at the kitchen table, a glass in her hand and laughing at something he had just said to her.

She looked more like a fashion plate than usual today, Davina thought, glancing dejectedly down at her own workmanlike outfit. Adele was in slacks and jumper as well, but they bore little resemblance to Davina's chain store apparel. Adele's black trousers and top had been made by a master hand and over them she wore a leopardskin jacket. Real leopardskin, Davina noted. No simulated fur for Adele.

She had thrown it back, perhaps because the room was warm, more likely, Davina thought uncharitably, to show off her excellent figure to better advantage. As the door opened, Adele glanced round disinterestedly and with no more than a casual wave of the hand, turned back to give Rex her full attention.

The two men, however, got to their feet, Rex to open two bottles of bitter lemon and Jim to pull out a chair to let Davina sit down. As Rex handed a glass to Davina and another to Peter, Adele watched with a mixture of amusement and contempt on her lovely face.

'I take it neither of the children is allowed anything stronger,' she drawled as Davina lifted the glass to her lips.

To her surprise, Rex came to the rescue. 'Davina's still got a headache and spirits would only make it worse.'

'In that case, she won't feel like coming tonight,' Adele stated flatly, and Davina gave her a glance of sheer surprise. If the notion weren't completely ridiculous, she would have said Adele was jealous. If she only knew the truth of the real situation between the two occupants of Nineveh Farm, she thought grimly, she would know there was no competition here!

But when Jim took her part too she saw the reason for Adele's antagonism towards her. She simply expected to be the centre of attention all the time and any woman was a threat to her egotism. When Jim added, 'It will do Davina good to get out for a change, and she's worked like a Trojan since she came to Nineveh. Look at this kitchen for a start.'

Adele gave an impatient shrug. 'It's no good asking my opinion. I don't believe I was ever inside the place before Rex bought it,' and she smiled at the big man sitting beside her. As she turned to give Rex the full benefit of her smile, she suddenly noticed that Peter, fascinated by the fur of her jacket, was softly stroking one of the sleeves.

'Take your hands away, you disgusting little boy!' she spat, then as Peter, startled by the shrewish attack, jumped and tilted his glass, Adele sprang to her feet and began shaking herself.

'Now look what he's done!' she demanded of the assembled company. 'I'm covered in lemonade!' and she began ineffectively to wipe off the spot or two which had landed on the sleeve of her coat.

Quickly Davina fetched a damp cloth and with a quiet, 'Stand still,' began to clean up the damage. It was with some relief that she heard Rex give a laugh and say in matter-of-fact tones, 'No harm done, Adele. See, there's not so much as a mark,' as he pushed Davina gently aside and smiled down at Adele. As he gently pressed her down into a chair he added to Peter, 'Go and see to George, Peter, and give him a rub down before he has his oats. Lunch will be ready in half an hour.'

Peter couldn't wait to make his escape and when Adele said sulkily, 'I wonder you let him hang around up here,' Davina met Jim's eyes and was surprised to see he was giving her a conspiratorial wink. After holding her glance for a moment he turned to his sister and said, 'Drink up, old girl. If Mrs Hepburn is to have a buffet supper ready by this evening she won't be too pleased if we're late for lunch.'

Jim got up as he spoke and with a whispered, 'I'll expect to see you later along with Rex,' went to help Adele to her feet. However, she had other ideas and was holding out both hands towards Rex. Davina watched as Rex took them, pulled her to her feet and with a casual arm thrown round her shapely body, guided her towards the door.

Giving a sigh of relief, Davina started to clear away the dirty glasses, wishing she could speak her mind about Adele's spiteful outburst when Peter had spilled his drink. But if Rex was developing a soft spot for the spoiled beauty, that would never do. She was in enough trouble with him already without adding jealousy to the list of her failings.

When man and boy came in for lunch, Davina was glad to see Peter seemed to have forgotten the unpleasant episode earlier, for he chattered quite happily all through the meal. He looked up from watching Rex roll a cigarette to ask, 'Have you decided about the Nativity play? Mrs Matthews asked me to ask you.' He turned to Rex. 'And she wants to know if you'll be one of the Kings, Gaffer. I'm going to be a shepherd,' he finished, a note of pride in the boyish voice.

Rex looked over his head to meet Davina's eyes and to her chagrin, a flush coloured her cheeks. A corner of Rex's straight mouth twitched before he turned to address the boy. 'I don't see why not. You can tell the Rector's mother we'll be at the next rehearsal, whenever that is.'

'Next Wednesday. And I told Mrs Matthews you'd let us have a sheep for the night,' said Peter, his blue eyes bright.

Rex reached over and ruffled the boy's hair. 'Take a lot for granted, don't you, young 'un? Okay, if it's that important to you. But it will have to be one of the rams. You'll have to train him to behave in church.'

Apparently this appealed to Peter's sense of humour, because he went away, a last slice of cake in his hand, and still giggling, to clean the tack. As Rex drained the teapot for a final cup of tea Davina burst out, 'How on earth am I to explain spending Christmas up here? We always go to Switzerland every Christmas.'

Rex gave her a satirical smile, drained his cup and got up. Just when she thought he was not going to trouble to answer he turned, an unpleasant glint in his eyes, to drawl, 'I'm sure your agile brain will think of something. By the way, we're invited to Thomas's place this evening. Be ready by seventhirty, and I understand food is laid on, so there's no need to get a meal before we go.'

Determined not to be the Cinderella of the party, Davina dressed with care. She had not worn the dress she had bought for her grandmother's birthday party since and she ironed it carefully before taking a long, leisurely bath. Tonight, her hair behaved itself and she was quite pleased with her appearance until she followed Rex into Jim's big drawing room and caught a glimpse of Adele holding court amid a circle of admiring males.

Tonight she was clad in a jade green dress of some clinging material, so cleverly cut that it looked as if she had been poured into it. As soon as she saw Rex, Adele deserted the group around her to walk over and greet him, raising her face in obvious expectation of a kiss.

Rex merely smiled beguilingly into the lovely face raised to his and said softly, 'That's a very seductive perfume you're wearing.'

A stab of jealousy tore through Davina's breast at his words and she watched as Adele tucked a hand through his arm and led him away, saying laughingly, 'Glad you like it.' How arrogantly sure of themselves they were, Davina thought, and turned to see that Jim had also witnessed the incident and was standing watching his sister's progress down the long room with an unusually serious expression in his eyes.

Jim, she could see, did not care for the relationship developing between Adele and Rex Fitzpaine and hoping her face had not been such a give-away as his own, she summoned up a smile. She had already seen one or two people she recognised from her previous visit here, and when Jim had supplied her with a soft drink, she left him to his duties as host and began to circulate.

Determined to put out of her mind the couple now dancing closely entwined on the space cleared at one end of the room, Davina stopped to speak to Tom Mulholland, partnered this evening by a pretty redhead whom he introduced to Davina as 'the sexiest nurse south of the Border.' She was also one of the nicest, Davina decided after five minutes' conversation, for Deborah Sawyer was easy to talk to and lost no time in complimenting her on her appearance.

'I looked for a dress like that everywhere this summer, but I daresay you bought it in London,' Deborah said, and at Davina's nod she added, 'Thought as much. Newcastle's a good place to shop, but unfortunately my off duty always seems to fall on their half day.'

This was the kind of frank, uncomplicated girly talk which Davina discovered suddenly she was missing, and she found herself unconsciously responding to Deborah's warm friendliness. They were only brought down to earth by Jim appearing at Davina's side to say, 'Can anyone join in?' and hear Tom say in reply, 'Thank goodness you've come, Jim. These two have forgotten I'm even here. Take Dav for a dance so I can get this one's attention for a couple of minutes,' and he pulled Deborah against his shoulder.

'Poor Tom,' Jim said as he led her away. 'He's been trying to get Deborah to make a date for months. Then I find you playing gooseberry!'

'But I thought . . .' Davina started, her eyes on Adele, then stopped as Jim turned to follow her glance to where his sister was making no secret of her special interest in the tall, handsome man holding her as they danced.

'Everyone for miles around has imagined themselves in love with Adele at one time or another,' Jim said in a sober voice. 'I'd hoped all that nonsense was over once she had a wedding ring on her finger, but I can see it starting all over again.'

'If you're worrying about Rex, I can assure you you've no need to,' Davina replied tartly. 'He's well able to take care of himself.'

She came down to earth with a bump as she found Jim's eyes on hers with something approaching surprise in their depths before he quickly changed the subject and began to talk trivial nonsense. By the time the dance was over and he had to go and see all his guests were supplied with drinks, Davina had almost forgotten how nearly she had given herself away and when Roy Comstone, a briming glass in his hand, appeared like a genie at her side, she was ready to turn and talk to him with her normal cool composure.

Roy lifted the glass and poured half its contents down his throat. 'You and Jim got a thing going?'

Taken by surprise, Davina laughed. 'I haven't a thing going with anyone. Not that it's any of your business.'

A quizzical eyebrow lifted and in no way put out by her straight from the shoulder reply, Roy said, 'Good! Now would you like to dance or shall I take you on a personally conducted tour of the bedrooms?'

At this Davina laughed outright. 'If that's on your mind, you'd better start looking for someone else,' she advised in a teasing voice, and Roy gave a theatrical sigh and replied, 'In that case, I'll finish this and we'll dance. At least that way I get to put my arms round you.'

By this time the room was crowded, but between them, Roy and Jim saw to it that Davina was never left alone. In fact the time passed more quickly than she realised, for when Rex appeared at her side and said, 'It's midnight—time we were leaving,' she looked down at her watch in surprise. About to say she was enjoying herself and would get Roy to give her a lift home, after a glance at Rex's face, she thought better of it. Collecting her coat, she thanked Jim, said goodbye and followed Rex outside.

Until they had passed through the dark and sleeping village, not a word was spoken, and when Rex broke the silence by asking, 'Trying to get in well with the family?' Davina jumped in her seat.

Her thoughts had been miles away, but his harsh, uncompromising question, coming like a douche of cold water, quickly brought her down to earth. 'Pardon me if I seem stupid, but I'm afraid I'm not quite with you.'

'Don't play games with me,' Rex warned. 'You know perfectly well what I mean. You spent at least half the evening with the Squire's elder son. It won't do you any good. I understand his father has as good as disowned him.'

'I can't think why,' Davina answered in a deceptively

innocent voice. 'After he got it through his head that I had no intention of sleeping with him he was perfectly charming.'

'And more than half cut too, I noticed,' Rex grated.

'I thought he held his liquor rather well,' Davina announced calmly, 'but since you were monopolising the best-looking female in the room, I'm surprised you had time to notice what I was doing.'

'Not jealous, by any chance?' came the taunting accusation.

Davina was glad of the darkness in the cab. She could control her voice if not her expression. 'Jealous? Me? But isn't my motto supposed to be "love 'em and leave 'em?" Once I knew you'd only made love to me out of a wish to wreak retribution, you surely didn't imagine I was going to nurse a broken heart?' and she gave a trill of contemptuous laughter which sounded so genuine it even surprised herself.

As if this last had caught him on the raw, Rex put his foot down hard on the accelerator and replied harshly, 'I had your measure correctly right from the beginning, it seems. Just remember, nothing's changed.'

Encouraged by her success in getting under his guard for once, Davina said rashly, 'If you're referring to rumours about us, you might find it a bit difficult after tonight to convince people everything wasn't completely above board at Nineveh. I wasn't the only one who noticed you and Adele Wickham with your arms wrapped around each other all evening.'

At that moment the field came into view and Rex braked so sharply that she slid forward on the seat. 'Thanks for the warning,' he said, and his voice held a grim note as he got out to open the gate.

The following morning brought an unexpected answer to Davina's problem about breaking the news to her family of her intention of spending Christmas at Camshaw. Mr Farr arrived as they were finishing breakfast with the mail, and this contained a letter from Davina's mother.

'You'll be sorry to hear that your grandmother had a heart attack a few days ago,' Mrs Williams wrote. 'Giles flew out, and as soon as she is well enough to be moved, he's arranged for her to be admitted to a London heart clinic. Of course this means there's no question this year of a big family party at Christmas. In fact it's Giles's opinion that it was all the excitement over her birthday party which brought this on. I'll let you know how she goes on,' and Mrs Williams ended with a few comments about 'making sure she kept warm and ate properly' which made Davina smile.

But her face was grave as she folded away the letter to be answered when she could find a moment. Almost impossible to imagine her indomitable grandmother laid up, and after such an active life she would hate being made to stay in bed.

She suddenly became aware that Rex was watching her face with his steady, decidedly unnerving gaze. 'Bad news?'

'Grandmother's had a heart attack.'

'I'm sorry. Is it bad?'

No doubting his sincerity, Davina thought as she replied, 'She's not well enough to travel, that's all I know. Mother says that when she is, Uncle Giles is going to bring her to London for treatment.'

'At least that settles your Christmas,' said Rex with one of his twisted smiles, 'and speaking of that reminds me—I suppose you know it's a tactical error to show your hand to your opponent?'

Still lost in troubled thoughts of her grandmother's illness as she was, it was a moment before Davina saw the danger light was flickering in his eyes.

'It was a mistake last night to point out that Adele's name could be linked with mine, so tonight I'm taking you out to dinner—in the best frequented restaurant in the district. And just for good measure,' Rex added, 'we'll start by going for a drink to the Shepherd and Crook. Be ready at seven,' he ended.

'But I don't want to go out with you,' Davina said promptly. 'In any case, it's Sunday. You'll not find anywhere open.'

'Don't you believe it. As a matter of fact Adele was only telling me last night of a spot only ten miles away which is very good and open seven days a week.'

'And what's she going to say when she hears you've taken

me?' Davina asked in desperation, her back to the wall.

'You can leave Adele to me,' Rex said in a hard voice as he got up and came round the table. Taking her chin in his hand, he jerked up her head until she was looking reluctantly right into his eyes.

As she stared speechlessly, Rex's hand travelled down to where the opening of her shirt gave a glimpse of the curve of her breasts. His fingers lingered for a moment, warm and vibrant, then he turned saying carelessly, 'Better be ready. You know me well enough by this time to be sure I mean what I say!' and he strode outside—rather like an avenging Heathcliff, Davina thought resentfully.

And to think she'd gone to bed last night thinking she'd actually scored off him! What an impulsive fool she'd been to show him the pitfall in his path. It was too late now to wish she'd been wiser, kept her mouth shut. Talk about being between the devil and the deep blue sea!

And there was no doubting who the devil was. Davina's hand went unconsciously to the spot his fingers had caressed. Were there no depths he wouldn't plumb?

That evening she deliberately lingered over her dressing and it was almost seven-fifteen when she came down to the lighted kitchen. She found Rex sitting at the big table quietly reading a newspaper as if completely unaware of her unpunctuality.

She had put a coat on over her long black and white pleated skirt and black top, for the evenings were now really cold. As Rex arose, presumably to hold the door, he suddenly gripped her by the shoulder and swung her round to face the light.

Davina flushed, but more with anger than embarrassment as his eyes went over her. 'Not bad,' he announced, 'but I think I prefer those velvet trousers you wear from time to time. They kind of do things to a man's blood pressure,' he ended with a mocking smile.

Davina's flush deepened, but this time with genuine vexation, for it had not occurred to her the trousers were particularly sexy. She'd not wear them again, she decided, glad that she'd chosen to dress in a swirling skirt which gave no hint of the delectable curves beneath.

Her voice was cold as she stood, still held by the shoulder. 'Are we going out, or do you intend to stay here discussing feminine fashions?' to which Rex responded by releasing her, giving a strange, almost reluctant laugh.

It was an unusual evening, but only the first of many, as Davina was to discover in the weeks that followed. Outside the house and especially in public, Rex treated her with an ostentatious gallantry which, while it might deceive others, only made her more aware that the ghost of Barr Patterson's near-tragedy stood constantly between them.

The days were now much shorter, the weather much colder, and Davina was thankful for the portable heater in her bedroom. She had unearthed an old table big enough for her to write on, and since Rex made it plain that she was no longer welcome in the study, she slipped away to get on with her stories whenever opportunity permitted.

Not that leisure was all that easy to come by, for the days seemed hardly long enough to fit in all the jobs Rex found for her to do. He was busy trying to finish the shelters for the sheep before the first snows, and when Peter did not come up after school, Davina found herself on occasion even expected to muck out the horse and any ewes who had been brought up to pens in the barn for observation.

She and Rex also went down every Wednesday to join in the preparation of the play to be performed in the village church on Christmas Eve, and had become friendly with the young vicar and his mother. Davina only saw Adele on her rare visits to Nineveh, but she suspected that Rex and the gay divorcee might be seeing one another in secret. Folding away one of Rex's thicker pullovers one morning, she had noticed several strands of long blonde hair caught in the weave.

Not that it was any of her business, Davina thought, but this piece of homespun philosophy did nothing to soothe the ache in her heart. If she ever began to think Rex was beginning to forgive and forget he would bring her back to earth with a bang. Like last night.

Her face burned as she recalled the rehearsal last night in the vicarage drawing room. Mrs Matthews had started the evening by announcing that owing to illness, the wife of the village postmaster would not be able to play the innkeeper's wife, and asked for a volunteer.

Immediately Rex had pushed Davina forward and proffered her services, and red of face, Davina had found the script thrust into her unwilling hands. As the rehearsal began, he had met her angry eyes with a bland smile and she had longed to hit him.

But she had been forced to control her temper until they were alone in the Land Rover, when she turned to him and demanded, 'You're miscast, do you know that? You would make a perfect Herod!'

Rex gave a laugh in which there was a hint of cruelty. 'Stop spitting like a little cat. I simply thought you're tailor-made for the part of a shrewish tavern-keeper—and it seems I'm right.' He glanced at her, and as they were passing the well lit Shepherd and Crook the cab was full of light.

'You look stony-hearted enough right this minute to turn away even a pregnant woman,' Rex went on, and Davina turned her head away, determined he should not know how his words had hurt her.

The first snow fell in early December and waking one morning to a white world, Davina stood at the window oblivious to the biting cold as her eyes took in the fairytale scene stretching out on every side. Snowflakes were still falling, like gentle blobs of cotton wool, and down the track Rex on horseback was shepherding about a dozen ewes.

For a few moments, admiring his easy seat and the lazy sway of his body to every movement of the animal beneath him, Davina forgot the feud which existed between them. As if he suddenly became aware of her fixed gaze, Rex looked up as he dismounted and catching sight of her standing at the window called up, 'Put breakfast back by half an hour.'

Trust him to spoil a happy moment, she thought resentfully, as she dragged her nightdress over her curls and began to scramble into her bra and pants. He might just for once have said, 'Isn't it a lovely morning?' or even, 'Hello, have you slept well?' Well, at least she wouldn't need to hurry her morning wash, she thought thankfully as she ran into the bathroom.

She was brandishing a toasting fork as if it were a bayonet when Rex, having discarded his boots in the outer porch, came into the warm kitchen. 'You look as if you wish you had me on the end of that,' he remarked with alarming discernment as he began to unzip his waterproof jacket, and at Davina's immediate, 'You've hit the nail right on the head!' he burst into a shout of laughter.

'What have I done now? You're as cross as two sticks, and on a lovely winter morning too. The sun's coming through, and the moor looks a picture,' he said, taking his place at the table.

As she slid a loaded plate in front of him Davina was uneasily aware of an unexpected camaraderie in his voice and since anything even verging on a softer manner usually meant he had another bitter pill for her to swallow, she was immediately on her guard.

As he buttered a piece of toast he remarked casually, 'I forgot to tell you yesterday, but we'll be having a visitor for a few days next week. No need to clear out another room, though. He can have my room and I'll sleep on one of the camp beds in the study.'

Nothing very sinister about a visitor, Davina thought, and her tense nerves relaxed again—but he might have told her who their visitor was going to be. But even in this unexpectedly friendly mood, it would be risking a snub to enquire. Rex had obviously told her all he thought it necessary for her to know by saying, 'Pour me some tea, please. You're forgetting your duties.'

The subject of the visitor was not mentioned again until the following Tuesday. As he got up from the breakfast table Rex announced casually, 'That guest I told you about—he's arriving this afternoon. I'm going into Carlisle this morning, so I shall pick him up and we should be here around four. Have the kettle boiling,' and he was gone before Davina, speechless with surprise, had pulled herself together. Not that it would make any difference if she had been given time to ask for more details, she thought resignedly as she went upstairs to change Rex's bed and tidy the room. At least a stranger about the place would make a pleasant change in the daily routine and Rex would be forced into playing the easygoing, undemanding employer for a day or two.

Only she would know how false it was, Davina thought as she baked two big tarts and got everything prepared for the evening meal. There was still plenty of time to spare by hurrying over the last chores for her to wash and change and she was putting the last touches to her make-up when she heard the Land Rover approaching the farmhouse.

She ran downstairs two at a time and had put the kettle on when the outer door opened and she turned to greet Rex's visitor. As he came in, her mouth went dry and her hand instinctively grasped a chair back as she felt the blood draining from her face and the familiar kitchen begin to spin round her.

She felt rather than saw Rex step forward quickly, and pulling a chair forward thrust her into it. As a big hand on the nape of her neck pushed her head down between her knees and she heard a familiar voice say accusingly, 'You never let me come here without warning her, King? Have you got some brandy? She looks like death!'

But Davina's vision was clearing and gathering all her courage she forced herself to sit upright. The hand on her neck was instantly withdrawn as she smiled faintly into Barr Patterson's anxious face as he looked down at her.

'Sorry about that, it was silly of me. Just the shock of seeing you so unexpectedly when I thought you thousands of miles away. But please, no brandy. I'd much rather have a cup of tea.'

Was that really her own voice, so weak and shaky? Davina thought, and cleared her throat nervously as Barr walked over with a pronounced limp to where the kettle was boiling furiously. 'Where do you keep the tea caddy?' he asked, and smiled, a smile she noted which had lost its former half apologetic suggestion of shy withdrawal.

Before she could answer Barr, a voice spoke harshly from behind her, and Rex strode over to the cupboard and began the business of warming the pot. Davina had for a second forgotten his presence, forgotten he was the author of this latest piece of vindictiveness, but as he busied himself with the tea making she saw his face was like a block of granite. She looked away quickly, met Barr's eyes and said the first thing that came into her head.

'What are you doing in England? Have you come to spend

Christmas with . . .' she had been about to say Rex and had stopped, unwilling to have to explain to Barr why she called his brother by what would appear to be a nickname.

'Yes, with the girl I'm going to marry,' Barr put in as she hesitated. 'I daresay King's told you I'm living at Penderoo Station with him and Uncle Fitz now, trying to learn farming. Well, I met Pam shortly after I got there. She's a nurse and was staying on a neighbouring station. Rex got her to come and help me get back on my feet and we found we'd a lot in common. When I popped the question, she wouldn't say yes until she'd been back to England to see her parents—she's English, you see, so it will mean a big change for her. I decided to come too, so her mother and father could judge for themselves what sort of guy Pam was considering hitching up with, and we've decided to get married right after Christmas so we can be back in Australia for New Year. I came up to tell King and ask him to be my best man. You could have knocked me down with a feather when he told me you were working for him. I hope he doesn't bully you. King can be quite a slavedriver when he likes,' and Barr cast an impish smile at his brother's expressionless face.

'Stop talking so much and give the lady her tea,' Rex ordered, and his voice was as expressionless as his face. Barr gave him a quick look, then turned to pour milk and tea into a cup and push it along the table towards Davina.

'Drink up. What have you been doing with yourself since I last saw you?' he asked. Then he added, 'Whatever it is, you're not so brown and fit as you were in Sydney.'

'Put that down to an English winter,' Davina answered quickly. 'Don't forget I was on holiday and the sun was shining the last time we met.' This was dangerous ground and she hurried on with, 'Tell me more about your Pam. And congratulations. I hope you'll be very happy.'

Barr needed little encouragement to extol the virtues of the absent Pam, and as he talked, Davina wondered what Rex was thinking. Had he known Barr was to become engaged? That his brother was no longer an object of pity? Or was he so obsessed with revenge that only punishing her was important to him?

Glancing at the stern face as Rex sipped his tea and smoked

a cigarette, Davina knew it needed someone a good deal more acute than herself to work that one out. Despite the success of his plan to walk in on her with his brother, he looked anything but pleased by the outcome. He had retired behind a seemingly impenetrable barrier, and knowing he was unlikely to let down his guard while she was present, Davina suggested as soon as the teapot was emptied that the two men should go and talk in the study and leave her to get on with the cooking.

Not until the following morning did she find herself alone with Barr. Rex had gone to put out extra feed for the stock and she was setting the breakfast table when Barr came into the kitchen.

'Sit down, I've got some tea on the go. I was going to let you sleep. We breakfast early.'

As she gave him the cup, Davina saw Barr was studying her thoughtfully and as he took the tea he caught her unawares.

'Is King giving you a bad time? I know what a thorny devil he can be, and when I found out he hadn't told you I was coming and saw the way you reacted to my arrival I began to wonder if he was making you a target for his eye-for-an-eye philosophy. Uncle Fitz is a hard man and he's raised King to be the same. My brother can be the best friend in the world, but he makes one hell of an enemy.'

Davina turned her back as she added more rashers of bacon to the pan. 'It could be he thinks you got a rotten deal, Barr. He's told me what happened to you after I left Australia. I'm sorry, truly I am.' She turned to face him. 'I wouldn't like to have it on my conscience as being truly at fault.'

Barr got to his feet and limping round the table captured her hands. 'You're not to blame yourself,' he ordered, and Davina blinked at the firmly commanding note in his voice, so at variance with all her recollections of him. Barr went on crisply, 'What happened was a build-up over several years, and you mustn't blame yourself because I chose to act like a fool. It taught me a lesson, and when I look back, I've come out of the mess a good deal better off than perhaps I deserve. I'm training now for what I've always hankered to do, and as a bonus, met the kind of girl I always dreamed about. So no more hang-ups, self-recriminations? For either of us,' and with these last words he leaned forward and pressed an unexpected kiss on her lips.

Just at that particular moment, Rex pushed open the door and came in. 'Is this a private party, or can anyone join in?' he asked with all his old mockery in voice and face, but letting go of Davina's hands Barr smiled at his brother and replied, 'That was merely a kiss between friends. Now as soon as we've eaten, how about showing me what you're up to? Uncle Fitz says your letters tell him nothing.'

Rex shot his brother a keen, analytical look before he turned to wash his hands, but to Davina's relief he made no further reference to the scene he had interrupted. Surely he must realise by now that Barr bore her no ill will, so perhaps he would give up his plan to make her stay until the six months were up.

The men were out all day, but as Rex had arranged for them to eat out in the evening, Davina was able to put in the whole afternoon on her own work. So far eight stories had been completed and with the exception of some minor alterations in two, all had been accepted. As she sat, pen in hand, staring out over the fields, she wondered what had happened to the fairy story Rex had appropriated. She was getting just a little tired of dreaming up romance for the younger readers, perhaps because she had discovered for herself that in real life, true love does not run smoothly—in fact, very much the reverse. Would things have turned out differently had she met Rex under happier circumstances? she wondered, and a long sigh escaped as she bent over her work again.

Dinner was to be a foursome, she discovered, when on arrival at the country club where Rex had taken her the first time they dined out, they found Adele Wickham waiting in the bar. She exerted herself to be charming as soon as she discovered that Barr was Rex Fitzpaine's half-brother, but she was so patently possessive that several times during the meal, Davina noticed Barr Patterson's gaze flitting from Adele's face to that of his older brother.

Lying in bed later that night, Davina reached a decision. No matter what Rex might think, this was the end of the road for her. Barr was settled and no longer the 'ship without a rudder' he had been when she first met him. Adele at least seemed not to care that the world knew who she'd chosen to be her second partner in the matrimonial stakes, and that being so, Catrin's future happiness no longer hung on a supposed association between herself and Rex.

There was absolutely nothing now to stop her shaking the dust of Nineveh Farm off her shoes and when Barr left, she would go too. But the following morning the old shepherd arrived at the house while Davina was only at the stage of relighting the kitchen fire and he was carrying a telegram in his hand.

'Mrs Wicks at the Post Office asked me to bring this up early,' he explained as Davina picked it up and saw it was addressed to Barr. He came into the kitchen at that moment, freshly shaved and already dressed, so silently she held it out to him.

Tearing the envelope open, Barr read the three lines and asked, 'Where's the nearest telephone?'

'Down in the village,' Davina answered as he handed her the telegram to read. 'Take the Land Rover. Here are the keys. Mr Farr will show you where to telephone,' and Barr slipped on one of Rex's anoraks, picked up the keys and pushed the old man out before him.

They had been gone some fifteen minutes when Rex returned to the house, and he had hardly finished reading the telegram when the roar of an engine heralded Barr's return. For a man with an artificial limb he could be pretty nimble, Davina noticed, as he swung out of the cab and began to walk towards the house.

Rex tapped the telegram. 'It just says there's been an accident. Did you get through to Pam? How bad is it?'

'Not too serious, I'm glad to say,' Barr answered quickly. 'Pam hasn't got a scratch, but her mother has a black eye, she says, and her father a broken leg and slight concussion. We'll have to postpone the wedding, of course, until he's up and about again. Look, can you run me into Carlisle as soon as we've eaten? I can tell it's shaken them all up, and even if Pam isn't hurt, I feel I ought to be with her.'

There was no time to weep over a lost opportunity as

Davina hurried to get the meal on the table, cut sandwiches and helped Barr collect his belongings before with a hasty goodbye kiss he was getting into the Land Rover beside Rex. Somehow she'd have to get to a station under her own steam, and what better occasion than now, when Rex was out of the way for two hours at the very least. She would have to leave a letter of explanation, of course, ask him to send on the trunk and her suitcase, but perhaps, in the light of recent events, Rex would be relieved to return and find her departure a fait accompli.

She worked fast. The trunk was packed and locked and her suitcase filled in record time. She was in the middle of stripping the bed when a voice immediately behind her demanded, 'And what, may I ask, do you think you're doing?'

She knew that particular note in Rex's smooth voice and her inside began to tremble. She lifted a defiant chin. 'I should have thought that was obvious,' she answered quickly.

Her mouth went dry as leaning one shoulder against the door frame Rex turned a deliberate gaze on to the trunk and suitcase standing side by side. There was a wealth of meaning in his insolent drawl as he said, 'How very unfortunate for you that I met Adele on her way to Carlisle. As soon as she heard about the accident, she offered to take Barr with her and save me a journey. I imagine all this,' he waved a hand towards the packing, the half stripped bed, 'means that while my back was turned, like the Arabs you intended folding your tents and silently stealing away?'

Davina could meet the hard eyes no longer and she looked away. 'It seemed the best plan,' she said in a low voice.

'What makes you think anything's changed?'

She looked up quickly. 'But of course it has. Barr has no hard feelings, why should you? What's more, he's happily engaged.'

'No thanks to you,' Rex replied. 'And you ought to know by now that I haven't a very forgiving nature like Barr.' He pushed himself off the door frame and strolled towards her. 'Now in his shoes I most certainly wouldn't have given you the kiss of peace. If you'd jilted me the way you did him, I'd more than likely have kissed you like this,' and he reached out to grasp her.

Seeing his intention, Davina backed hastily away, completely overlooking the fact that the bed was right behind her. As the edge caught her behind the knees, she overbalanced in a tangle of arms and legs and seconds later felt the weight of Rex's body as he lay down beside her.

The mocking eyes were only inches from her own as he said provocatively, 'On occasion you can be a most accommodating girl,' before hard lips came down on hers. From the moment his mouth met her softly parted lips the battle was lost, and when at last he took his lips away it was only to say in grim smiling tones, 'Have everything back where it was by lunchtime,' before he got up and went away.

Davina sat on the edge of the bed and wiped away the slow tears coursing down her face. She knew miserably that she would do exactly as she was told. Not because she was afraid of Rex, not because she wanted to safeguard Catrin's future, but simply because she was so much in love, she did not want to leave the cause of all her recent misfortunes. To her eternal shame, Adele or no Adele, she knew she would stay at Nineveh until Rex had no further use for her.

CHAPTER TEN

STILL feeling sick with misery, Davina slowly undid her trunk, going over the scene which had just taken place. After her enthusiastic response to his lovemaking, Rex could be under no misapprehensions whatsoever about her feelings towards him and no doubt would take full advantage of her weakness. She, Davina Williams, who had always secretly despised girls who considered the world well lost for love, was just as foolish, it seemed, when it came to the crunch.

She put off her descent to the kitchen quarters until a glance at her watch showed her she could delay no longer. While she had been unpacking it had started to snow again, and she could almost guess word for word Rex's comment were he to find nothing hot to eat on a day like this.

But one o'clock came and went with no sign of either him or Mr Farr. Davina looked anxiously out of the kitchen window but could see that there was no sign of a let-up, for the snow was falling as fast as ever. She thought she could see a movement in the doorway leading to the barn and grabbing her thickest waterproof jacket she put it on and ran across the yard.

Peter McKay was standing just inside the barn and he turned to speak to the old shepherd who was attending to one of the penned ewes. 'Here's Miss,' he called over his shoulder, holding the door wider for Davina to come in out of the cold.

'What are you doing here at this time of day?' Davina demanded, then cutting short Peter's explanation that the heating boiler at the village school had broken down and given them all an unexpected holiday, she turned to ask the old man, 'Where's Mr Fitzpaine?'

He gave the ewe a pat, walked slowly out of the pen and slowly closed the door, while alarm rippled down Davina's spine. 'He went up a while ago to see all was right on account of I thought we'd more snow on't way, miss,' the shepherd said slowly and unemotionally, 'but he did say as how he'd be back dinner time.'

They all heard the clatter of George's metal shoes on the cobbles, and with a shout of, 'Here he is!' Peter dived for the door.

But when Davina followed the boy only the horse, his reins dangling, was coming towards the barn door. Rex could not have dismounted in the time and she was conscious of a feeling like a gigantic hand squeezing all the blood out of her body as she fought against a sick faintness.

She was brought to her senses by the old man grasping her elbow. 'Looks as if yon pony's run off. Gaffer'll have a long walk home.'

'No, there's been some kind of an accident. Rex is too good a horseman to lose hold of the reins. I'll get the Land Rover and go up the track.'

The old man shook his head. 'No use, miss. Snow's banked pretty high still from the last fall and this isn't going to make it easier.'

'Then I'll have to ride up.' Davina was suddenly ice cold. 'Do you think you could go for help, Mr Farr?'

'I'll come with you,' Peter broke in. 'George will carry us

both. Gaffer's too big a chap for a little 'un like you to manage, miss.'

'The boy's right,' the shepherd added his voice to Peter's, and as Davina hesitated, he picked up his crook and called to his dog. 'I'll get going. The sooner I'm on the road the better.'

It seemed inhuman to let a man his age walk the long, unsheltered road to Camshaw, but Davina was on the horns of a dilemma. She couldn't go in two different directions at once and the old man couldn't drive. As if aware of her divided duties, he set off at once, and suddenly remembering that some sort of first aid might be needed, with a, 'Wait here,' to Peter, Davina ran back to the house and collected the first aid box and as an afterthought the sleeping bag still on the camp bed where Rex had slept last night.

Peter McKay was already in the saddle when she emerged. She threw the bag across the horse's rump, put her foot on Peter's and sprang up behind the boy. As soon as he knew she was not likely to slip off, Peter turned George's head towards the track and set off to follow the hoof marks, already beginning to be covered as the snow continued to fall.

In some places, the snow lay in drifts as high as their knees and Davina examined each one carefully as they passed. If by chance Rex had misjudged the iciness of the track and been thrown, he could be lying unconscious in one of these drifts. Davina shuddered at remembered tales of death from exposure in her native Wales when a shout from Peter brought her head round to stare over his shoulder. 'Quick, miss, there he is!'

She looked ahead and her heart quickened, for the snow was trampled and stained with what looked undoubtedly like blood and in the middle, looking like a pile of discarded clothing, lay Rex. As soon as Peter had brought the horse to a standstill, Davina dropped to the ground, her feet slipping on the snow as she hurried to reach the unconscious man.

Rex was lying on his face, and as she reached his side, she could see blood was oozing sluggishly from a wound high on his left thigh. She turned to say, 'Give me the sleeping bag,' and found that Peter had already tethered the horse and was reaching up for the bag. Between them they unzipped it and laying it out on the snow began to roll Rex gently on to the covering.

One look at his face and Davina drew in a horrified breath, for already his lips were blue. His eyes were closed and a huge purpling bruise on his left forehead told their own tale, and the movement necessary to roll him on to the sleeping bag had made the wound on his leg begin to bleed more freely.

As she dragged the silk scarf from about her neck to form a tourniquet she said, 'Do you think you could ride back and see if you can get to Mr Farr? Tell him Mr Fitzpaine will need a doctor,' she added, and without a word, his usually healthy tanned face pale with shock, Peter scrambled back into the saddle and was gone. Left alone, Davina made sure the bleeding had been stopped, put a large dressing on the deep laceration in Rex's leg and pulling the sleeping bag over him, zipped it as far up as she could.

Until someone came it was essential to keep him as warm as possible, one tiny portion of her brain was saying, and another, 'Time the tourniquet. If no one comes within twenty minutes you'll have to loosen it.' Wishing Rex would give just one small sign of life, she lay full length and put her arms right round him, hoping that a little of her body warmth would penetrate and perhaps drive that death-like look from his face.

Frequent glances at her wrist watch told her it was only twelve minutes, but to Davina it seemed like hours when she heard voices and the sound of several pairs of feet told her that a relief party had arrived.

She looked up and saw that not only Mr Farr but Jim Thomas and three burly farmhands were coming along the track. Two of them were carrying a sort of hurdle, Davina noticed as, feeling slightly foolish, she got to her feet.

'Good thing I was up this way,' Jim greeted her. 'What's the damage?' and he knelt down and slipping a hand under the cover, took Rex's pulse.

'He's got a horrible gash in his leg. Look, he must have come off on that flint,' Davina pointed to a blood-stained stone sticking up out of the snow. 'I put on a tourniquet about fifteen minutes ago. But I can't tell if he's broken anything.'

'Not to worry. You've done marvels. We'll carry him back to the farm and then I'll run him straight to our little community hospital. There'll be someone there this time of day who can patch him up. Probably Tom. He's on duty today, I know.'

Davina watched as two of the farmhands lifted Rex, sleeping bag as well, on to the hurdle, then said slowly, 'You'll let me know, Jim?'

'Course I will. As soon as he's been attended to,' Jim answered cheerfully, taking his corner of the hurdle, and the men set off with their burden.

She was left suddenly conscious of being soaking wet and shivering with cold. The old man, waiting with stoical resignation in the driving snow, saw she had registered his presence and smiled encouragingly.

'Let's get you home now, missie. I told the lad to stable the horse. Fair shook up, he were, at seeing Gaffer had taken a fall. We could all do with something hot to warm our insides. Off we go!' and putting one horny hand under Davina's upper arm, the old man marched her back along the track at a brisk trot.

Peter was sitting glumly in the kitchen waiting, but a, 'Come along, lad. Take missie's coat. I'll pour the soup,' roused the boy to activity.

Davina found herself stripped of her anorak and wet footwear and pushed into a chair beside the fire. She gave a groan as feeling began to return to her frozen fingers and as he gave her a cup of hot soup the old shepherd said, 'Get that down you, miss. Then I suggest a hot bath. Peter and me'll manage fine.'

When Davina emerged from the bathroom some time later, warm again and clad in thick, dry clothing, the old shepherd had cleared away the lunch and he and Peter were washing up. The snow, Davina saw, had stopped and a fitful sun was trying to peep between the clouds.

Mr Farr saw the direction of her gaze. 'Me and the boy will just see everything in the barn is all right, then I daresay you'll be wanting to get to the hospital. We'll come and show you where it is.'

Thank goodness Rex had fitted snow chains, Davina

thought as she fought to steer the car down the winding moorland road. She could see now the sense of the posts on either side, for without them she would have had difficulty in the gathering dusk of an early winter afternoon of keeping to the road. They were just on the outskirts of Camshaw when Jim Thomas's station wagon came into view and he honked for her to stop.

'Tom was there, and one of the visiting consultants from Carlisle. Rex was lucky, because it was clinic day and he's having the very best treatment. Want me to come with you?'

'Good idea, Mr Thomas.' Mr Farr was already climbing down from the cab. 'Me and the boy were only along to show miss the way to the hospital. She can follow you.'

His manner brooked no argument and Davina sat alone in the Land Rover and waited for Jim to turn. Once at the hospital they were met by the Sister, who smiled at Jim and when she heard who Davina was said, 'Mr Fitzpaine's doing fine. You can go in and look at him—but mind you, he's not properly round yet.'

Davina turned to Jim, but for once he was strangely backward. 'Go on, I'll wait for you here.'

Following the Sister into a small six-bedded ward, Davina saw Rex had been put in the bed nearest the door and was lying with his head turned away.

She walked round the bed and pulling up a chair sat down gingerly. Rex's eyes were closed, but his breathing was healthily regular and the blue which had so frightened her had gone from his lips.

In fact, she thought, leaning an elbow on the bed to study his face more closely, he looked curiously young in the white hospital gown, and if one ignored the bruise on his forehead as if he had just fallen asleep. Unable to resist the temptation, she had given his cheek a butterfly kiss when Rex's eyelids quivered and then lifted.

There was a silence as he blinked, made an obvious effort to focus his eyes and then smiled, not the kind of sardonic curl of the lips to which Davina was accustomed but a tender smile, one with infinite allure that made her draw in her breath. He reached out a hand and as she instinctively took it between her own he said in a faint, faraway voice, 'Hello, darling! Fancy seeing you here. Like a raw beginner, I came off.' He stopped to yawn, 'Lord, I'm tired,' and his eyes slowly closed.

Davina hardly heard the ward Sister's voice saying, 'He'll sleep now, probably for hours. Nothing you can do by staying. Come along tomorrow afternoon,' before, her mind in a whirl, she was outside the ward doors. She was only barely aware of Jim's hand steering her outside, his rather anxious, 'Sure you're all right?' as he helped her into the Land Rover. She pulled her thoughts back from a seventh heaven where they had been floating ever since she had seen Rex's smile and heard his loving words to say, 'I'm fine, and thanks for all you've done, Jim,' before starting the journey back to the lonely farmhouse.

But it didn't seem lonely tonight, she thought, for every part of it held reminders of Rex. A boot lying on its side in the porch, his spare work jacket on the hook behind the door, a packet of tobacco still unopened on the dresser, and going into the study, all his books and papers as if he were about to come in and sit down.

Which if all went well, he would be doing very soon, Davina thought, and wondered when the doctors would let Rex come home. Home! She had never in her wildest dreams imagined thinking of Nineveh Farm as 'home'. Yet didn't people make a home? Four walls and a roof would be home if Rex was there to share it with her.

Next morning Davina worked with but one thought in mind—the afternoon's visit to the hospital. She had found out visiting hours began at two, but she was at the hospital long before that, a bag containing Rex's shaving things, clean pyjamas and dressing gown in one hand, a bundle of magazines and books in the other. She was in the waiting room patiently watching the clock when a nurse came in. 'Sister would like to see you.'

Puzzled, Davina followed the girl into the ward Sister's glassed-in cubicle. 'Mr Fitzpaine *is* going on all right?' she asked as the Sister pushed forward a chair.

'With Mr Ballard, not to mention our own Dr Mulholland, to patch him up, of course he's all right!' Even her cap seemed to crackle with indignation as she took the bag from

Davina's hand and gave it to the waiting nurse. 'However, I feel after concussion, one visitor at a time is quite enough. I wonder therefore if you'd mind waiting in the waiting room until Mr Fitzpaine's fiancée has gone. She told me she only had a few minutes as she'd an appointment, so I stretched the rules and let her go in and see him ahead of time,' the Sister ended.

Davina, a sick feeling in the pit of her stomach, was looking through the glass into the ward beyond where at the nearest bed, two people seemed to be oblivious to their surroundings. Adele had drawn a chair close to the bed and with her head almost touching Rex's was talking earnestly. As he smiled and nodded, Davina turned away and said in a wooden voice, 'Thank you, Sister.' She saw a look of surprise cross the ward Sister's face as she got to her feet and escaped to hide her despair in the now crowded waiting room.

At least a tear or two was to be expected in hospital, Davina thought, as she blew her nose and wiped her eyes, wishing she could have walked out there and then. But the Sister knew she was here and might ask embarrassing questions, for it was certain now that yesterday Rex must have mistaken her in his only half-conscious state for Adele. It was even possible he had no recollection whatsoever of that episode which had made such an impression on her mind. What a fool she'd been, Davina thought, after all that had gone before to even dream Rex could have had such a dramatic change of heart.

Five minutes later, with a click of high heels, Adele hurried past the open door of the waiting room, and Davina got up slowly to watch her walk briskly down the corridor and push open the swing doors. Even from the back, Adele looked like a fashion plate in a gold tweed coat with a blonde mink collar no lovelier than the long golden hair held back by a knot of ribbon. Glancing down at her green trouser suit with its matching polo neck woollen top, Davina knew she couldn't hope to compete when it came to clothes with Adele. Not that it mattered now, she thought, as she prepared to face Rex.

Her reluctance to face him made her usually transparent features turn into an expressionless mask, though as she concentrated on keeping a guard over her bruised feelings, Davina was not aware she was acting out of character. She walked to the end of the bed and standing stiffly laid the books and magazines on his bed table.

As she asked formally, 'Are you feeling better?' Rex eyed her thoughtfully, then, 'Come and sit down,' he urged, and patted the chair which Adele had so recently occupied.

Davina only just managed to control a shiver of distaste as she said hurriedly, 'No, I mustn't stop. I've a lot to do while I'm near the shops.' She was suddenly aware of small things about Rex, the bruise on his forehead beginning to go yellow at the outer edges, the lipstick on his right cheek ... Quickly she looked away. 'I don't know when I'll be able to get in again, so I must stock up a bit.'

There was an uneasy silence as she realised how lame that sounded, for Rex knew as well as she did what time the shops closed. She rushed on, 'I want to get back before it's dark, because Mr Farr's holding the fort and he must have a decent meal before I take him home. He was the one who fetched help yesterday, you know,' she ended, miserably aware of babbling like a schoolgirl.

Stealing a glance at his face, she saw that a stern, uncompromising look had replaced Rex's first welcoming smile. He said quite levelly, however, and with only a hint of the old mockery in his voice, 'I mustn't keep you, then. Off you go, and thanks for the reading matter. They may keep me in a day or two, so I'm afraid I must rely on you and Farr to keep things ticking over until I'm on my feet again.'

Did even asking this of her go against his better judgment? Davina wondered, and hitched her shoulder bag higher as she prepared to leave. 'Don't worry. Jim will give me a hand if I get into difficulties,' she said thoughtlessly, and saw a flash of real anger cross Rex's face before she turned and fled.

She had the shopping done and loaded into the Land Rover in record time. Suddenly aware that in order to be at the hospital early she had missed lunch, she went into a café near the parking lot and asked for a cup of tea.

Suddenly the picture of Rex and Adele, their heads together, exchanging smiles, could be dismissed no longer and she was haunted by a feeling of deprivation. Stirring the contents of her teacup round and round in bitter self-analysis, she faced the end of all her hopes. Despite all his taunts and attempts to make life difficult for her of late she now knew she had subconsciously clung to the belief that Rex's behaviour during the earlier part of her stay at Nineveh had not all been play-acting.

Now she could delude herself no longer. All that tenderness, all the passion he had deliberately aroused in her had been as he had stated—solely to teach her a lesson she'd never forget. Well, he had succeeded, perhaps even beyond his dreams. If the cup in front of her had contained arsenic instead of sugar, she would have drunk it gratefully, she thought, but laid down her spoon with a sigh. Melodramatic gestures were just for books, not for real life. What was that quotation? she thought, as she got up to pay the bill. 'Men have died and the worms have eaten them, But not for love'—that was it.

In real life you have to soldier on, Davina thought as she drove back to feed the tough old man. It was balm to a sore heart therefore to see the welcoming light streaming out across the farmyard as she pulled up, and she went inside to find not only the old shepherd but Jim Thomas waiting for her to return.

The table was laid, the kettle steaming, and as he relieved her of the shopping bags Jim said, 'I ran the old bus into the shed. Hope you don't mind. And we've been raiding your larder. Old Bill and I thought you'd be tired after coping with all this snow, so we've got a meal ready.'

Davina smiled, choked by this unexpected kindliness. 'Old Bill' she took to mean Mr Farr. She'd never heard his first name that she could remember. As she turned to thank the old man he said, 'I hear Gaffer's coming along all right. I don't doubt he's giving them pretty nurses a run for their money.'

Accepting a cup of tea, Davina did not reply. Jim gave her a searching look, then turned casually to the old shepherd and said, 'So my sister tells me. She called in before visiting began. Did you see her?' he asked Davina. Then to her re-

178

lief he went on, 'Trust Adele to get them to break the rules for her,' with brotherly frankness.

Apparently he wasn't yet aware of the understanding between Rex and his sister, Davina thought as she reluctantly let Jim cut her a slice of pork pie. Refusing salad or pickle, she forced herself to chew a mouthful, deciding to keep this piece of information to herself. No doubt Rex would prefer to make an announcement of his intentions in his own good time.

The meal over, Jim, with an evening surgery, took Mr Farr down to the village leaving Davina to face the long evening alone. With no happy promise of tomorrow it seemed uncomfortably silent and she found her thoughts returning relentlessly to the scene she had witnessed that afternoon.

Determined to put it out of her head at all costs, she fetched her transistor radio, made up the fire and collecting paper and a pen, began on the last of her commissioned stories. But somehow she couldn't write about true love tonight and after spoiling several sheets of perfectly good paper she began to bring to mind another of the stories with which as a child she had entertained her younger sister.

By the time she finished writing it was nearly midnight and she shuffled her rough manuscript together in some surprise, checking her watch by the mantel clock. At least there was no need to be up with the lark and no need either, she thought grimly, to hurry through her housework to go hospital visiting. Adele could do that. And it would undoubtedly be more to Rex's liking than a visit from his 'housekeeper'.

She gave herself no time the following day to mope. Indoor jobs done, she volunteered to saddle the horse and cart extra feed for the ewes to the far pasture, and the old shepherd, a curiously knowing gleam in his shrewd dark eyes, said, 'I'd be grateful, missie. Just so long as you don't come off yon horse,' as Davina laughed back, and shook her head.

'I'll be extra careful, Mr Farr,' she promised as the shepherd began to load the sledge with the concentrated fodder, saying, 'Us don't want no twin lamb disease on Nineveh,' as Davina led out the horse and hitched him up.

'Not much likelihood of that with you about!' she called over her shoulder. 'I'll be back in fifteen minutes.' But as she turned the last of the feed into sheep troughs she found the old man at her elbow.

'I'll go back for more,' she began, but he caught her arm and pointed.

'You've better eyesight nor mine. Is yon creature on her back?'

Davina's eyes followed the pointing finger and after a moment she turned. 'Yes, she's having a roll.'

'Roll be blowed! If us don't turn her, she'll die,' and the old shepherd set off across the snowy field.

Davina gave his retreating back a resigned look before she followed. Rex had said he relied on her to keep things ticking over. Had he visualised a situation like this? she wondered as, reaching the stricken animal, she listened to the shepherd's instructions.

By the time supper had been cooked and eaten and the old man dropped at the Shepherd and Crook Davina's eyes were beginning to feel heavy. She had only just garaged the Land Rover, however, when Jim Thomas drove into the yard and pulled up beside her.

'Got a cup of coffee for a weary vet?' he asked, leaning out of the window.

'I can just about manage that.' Davina gave him a tired smile and led the way towards the porch door. As she turned from the dresser with a cup and saucer in either hand, she noticed Jim had pulled off his sheepskin jacket and from the thoughtful look on his usually cheerful face, he had something on his mind.

But until the cups had been emptied he talked about amusing clients, farmers with out-of-date cures, old ladies with spoiled pets, children with their variety of hamsters, rabbits and gerbils with which he was called upon to cope. He had just had Davina laughing in spite of her feeling of bone weariness over a white rat which had escaped into a waiting room full of cats and nervous women owners when he suddenly dried up, and she looked across the table at him, curious to hear what was coming next.

'As you've no phone up here, Rex rang through to me half an hour ago. He expected you to go in to see him this afternoon.'

Here at last was the real reason for the visit. Davina found herself saying calmly, 'He can't expect Mr Farr at his age to do everything alone. I had to give a hand outside.'

Jim seemed to accept this. 'Look, I've an afternoon free tomorrow. Tell the old chap if he wants help with giving the flock their weekly foot bath to leave it until after lunch. Then you can take Rex some clothes when you go in. He says if they don't let him out in a couple of days he'll sign himself out. He sounded a bit restless,' Jim added, and grinned. 'Not the type, is he, to take to blanket baths and bedpans?'

'If I get the things packed now your sister could take them in to Rex,' Davina said decidedly, getting to her feet, but Jim stopped her with a, 'Sorry, but Adele's a bit preoccupied just now and if I help Farr, that only leaves you.'

Standing in silence, Davina wondered about Adele's 'preoccupation'. Probably merely the arrangement of an engagement party, she thought uncharitably, to be brought out of these unpleasant musings by Jim clearing his throat in an undeniably embarrassed manner. As she looked up to meet his eyes he gave her a sympathetic smile and said, 'None of my business, but what goes on? When we walked up that track out there to see what we could do to help Rex, the reason why I've never been able to make first base with you became very clear. You're in love with him, aren't you?'

Davina's pale, tired face flushed with mortification. 'Is it as obvious as all that?'

'Only to me, I suppose. But why the hassle? There's no law that says you can't marry a step. Or is Rex totally blind?'

Davina's mouth curled in a wry smile. 'Thanks for the compliment, but Rex seems to be a gentleman who prefers blondes.' She couldn't put it plainer than that without actually mentioning Adele by name, for it was abundantly clear that Jim had not yet been told of how matters stood between his sister and the owner of Nineveh Farm.

It was in a decidedly uncompromising frame of mind that Davina set out the following afternoon to take a suitcase of clothes along to the hospital. She had deliberately delayed leaving until Jim's arrival and when the engine of the Land Rover spluttered and died, she knew she was going to be very late indeed in arriving at the hospital.

A glance at the dashboard had revealed that the indicator on the fuel gauge was pointing to 'empty'. Preoccupied with personal problems, she had quite forgotten to fill up the tank. Glad that at least it had stopped snowing, she got out to walk to the nearest garage.

By the time she had borrowed a gallon can, walked back to the car and driven to the hospital it was already dark. Most of the afternoon visitors had gone and Rex was sitting, propped up by several pillows, a thunderous frown on his face.

He gave a meaning glance up at the ward clock and with a dangerous note in his voice asked softly, 'Where've you been? Visiting is over in ten minutes and I want to arrange with you about tomorrow. I've told Tom Mulholland I'm not staying another minute longer being clucked over as if I'm about to cock up my toes. He says the specialist comes at ten and I've agreed to wait and let him look at me before I leave. Be here at eleven—and be sure you're on time.'

If she hadn't been so angry, Davina would have burst into laughter, for Jim's comment about Rex and 'blanket baths and bedpans' had hit the spot. Under the angry commands was a note of desperation, but her momentary feeling of sympathy for the big man in the bed was dispelled as she set down the suitcase and her eye caught the bold handwriting on the card propped against a vase of multi-coloured carnations on Rex's bedside locker.

Davina's eyes sparkling with indignation as she straightened. 'Just be glad I'm here at all. I'm not your slave, and don't forget it!'

She was quite proud of having just once had the last word as she swung round and left him. How dared Rex, revenge or no revenge, speak to her in such monitory tones when he had Adele writing that she was 'eternally in your debt,' and sending him expensive out-of-season flowers! And why wasn't *she* picking Rex up tomorrow? Davina shrugged her shoulders in despair. None of it made sense any more.

No more sense than Sister's warning as she intercepted Davina. 'We don't like Mr Fitzpaine going out so soon, but he insists. Here's his outpatient appointment card. Keep an eye on him, and above all no walking or horse riding. Dr Mulholland says he'll be in touch about the sutures.'

As the ward Sister walked away a little light was beginning to dawn. So Rex hadn't even had his stitches out yet, and however much he disliked hospital routine this couldn't be the only reason for his anxiety to get back to Nineveh. Were he and Adele planning to try and get her divorce speeded up? If so this explained his insistence on virtually discharging himself from the doctor's care.

Davina was in the waiting room on the dot of eleven the following morning, wondering how on earth she was to restrict Rex's activities once he was back at the farm. But apparently he had no intention of abusing his freedom, for to her surprise he walked to the Land Rover with barely the hint of a limp, threw his case into the back, gave a huge sigh and said, 'Thank God! Fresh air at last,' before getting into the passenger seat.

Silently she climbed behind the wheel and started the engine. But before she could engage the gears, he demanded, 'What did happen to you yesterday?'

She turned to meet the hard eyes, but a gleam in their depths hinted at the suspicion of an olive branch. Suddenly, she didn't want to fight and her customary sense of humour got the better of her. With a dimple in her cheek she answered, 'Ran out of petrol.'

There was resignation in Rex's drawl. 'I suppose I might have guessed. How like a woman! Anyway, you're forgiven for having me worrying about you lying somewhere in a ditch,' he ended, and his hand came down on the denim covering the thigh almost touching his own. Trying to make up her mind how to deal with this totally unexpected gesture, Davina was motionless, when suddenly the hand was removed and, 'Are we going to sit here all the rest of the morning?' Rex enquired in a harsh voice.

Back to normal, she thought, as she let the handbrake off. Rather to her surprise, however, Rex kept up a friendly conversation all the way back to Nineveh, their only unharmonious moment coming when Davina, with the ward Sister's instructions in her mind, nipped smartly out to open the gate before he had time to uncoil his long legs.

'I'm not completely helpless,' he barked as she got in again.

'No one said you were, but that leg must be a bit stiff still,' she said in a gentle voice. With only a, 'Don't try and treat me like an invalid,' Rex let the episode pass, and he didn't speak again until Davina braked outside the porch door.

Peter McKay was cleaning some of the horse's tack and the old shepherd was placidly smoking beside a roaring fire, almost, Davina thought with amusement, as if they belonged to Nineveh Farm by right. As soon as the inner door had opened to reveal Rex, the boy sprang up with a light almost of hero-worship in his blue eyes as he ran round the table.

Rex put out a long arm and held him off. 'Steady, young man! I'm not up to wrestling yet.'

'Can I see your stitches?' Peter demanded, in no way put out by being kept at arm's length. Peter even grinned when Rex said dourly, 'No, you may not,' before turning to greet the old man.

'Everything all right, Mr Farr? Stupid of me, wasn't it, to come a cropper. I thought one of the ewes was in trouble and was turning back to have another look.'

The shepherd took his pipe out of his mouth and said, 'I had the whole lot up for Mr Thomas to have a look at this afternoon. Seemed to me there wasn't none missing. Only two in't barn, that is. But you knew about them, Gaffer, afore you were took bad.'

'That's fine,' Rex replied, and drawing out a chair, he sat down and stretched out his injured leg. As if this might be taken as a sign of weakness he looked across at Davina and said, 'What about something to eat? I haven't been offered a decent cup of tea for days,' he finished, and as Davina turned she was smiling.

The sheer pleasure of seeing Rex occupying his usual chair had almost driven thoughts of Adele to the back of her mind, but now they returned and as she began scrambling eggs and making toast, she wondered what had happened to the gay divorcee. It was strange she had not put in an appearance—but then Adele was a law unto herself.

It was odd behaviour even by her standards, Davina decided, for surely collecting Rex and bringing him up to Nineveh was more important than arranging a celebration party. Perhaps Adele would be turning up later with, no doubt, a perfectly plausible explanation for her absence.

But the afternoon passed, supper prepared and eaten and Peter and the old man restored to their respective homes with still no sign of Adele Wickham's sleek sports car, and it did not appear as if Rex was expecting her, for he threw a last cigarette away as the clock chimed nine and announced his intention of having an early night.

Pleased that she had the forethought to pull the curtains in his bedroom and turn on the portable heater before she went to start the Land Rover, Davina asked in a casual voice if he would like a last hot drink when he was in bed, and was unprepared for the sudden gleam which appeared in Rex's deep-set eyes.

'Thanks, but no, thanks. I'd welcome a cup of tea in the morning around six, though.'

'You're never thinking of getting up at that hour?' Davina asked before she could control her rash tongue, to be greeted with an impatient, 'Don't you start fussing, for heaven's sake!' Then as he was about to shut the door, 'Anyway, the Florence Nightingale bit doesn't suit your image.'

As she angrily began to tidy the kitchen and set a tray for the morning she thought how satisfying it would have been to have hurled something heavy in Rex's direction, for that last remark had been said purposely to catch her on the raw. At least temper cured an urge to burst into tears, she thought as she sat down to write to her mother before getting ready for bed herself. Not for the first time since she had dis- covered Rex Fitzpaine's relationship to Barr Patterson, Dav- ina wished she could have wept out the whole miserable saga on her mother's sympathetic shoulder. Helen Williams had thought Rex a charming man during the days he had spent under her mother's roof. What would she think of him if she knew the kind of punishment he was meting out to her be- loved elder daughter?

But when she carried in the tea tray the following morning and she caught a glimpse of Rex's drawn face Davina was glad she had delayed awakening him until after seven. Ex- pecting an abrasive comment, she was surprised to find he made no remark about 'disobedient employees', but simply sat up to take the cup she was holding out.

He drank the strong, hot brew with relish and as he held out the cup for a refill his eyes were on Davina's damp curls. 'Left me any water for a bath?'

'I'd give it half an hour to get really hot again. Don't worry —I don't mind keeping breakfast back,' and Davina picked up the tray and whisked herself out of the room, inordinately pleased by the small victory.

Rex lingered over his breakfast and showed no sign of being in any hurry to get back to his beloved sheep, until he saw Davina begin to put on her waterproof over trousers preparatory to going out. As his eyebrows shot up questioningly she said, 'The track is negotiable for the time being, so I'm going to take a double lot of extra feed up for the sheep.'

'My chore, I think.' Rex twitched off her woollen cap with the words and put her anorak out of reach. 'The leg's quite up to driving this morning, so you stick to household chores. You can check the generator if you really want to help,' he added as he shrugged into a parka and was gone.

Anxiously Davina watched him cross the yard, almost wishing Adele were there to make him behave with a modicum of common sense. What would that hospital Sister say if she could see her patient right this moment? At least he wasn't limping today, she noticed as she turned to get on with her work.

All the morning, the sky grew steadily darker, and as well as checking the generator, Davina brought plenty of fuel into the outer porch and put a spare Calor gas cylinder in the larder in case of emergency. She was not surprised to hear as lunch was eaten that on the old shepherd's advice, the sheep had been moved nearer the house. 'You could be snowed in for days,' Mr Farr informed them with all the relish of a Jeremiah, and his bright, knowing eyes switching from Davina's face to that of the tall man sitting at the head of the table.

It was beginning to go dark as the first snowflakes began to fall. Wishing Rex would come in and rest, Davina made up the fire and then put on all the portable gas heaters, because if the old man was right, they were in for one of the coldest nights of the winter. She heard the Land Rover roar away down the lane and guessed Rex was taking the shepherd home before the road became impassable, and half an hour later her face lit up with unconcealed relief as she heard his return.

He came into the kitchen shaking snow in every direction. 'You must be frozen,' she said, and leaving the scone mixture she turned to put on the kettle. 'I'll soon have these in the oven,' she began, then stopped as Rex threw down his coat and came to stand right in her path, a curiously triumphant expression on his face.

His long arms came out to imprison her as he said, 'Now, Miss Williams, I've got you where I want you at last. We are about to be cut off for several days, by the look of things.'

So he *was* going to make the most of their enforced imprisonment and take up where he had left off the morning of his accident, Davina thought, and her anger lent her strength she didn't know she possessed. Eyes sparkling with fury, she put two floury hands against his dark pullover and pushed him away, flinging back her head to ask, 'And what is Adele going to say when I tell her how you behave behind her back?'

Surprise crossed Rex's face, but he wasn't startled enough to let Davina go completely. His hands closed over her upper arms and holding her firmly he gave her a small shake. 'What's Adele got to do with us?'

'Everything, I imagine, since you're engaged to be married.'

Apart from his brows twitching together, Rex was completely motionless after she had spat out her challenge. Then he looked down to ask in a deep, soft drawl, 'Since when?'

Davina tried to pull away from the firm hold, but his hands were clamped firmly. Still a prisoner, she shrugged. 'How should I know? You were holding hands with her the other afternoon, and Sister told me your fiancée was with you.' Trying to sound supremely unconcerned as she replied to Rex's laconic question, she was annoyed to find her voice wobbled ominously with the last words.

Rex gave a short laugh. 'How typical of Adele! So that's how she managed to get in to see me before visiting hours. I suppose I might have guessed. It never occurred to her that she might be complicating things for me.'

This was hardly the sort of thing one expected from a

newly engaged man and Davina's eyes opened wide. Rex looked down into them and for perhaps the first time since they'd met, his glance held a hint of apology.

'I've been trying to get her to see sense and go back to that husband of hers for some time. She's the kind of woman who needs the sort of life he can offer—a social round with no expense spared. She's not the sort to rough it in the country and above all she needs a man around, preferably one who won't stand too much nonsense. Wickham seemed to me to fit the bill and it was simply a case of getting Adele to see which side her bread was buttered, if you'll pardon the expression. Apparently I got through to her—and just in time too. The day after she rang him up and asked him to take her back, she found out he'll be getting a title in the next Honours List. Adele was holding my hand simply by way of thanks. Strange, but the thought of being Lady Wickham is her idea of heaven.'

As she tried to absorb this information, Davina stood quite still until the spluttering of the kettle behind her caused Rex to say a soft 'damn' as he released her to lift it off the flame. He turned back to look down at Davina's thoughtful face and say commandingly, 'That reminds me, why didn't you tell me your part in the rescue? Farr told me this afternoon that but for your quick thinking I'd have lost a lot of blood.'

'One acts instinctively in an emergency,' she hedged, but Rex swung her round so that the light fell full on her face.

'Do you instinctively embrace all the people you administer to?' Rex asked, and as she began to blush added, 'Yes, it wasn't cricket, was it, the old man giving you away like that. But he knows how I feel about you and he's doing his best to play Cupid.'

The flush died as Davina looked a question. She said slowly, 'How you feel about me? He can hardly know the truth or he'd be playing Mephistopheles, not Cupid,' she ended bitterly.

To her surprise, Rex dragged her into his arms and his voice above her head held a note of remorse. 'Oh, Davina, have you forgotten the morning I had my accident? What happened before I left the house? I thought I'd made myself plain.'

'Plain that you found me physically attractive, yes.' Davina's voice was muffled.

'Physically and mentally. Now I know why the police leave hostages alone with their captors. It becomes increasingly difficult to regard their feelings with indifference.'

'Yet only a few days ago you brought your brother up here without warning me. Did you imagine I'd enjoy seeing his disability?' Davina demanded, and struggled to escape his hold. Rex gave an odd laugh, pulled her even closer and laid his cheek on top of her head.

'Try to understand.' Davina stayed motionless, for he was actually pleading and she could hardly believe her ears. 'Mother's behaviour didn't exactly give me a high regard for your sex and I'd been feeding my hatred of you as the cause of Barr's attempted suicide for a long time. But you were not a bit as I expected, and the first hint I got from your attitude to your family that you were not just another heartless good time girl was borne out by the way you got down to tackling this place. I'd bought it mainly for its dilapidation and was expecting tears and recriminations, but not a bit of it. Even when I told you precisely why I'd brought you up here and forced you into staying, you still kept that firm little chin gallantly in the air. Though I wouldn't admit it even to myself, you'd got right under my skin.'

Davina moved and as Rex raised his head, she looked up to meet his eyes. 'No one would have guessed. You were hateful,' she stated flatly, keeping every trace of feeling out of voice and look.

'And I invited Barr here more to pinch myself than you,' Rex went on, looking down at her from his great height. 'But if I'd had any idea of how genuinely upset you'd be . . .' His voice trailed off as they stared into one another's eyes.

Davina could not resist that look. She reached up and stroked his face. 'Trying to make me believe that melted your hard heart?'

'It had melted long before.' There was a smile in Rex's eyes. 'The ice had been chipped away bit by bit by a chit of a girl I could break in half with one hand tied.'

As if to add weight to this statement, he wound one long arm round Davina's waist and cupped her chin in his other

189

hand. 'I got so that I was afraid to be in the same room with you,' he confessed.

Her smile held disbelief. 'You—afraid?'

'It's true. When I wasn't longing to break your neck for being so confoundedly attractive, I wanted to make love to you. Do you wonder I was "hateful", as you put it? It hadn't been part of my plan that *I* should fall in love with *you*.'

'Does that mean I'm forgiven for my supposed misdeeds?'

Rex gave her a rueful smile. 'Yes, Barr put me right about that too when he put two and two together and found out I'd deliberately looked you up. But I'd begun to wonder on my own account if I hadn't got the whole thing wrong. Can you ever forgive me, my delightful Welsh Witch?'

Davina's dimple peeped as she drew his head down. 'That depends,' she answered, and kissed him quickly, a butter-fly kiss on his firm mouth.

One corner was curling in a smile that was making her heart turn over.

'On what?' Rex asked.

She pulled his head down and whispered in his ear. He gave a crow of laughter, ruffled her curls and said, unholy joy in his voice, 'Why, you little devil! Poor Lionel doesn't know what he's in for. You'll turn Penderoo Station upside down. But it will be worth it,' he ended as his mouth came down to find hers, and the snow continued to fall outside, shutting the two of them in their winter wonderland.

By popular demand...

24 original novels from this series—by 7 of the world's greatest romance authors.

These back issues have been out of print for some time. So don't miss out; order your copies now!

Harlequin Reader Service
ORDER FORM

Mail coupon to:
Harlequin Reader Service
M.P.O. Box 707
Niagara Falls, New York 14302

Canadian Residents send to:
649 Ontario St.
Stratford, Ont. N5A 6W2

Please send me by return mail the Harlequin Presents that I have checked.
I am enclosing $1.25 for each book ordered.

Please check volumes requested:

☐ 38	☐ 46	☐ 54
☐ 39	☐ 47	☐ 55
☐ 40	☐ 48	☐ 56
☐ 41	☐ 49	☐ 57
☐ 42	☐ 50	☐ 58
☐ 43	☐ 51	☐ 59
☐ 44	☐ 52	☐ 60
☐ 45	☐ 53	☐ 61

Number of books ordered_____ @ $1.25 each = $ _____

N.Y. and N.J. residents add appropriate sales tax $ _____

Postage and handling = $ _____ .25

TOTAL = $ _____

NAME _____
(please print)

ADDRESS _____

CITY _____

STATE/PROV. _____   ZIP/POSTAL CODE _____

ROM 2158